ELECTRON THEORIES AND PROPERTIES OF SOLID MATERIALS

K. Srinivasan

Clever Fox
PUBLISHING

Chennai • Bangalore

CLEVER FOX PUBLISHING
Chennai, India

Published by CLEVER FOX PUBLISHING 2022

ISBN: 978-93-56481-77-0

DEDICATION

To my beloved parents

CONTENTS

CONTENT DETAILS

PREFACE

Materials play a vital role in the development and advancement of human civilization right from the origin of life on this mother earth due to their inherent properties which can be put to use by humans. It may be for their welfare or for satisfying their ego by achieving whatever they want and prove to others their superiority and suzenarity. In this information age this will be possible only if they do information processing very quickly, precisely and safely. This makes the role of electronic materials very crucial. As engineered materials they have changed the way we communicate, analyze ,travel recuperate, manufacture etc.

The properties of materials can be broadly divided into two kinds namely electronic and mechanical. The former is dependent on electrons in an atom [subatomic level] and their interaction with external stimuli such as electric, magnetic, thermal and optical fields, while the later depend on imperfections at the atomic level such as vacancies and dislocations. Our concern in this book is the former. Chapter 1 is introductoy. To understand the electronic properties theories have been formulated and these are discussed in the book in chapter2, 3&4.Chapter 5 describes the various properties based on the theories Electronic properties of materials at the microscopic level obey simple laws and can be related to macroscopic behavior of an assembly of atoms called solids. It helps in synthesis of new materials by novel methods to suit the specific requirements of each application. Chapter 6 is on various materials suitable for electronic devices and production on industrial scale. Recent developments are highlighted in chapte7. 11 appendices follow these. These give some basic but essential information to arouse the curiosity of the readers.

It is not so much the knowledge of specific values of properties but the fundamentals that govern such properties that will be useful and helpful to beginners in the field in the long range since today`s materials of choice are not tomorrow`s materials of choice. Things become obsolete. Current materials have been included as an illustration. Tables are added to have a feel for numerical values of properties.

Synthesis and production methods such as single crystal growth, zone refining, epitaxial growth, tape casting, wire drawing ,powder processing etc. have been dealt with in length. Applications have been mentioned.

About 200 questions and 110 numerical problems are included to help the young readers. The problems aid the students in design of applications and devices used in our daily life and activities. More than adequate number of illustrations help in clear understanding of the subject. Equal emphasis has been given on the know how and the know why of the subject matter.

ACKNOWLEDGEMENTS

First and foremost I thank Prof. E. G. Ramachandran who taught me a course on Theory of Metals way back in 1974 at IIT, Madras during my B. Tech Metallurgical programme. Secondly I record my gratitude to Prof. T. Ramchandran who requested me to handle a course on Physics of Materials at the suggestion of Prof.N.Venkatraman,my friend,philosopher and guide at NITK,Surathkal. This led me to teach the course under various names for around 20 years. I express my gratefulness to Prof. S. Ranganathan of I.I.Sc, Bangalore who gave my academic life a meaning , purpose and focus. I should place here my appreciation of my students, who took seminar topics in this area. I thank my family members for their co-operation during the entire period of preparation of the book. I dedicate the book to my energetic and enthusiastic parents. It is highly appropriate and apt to express my thanks to the proprietors of Laxmi Computer Services for composing the manuscript and Ms. R. A. Suganya for all the drawings done.

1

INTRODUCTION

Dual nature of electrons is a well established concept in science and its application in human life is truly mind boggling. An electron can be considered as a particle as well as a wave, but equations defining both cannot be applied simultaneously. In some cases the particle concept is used while in some other situations wave concept is used. This made the famous physicist Bragg to quip in a lighter vein that ELECTRONS ARE PARTICLES ON MONDAYS, WEDNESDAYS AND FRIDAYS AND WAVES ON TUESDAYS THURSDAYSAND SATURDAYS. In any case the duality apparently does not affect the various phenomenon associated with electrons and their applications in everyday life of so many thousands of humans under or on or above the earth. The waves associated with electrons are called MATTER WAVES and are different from ELECTRMAGNETIC WAVES which are associated with the particles called PHOTONS (light) and ELASTIC WAVES associated with PHONONS (sound).

The wavelength associated with electrons depends on the velocity with which it moves. It is governed by the postulate of de Broglie. The position of an electron cannot be determined accurately. There is always an inaccuracy as given by Heisenberg`s Uncertainty principle. Only the probability of finding an electron in a particular position can be given. An electron moving freely in space without any external influence such as an electric field can posses any energy value from zero to infinity. But it is not so for an electron in an atom. It can possess only certain sharp energy values. The same electron in a group of atoms can have a spread in its energy values. That is to say that the behavior would be different in an individual atom and in an assembly of atoms. It is illustrated in Figs 1.1 & 1.2 where energy values in an individual atom and an assembly of atoms are shown with respect to inter atomic spacing and reciprocal of inter atomic spacing. As two atoms are brought together the outer orbits overlap and sharp energy levels spread out. This is due to the interaction of the electric field of all the electrons and ions in a solid which is nothing but an assembly of atoms. The electrical, thermal, magnetic and optical properties of a solid are thus determined by the behavior of the outermost (valence) electrons [number, mobility, energy etc.] of the solid. These properties are called ELECTRONIC PROPERTIES in contrast to MECHANICAL PROPERTIES (strength, toughness, fatigue resistance, creep resistance etc.) which are influenced by VACANCIES AND IMPURITIES [number, mobility, energy etc]. Applications base on electronic properties are varied and numerous with far reaching implications and influence. Manufacture of various electronic materials and devices are complex, time consuming, challenging and tedious. The frontiers are ever widening and the possibilities never exhausting.

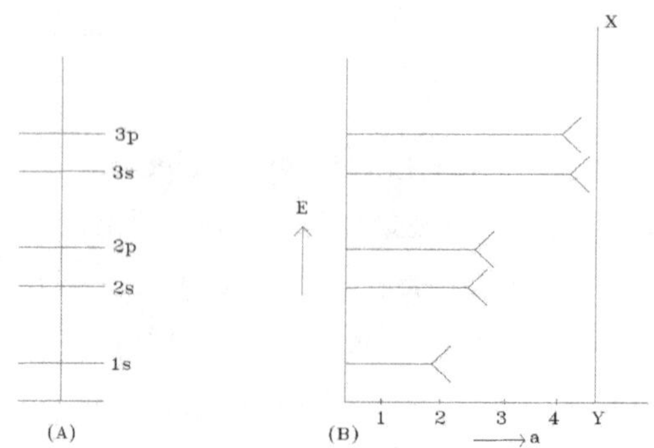

Fig. 1.1 Energy of electrons against inter atomic distance in solid compared with energy in free atom.

Statistics

A system of particles can be mathematically handled with quantitative equations using statistical techniques.

For a group of atoms or molecules obeying the rules of classical mechanics Maxwell-Boltzman statistics should be applied. But for subatomic particles obeying laws of quantum mechanics such as Fermions. One should apply Fermi-Dirac statistics.and for Bosons one should use Bose-Einstein statistics.

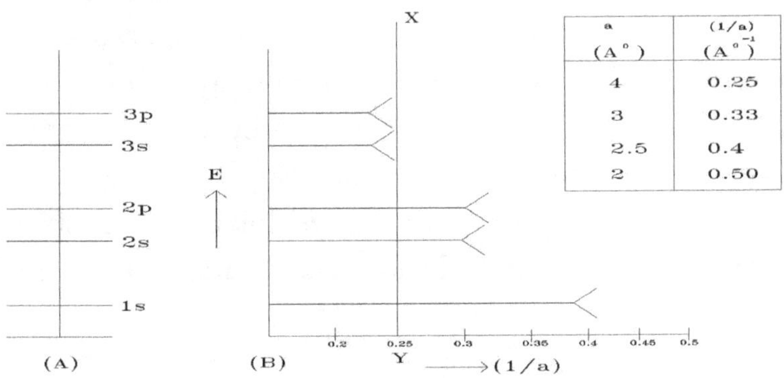

Fig. 1.2 Energy of electrons against reciprocal of interatomic distance in solid compared with energy in free atom.

Energy

High energy state is unstable and it will spontaneously go to a low energy state. Total energy remains the same but one type of energy can get converted to another type. ordered state is high energy state and move to disordered state which is a low energy state.There are three equations for energy one relating frequency another to temperature and the third to the square of light velocity. One should use the appropriate equation depending on the situation.

Bonding

Electronic properties depen on the types of materials namely metals ceramics or polymers and their combinations called composites. In turn they will depend on bonding, structure and texture. Metals have non directional metallic bonding. Polymers have covalent bonding in large and long molecules and between one molecule and another have van der waals bonding. Ceramics have either covalent or ionic bonding or a mixture of the two. Covalent bonding is the strongest, ionic the next strongest and metallic the next strongest bond. Van der wals is the weakest of the four types of bonding. Covalent bonding can exist among the different types of atoms, say carbon and carbon, hydrogen and hydrogen, carbon and hydrogen etc. Metallic bond exists among the same metallic elements of equal size or between different metallic elements of similar size. Ionic bond exists between two different sized ions namely anions and cations. Ionic bonds are nondirectional

Electronic Structure

Structure can be macro, micro,nano ,crystal, atomic, ionic,electronic and nuclear, in the order of decreasing size. Electronic structure has a significant effect on electronic properties. It depends on how the electrons get filled on the basis of energy. Theoretically one would expect it to be 1s 2s 2p 3s 3p 3d 4s 4p 4d 4f 5s 5p 5d 5f 6s 6p 6d 6f 7s.... ....in the decreasing order.But it goes as follows:1s 2s 2p 3s 3p 4s 4p 3d 5s 4d 5p 6s 4f 5d 6p 7s 5f 6d.....ie 4s is filled before 3d 5s before 4d and 4f etc. This has a very important effect on electronic properties of various types of materials.

Crystal structure

It plays an important role. Metals are crystalline. They usually crystallise in close packed bcc, fcc and hcp structures It has to do with energy and stability. Metallic alloys can be solid solutions (substitutional or intestinal) or compounds or a mechanical mixture of the two at room temperature and liquid above melting point. Only five atoms can get into tetra and octahedral voids in metals These atoms are small in size . Their radius in Angstroms are C(0.77) N(0.71) H(0.46) O(0.60) and B(0.97) Ceramics can be crystalline or non crystalline or semi crystalline. They are inorganic. Ceramics come in a variety of crystal structures, in any of the 14 Brava is lattices. Similarly for polymers. Polymers can be organic (C backbone) or inorganic (Si) backbone). They can be thermoplastic or thermoset or rubbers . Amorphous metals are called metallic glasses. They have interesting electrical and magnetic properties.

Microstructure

Microstructure plays a decisive role in influencing electronic properties. Grains, grain boundaries, single or polycrystalline, single phase or dual phase or multiphase, voids, inclusions, impurities, dopants - all of them will have a bearing on electronic properties. In single crystal no grain boundaries will be present. In polycrystalline materials grain boundaries are present and will be a sink for impurities and imperfections. They will scatter electrons. They will pini down domain walls. The solid state devices made with these may not work or work suboptimally. Coarse grained material will have smaller length of grain boundary while fine grained material will have longer lengths. The electronic materials should be super pure and crystallographically perfect without dislocations etc. Microstructure can be modified by alloying and heat treatment. Opposite to single crystal (without grain boundaries)is the fine grained polycrystalline. The later will have high strength and toughness. The long grain boundaries will stop the dislocations in a pileup making it difficult for further movement thereby increasing strength. Also the grain boundaries will arrest the propagation of cracks and prevent their growth before damaging there by increasing toughness.

Texture

Texture also called preferred orientation has an appreciable effect on electronic properties that are anisotropic. One may have a high value for a property in a particular crystal direction. There are two types of texture namely annealing or recrystallization texture and deformation texture. The former occurs after annealing and the later after deformation. One can have texture in wire or sheet. In the former the grains in the wire have a particular crystallographic direction say <111> parallel to the axis of the wire. It Is called <111> texture. In the later grains may have a crystallographic plane parallel to the rolling plane of sheet say {100} and a crystallographic direction say <010> parallel to the rolling direction. It is called {100} <010> texture. It is termed as cube texture. {110} <100> texture is called cube on edge texture. Both are important in magnetic materials like iron. All crystal structures like BCC, FCC, HCP etc can have texture. It is important in magnetic materials. Easy direction of magnetisation is useful in such materials.

Nanostructure

Nanoparticles are cluster of molecule of atoms. They will be less than 100 nm in size. As the size decreases reactivity increases The stability of the particle depends on the number of atoms. That number which gives stability is called a magic number. The crystal structure of bulk material will change to an icosahedral shaped structure at the nanometer. These nanomaterials possess interesting electronic properties.

Dual nature of matter

A particle moving with velocity will create waves. It is given by the de Broglie equation. But it's effect will be significant for very very light mass for example electrons not for macroscopic masses such as planets or for that matter humans or animals. The above equation along with Heisenburgh`s uncertainty principle, Schrodinger`s wave equation, Pauli's exclusion principle and Hund`rule form the basis for quantum mechanical treatment of electronic properties of materials. Electron diffraction is useful for determining the boundaries of Brillouin zones. Neutron diffraction is used for understanding antiferromagnetism. The conditions for diffraction from SC, BCC, FCC, DC and HCP crystals remain the same as for X-ray diffraction. Moreover Electron and Neutron radiography are used for NDT like X-rays.

Organic materials

Of late, a lot of interest has been shown by researchers to use organic molecules showing interesting electronic properties. Organic superconductors, semiconductors, lasers are coming into use and the future holds a lot of promise and new opportunities.

Quantum computers have been developed and switching speeds of femtoseconds have been reached. Biological computers are in their infancy. Miniaturisation is progressing very rapidly. Speed of computing is rising. Parallel processing and optical switching together will make computations very very quick and fast.

Electronic waste

It is also called e-waste. Plenty of electronic goods and appliances are discarded every year. By recycling several precious materials can be recovered at low cost and reused. Toxic elements like arsenic, antimony, mercury, lead etc can be prevented from contaminating the environment. The health and wellbeing of humans, animals and plants can be ensured.

In the following chapters of the present book a brief description of the electron theory, properties, materials and production techniques has been attempted to address the need of beginners in the field of Materials Engineering and Materials Science.

2

FREE ELECTRON THEORY

2.1 CLASSICAL APPROACH

Classical free electron theory was proposed at the beginning of the twentieth century based on the existence of bonding between atoms in a metal called the METALLIC BOND. According to the above theory valence electrons of a metal called FREE ELECTRONS drift in an electric field of the ions comprising of the nucleus and the tightly bound electrons of the metallic solid. The valence electrons are considered as a sea or a gas enveloping the lattice of regularly arranged ions. This electro gas is common to all ions and is not attached to any particular ion or group of ions. It can be treated by the classical MAXWELL-BOLTZMAN statistics similar to an ordinary gas consisting of molecules. This treatment was not adequate to explain the behavior and properties of metals. This led to the application of quantum theory in the second quarter of the twentieth century.

2.2 QUANTUM THEORY APPROACH

The valence electrons are still treated like a gas of charged particles with small mass, but instead of applying the classical M-B Statistics FERMI-DIRAC Statics is applied. The valence electrons are collectively treated like a gas but they have to obey the Heisenberg`s uncertainty principle [only the probability of position of electron can be given ] and the Pauli`s exclusion principle[no two electrons have all their four quantum numbers same].The implication of this is described below: In the momentum diagram if one plots the momentum values for various valence electrons at the temperature of absolute zero one gets a sphere unlike the classical case where all points fall on the origin. This is illustrated in Figs 2.1(a) & 2.1(b). At room temperature it will be as shown in Figs 2.2(a) & (b). At a temperature higher than room temperature it will be as shown in Figs 2.3(a) & (b).

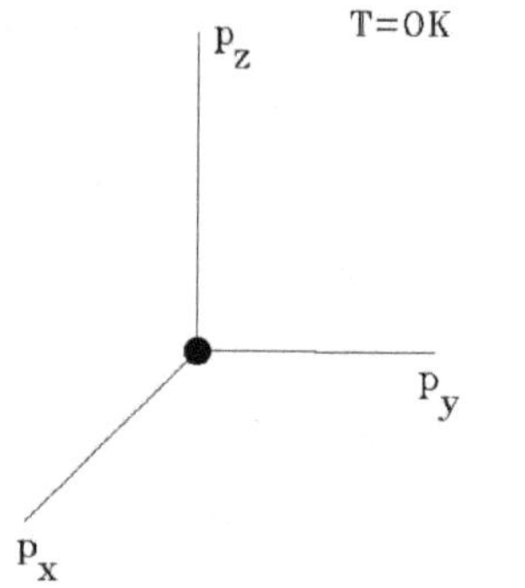

Fig. 2.1(a) Classical FET

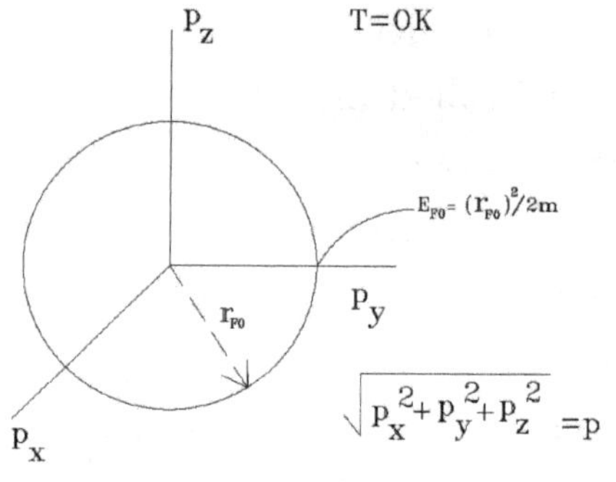

Fig. 2.1(b) Quantum FET

At absolute zero the energy of electrons is not zero as give by classical theory but is spread over a range of values from zero to a maximum .The maximum energy is called FERMI ENERGY. At a higher temperature this maximum will increase. It can be represented as

$$\mathbf{E_{FT}=E_{F0}+kT}$$

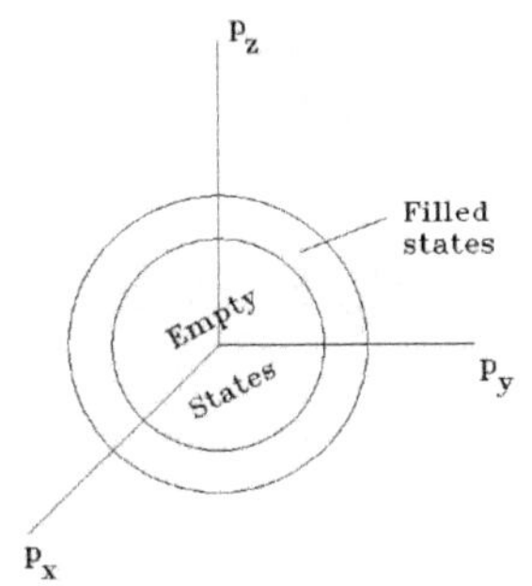

Fig.2.2(a) According to CFET–Distribution of Electrons at Room Temperature(T_1)

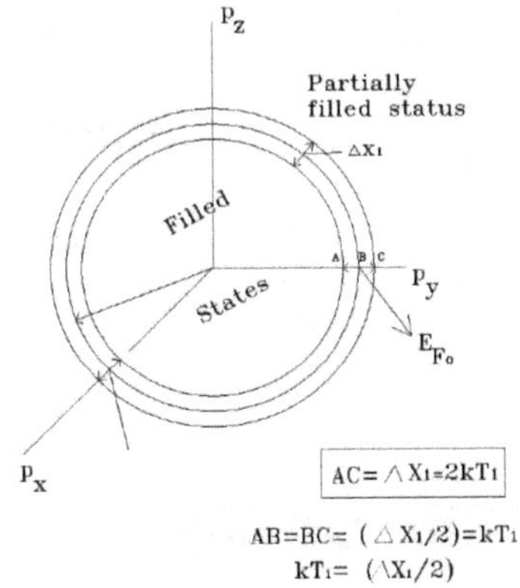

Fig.2.2(b) According to QFET – Distribution of Electrons at Room Temperature(T_1)

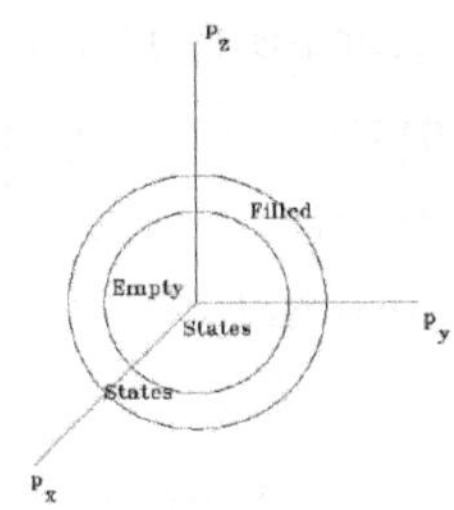

Fig. 2.3(a) According to CFET – Distribution of Electrons at T2 > Room Temperature (T1)

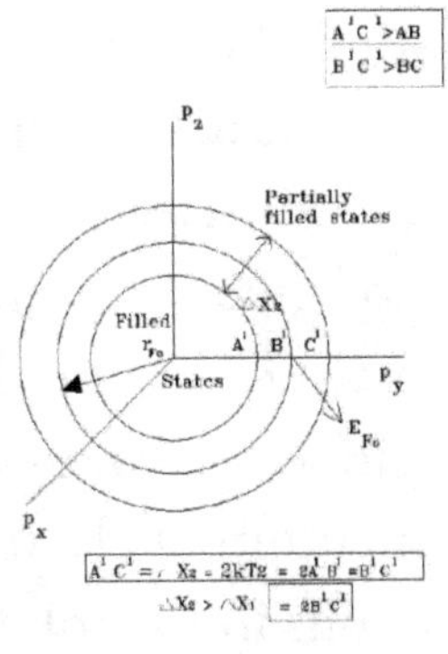

Fig. 2.3(b) According to QFET – Distribution of Electrons at T2 > Room Temperature (T1)

The sphere one obtains in the momentum diagram is called the FERMI SPHERE and its volume is given by

$$(4/3)(\pi)(p_m)^3$$

the and temperature corresponding to the Fermi energy is called FERMI TEMPERATURE.

$$E_F=k(T_F)$$

2.2.1 FERMI ENERGY

Consider a cubic solid of dimensions $L_{x,}$ L_y & L_z equal to L. The volume (V)of the solid is L x L x L = L^3. The maximum uncertainty in the position of an electron in the solid in x direction is L. The minimum uncertainty in momentum in the same direction is (h/L).Similarly in y and z directions. Total uncertainty in momentum is $(h/L)^3 = (h^3)/(V)$. In momentum diagram this uncertainty is represented as a cubic cell of side (h/L).The momentum vector starting from origin and ending inside this cell will represent the momentum value possessed by two electrons only due to Pauli exclusion principle. The two electrons can possess any of the momentum value falling inside this cell due to Heisenberg's uncertainty principle. Similarly there will be cells around the origin of the momentum diagram representing the momentum values of all the electrons (taken in pairs) in the cubic solid considered. All these uncertainty cells will have a volume of $(h/L)^3$. Assuming there are N_e electrons there will be $(N_e/2)$ cells representing the number of quantum states. Total volume will be $(N_e/2)[(h)^3/V]$. In the most general case they will form a sphere of radius p_{max} around the origin with a volume of $(4/3)(\pi)(p_{ma}x)^3$ where p_{max} is the maximum momentum of electrons corresponding to the highest energy of the electrons in the solid called Fermi energy E_F.

$$E_F=E_{max}=[(p_{max})^2/2m]=(3/\pi)^{2/3}(Ne/V)^{2/3}[(h)^2/(8m)]$$

Due to uncertainty energy can be considered as varying from zero to maximum continuously [(h/L) is extremely very small].The maximum energy of electrons in a solid E_F is a constant for a given metal. It does not depend on the size of the solid (volume) considered but on the ratio of (N_e/V).This a constant for a given metal. The values of E_F for some metals are listed in Table 2.1. The total energy of an assembly of N_e electrons in a metallic solid at absolute zero is equal to $(3/5)(N_e)(E_F)$. The mean (average) energy of one electron is about $(3/5)(E_F)$.

An increase in temperature will increase the energy of any and all the electrons without restriction in classical FET. In quantum FET only empty states can be occupied if available. Already completely filled states (2 electrons per state) cannot be occupied. Therefore electrons on the Fermi surface only can take part in the process as empty states are available for them. If temperature is T, the energy of electron with energy E_{F0} on Fermi surface at 0K will increase to E_{F0}+kT and this maximum energy becomes the new Fermi energy E_{FT}. The values of kT are listed in Table 2.2

Table 2.1 Fermi energy of metals

Metal	Ag	Al	Au	Be	Ca	Cs	Cu	K	Na	Li	Zn	Fe
Fermi energy(E_F)eV	5.5	11.8	5.5	12.0	3.0	1.6	7.0	1.9	3.2	4.7	11.0	4.7

Table 2.2 Variation of energy with temperature

T(K)	300	600	900	1200	2400	4800	6000
E(eV)	0.025	0.05	0.075	0.01	0.02	0.04	0.5

(E_F+kT) and(E_F-kT) will represent the bounding spherical surfaces of the energy values. Those electrons present within can occupy the empty states available. It will be difficult for an electron with energy less than (E_F-kT) to come to the Fermi surface at a temperature T. Therefore all the valence electrons will not participate in the process but only the Fermi electrons will. The Fermi electrons are only a small fraction of all the valence electrons.

2.2.2 FERMI DISTRIBUTION FUNCTION

Electrons are mathematically treated with Fermi-Dirac statistics and their distribution at a given temperature over various energy vales is given by the following function called the Fermi distribution function:

$$\mathbf{f(E)=(1)/\{EXP\{(E-E_F)/kt\}+[1]\}}$$

At absolute zero

$E < E_F$

$$f(E) = [1]/[(1/\infty)+1]$$

$$= 1$$

$E > E_F$

$$f(E) = (1/\infty)$$

$$= 0$$

$E = E_F$

$$f(E) = 1/[0+1]$$

$$=1$$

It is shown in Fig 2.4(a)

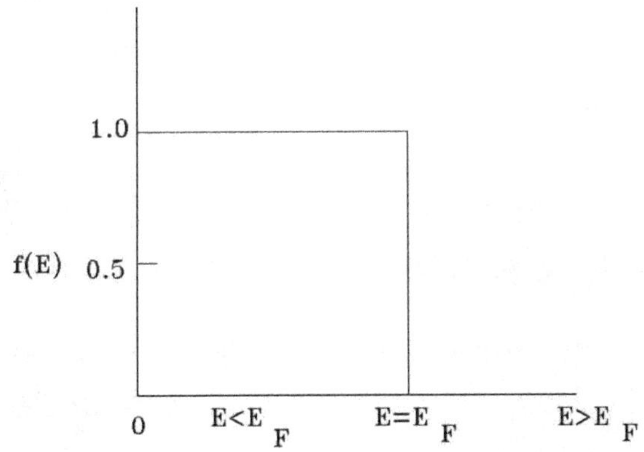

Fig. 2.4(a) Fermi Distribution Function Vs Energy at k

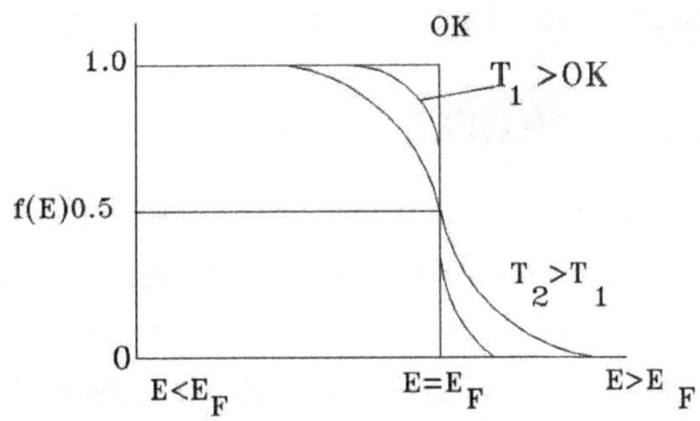

Fig. 2.4(b) Fermi Distribution Function Vs Energy at Diffrent Temptures

At a temperature T three cases can be considered as follows:

$E = E_F$

$$f(E) = (1)/(1)+(1)$$

$$= 0.5$$

$E >>>>> E_F$

$$f(E) = (1)/(\infty+1) = 0$$

$E <<<<< E_F$

$$f(E) = 1$$

The above variation of f(E) with energy at different temperatures is illustrated in Fig2.4(b)

2.2.3 SUCCESSES& FAILURES OF QFET

The quantum free electron theory was able to explain qualitatively and quantitatively the specific heat of metals, photoelectric effect, para and dia magnetism. It can explain electrical and thermal conductivity only qualitatively. It cannot explain ferro, ferri and anti ferro magnetism of materials. It was not also able to explain Super &Semi conduction of materials.

2.2.4 LIMITATIONS OF QFET

The periodic potential variation in the ionic lattice was not taken into consideration in the theory. The repulsion between the electrons in the sea of free electrons is not taken into account. The ion-electron, the electron-electron and the ion-ion interactions are totally neglected.

2 .2.5 DENSITY OF STATES IN QFET

The density of states of electrons is directly proportional to the square root of energy of electrons. The curve is parabolic as shown in Fig 2.5 where the energy is taken on the x-axis and density of states on they-axis. The area under the curve up to an energy E is the total number of states filled up to that energy. There will be two electrons per state and therefore total number of electrons will be twice the number of states. In a metal with a Fermi energy of $\mathbf{E}_{FO}$ at a temperature of absolute zero the density of states of electrons that will be filled is shown in Fig 2.6(a). The nature of the filled density of states at two other different temperatures is shown in Fig 2.6(b).

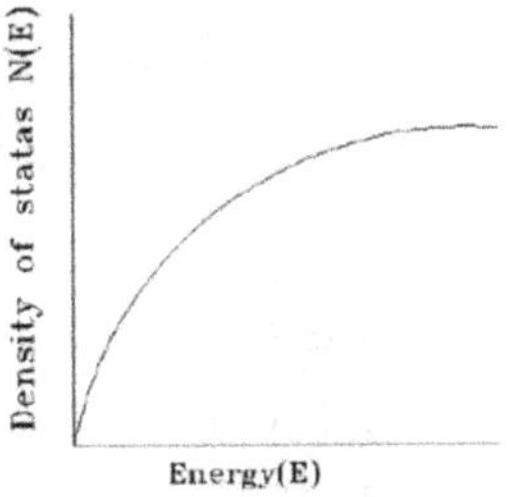

Fig2.5 Plot of Density of states N(E) against Energy (E)[Sctamatic]

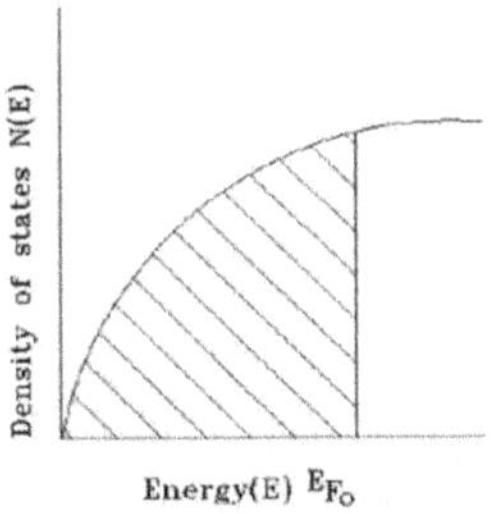

Fig2.6(a) Plot of Density of states in a metal with Fermi Energy E_{F_0} at OK

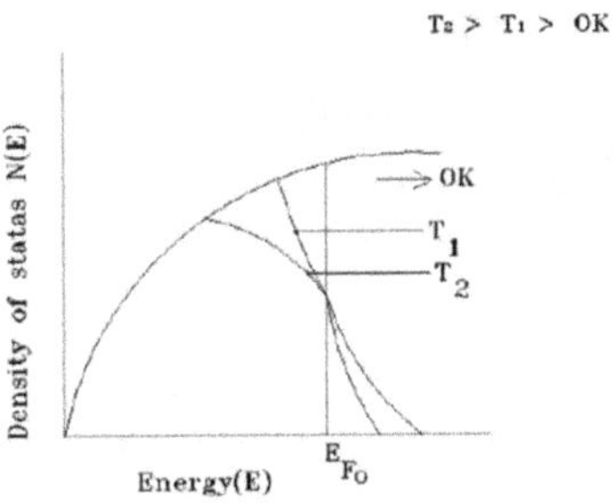

Fig2.6(b) Plot of Density of states in a metal with Fermi Energy E_{F_0} at three differant temperatures.

2.3 KRONIG-PENNEY MODEL

Kronig & Penney, two physicists attempted modeling and simulating the actual problem in metals. They considered the periodically varying potential in a metal and formulated their problem. The actual electron is neither totally free nor totally bound but existing between the two extremes. They assumed a potential well of depth V_0 and a breath 'a'. The thickness of the wall of the well is 'b'.The diameter of the ion (a+b) represents the inter atomic distance, i.e. the distance between the centres of two atoms in a metal. In this model the SCHRODINGRER'S wave equation should be satisfied in two different regions simultaneously, shown in Fig 2.7 as regions

I & II. Without going into complex mathematical equations the qualitative picture and results are summarized below. One can think of four possibilities in the metal. (1) Potential is infinite implying that the electro is very tightly bond (2) Potential is large meaning the electron is tightly bound (3) Potential is small indicating that the electron is loosely bound and (4) Potential is zero signaling that it is a free electron and not bound at all. In the first case energy levels in the metal are sharp as in Fig 2.8(a). In the second and third cases one get allowed and forbidden bands of energy values as in Figs 2.8(b) & (c).The width of allowed bands are large in the third case. In the last case for the free electron nothing is forbidden and it can possess any value. The energy varies continuously as in Fig 2.8(d).

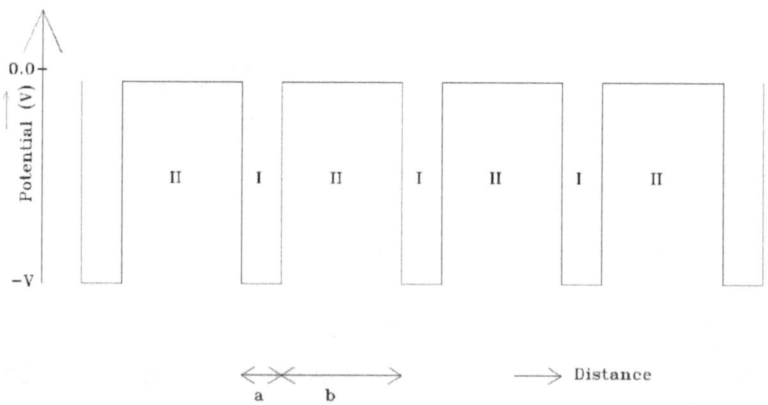

Fig2.7 Schematic of potertial against distance according to Kronig-Penney Model.

The model though less sophisticated in its over simplification of the periodically varying potential in a metal, brings out in its results the remarkable features that there are permitted and forbidden energy values for the electron. Also by varying the depth and breadth of the potential well and the width of the wall of the well one can fine tune the size of the metal atoms, the valence of the metal etc. that occur in reality. It makes quantification possibleas given below:

$$\mathbf{P = (mbaV_0)(2\pi/h)^2}$$

Where P is potential barrier strength

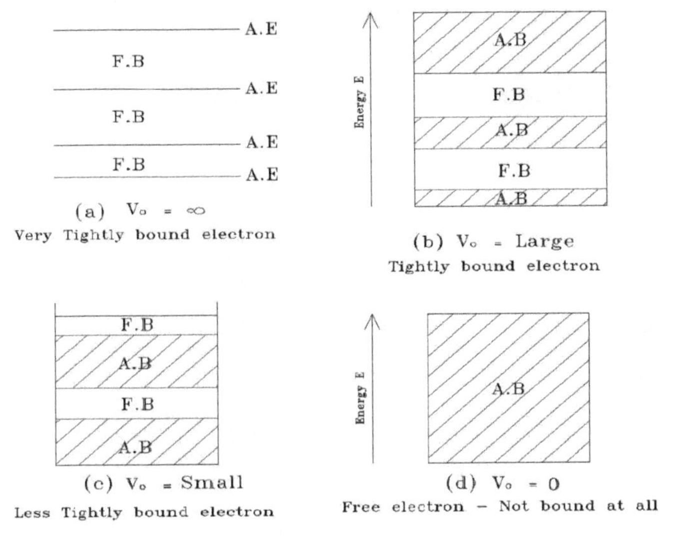

Fig.2.8 Four Special cases of K–P Model.

Semi quantification is possible between bonding of electrons to the lattice and size of the energy gap. For atoms that are more electronegative V_0 & P are large and allowed bands are narrow while forbidden bands are wider. An empirical relationship exists between energy gap and electro negativity of constituent atoms of the solid. It is shown as follows:

$$\mathbf{E_g=(-15)+3.75[\sqrt{(X_A-17.5)}]+[\sqrt{(X_B-17.5)}]}$$

where X_A & X_B are electro negativities of atoms A & B in the solid.

The K-P model is one among many and is successful in describing the properties of solids in an elegant way .But it is not quite accurate.

2.4 REAL SOLIDS

In a real solid (metal) the variation of potential is not what is assumed in the K-P model. It is as shown in Fig 2.9 (a) & (b) for mono valent and multi valent metals. The potential is given below where e is charge [protons in nucleus and electrons in valence orbit] and r is distance between charges [here electron and nucleus] and Z is valence.

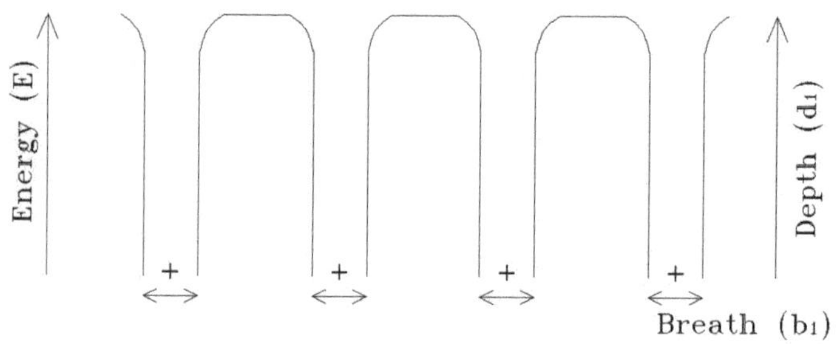

Fig2.9(a) Mono valent Metal – narrow and shallow potential well

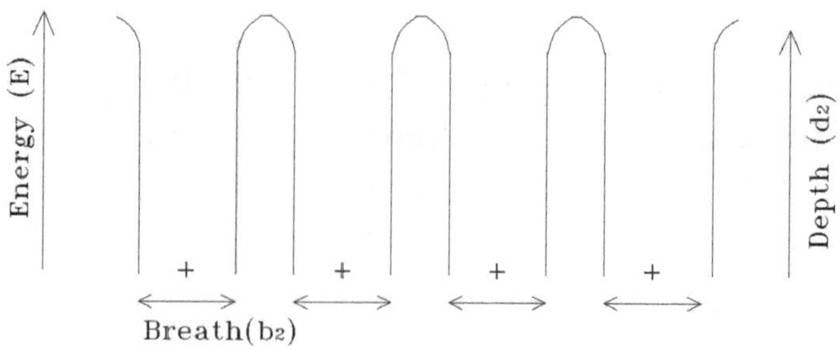

Fig.2.9(b) Multi valent Metal – Broad and Deeper potential well [$b_2 >> b_1$ & $d_2 >> d_1$]

$$V=-[Z(e)^2/(r)^2]$$

In a monovalent metal the potential well is narrow and shallow. In multivalent metals it is broad and deep. It depends on the atomic number also. The actual situation can be imagined from the Figs 2.10(a)(b)(c) & (d)) drawn schematically for illustration. The first one is for a solid with low atomic number and low valence. The second one is for a solid with high atomic number and low valence. The third is for a solid with low atomic number and high valence and the fourth is for a solid with high atomic number and high valence. Fig 2.11(a) & (b) show the width of allowed and forbidden bands in mono and multivalent solids .In a monovalent metal the energy barrier is small in contrast to a multivalent metal. In the latter the attractive force of the ionized atom and valence electron is large causing deeper energy well. It is broader also due to size of atom being large. The forbidden bands are wider and allowed bands are narrower in multivalent metals compared to monovalent metals.

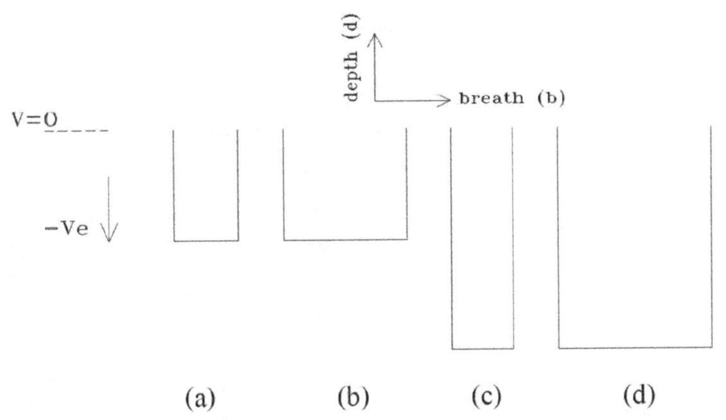

Fig.2.10 potential well (a) b and d small

(b) b small & d more

(c) b more & d small

(d) b more & d more

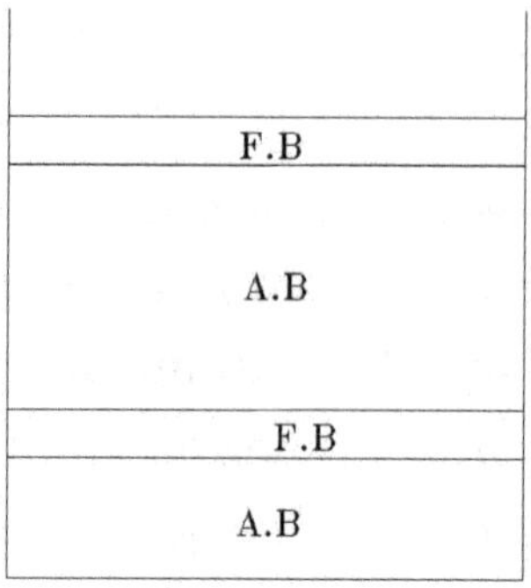

Fig.2.11(a) Mono valent Metal – Forbidden energy bands are narrow

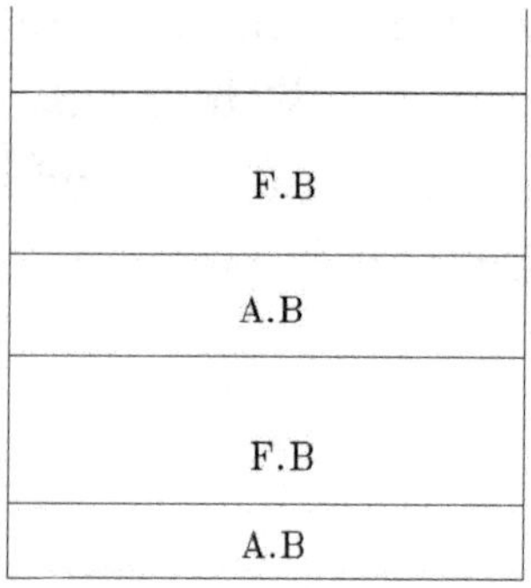

Fig.2.11(b) Multi valent Metal – Forbidden energy bands are broader

3

BRILLUOIN ZONE THEORY

3.1 INTRODUCTION

Inside a metal there is a periodic repetitive arrangement of positively charged ions through which the valence electrons move. It is illustrated in a 2D hypothetical metal as shown in Fig 3.1. Cosequently the potential across a straight row of atoms varies as shown in Fig 3.2. Movement of electrons in a crystal cannot happen under certain conditions. This can be pictured very elegantly by considering the matter waves associated with moving electrons .These waves undergo diffraction and are bound by Bragg's condition of diffraction given by $n\lambda = 2d\ Sin\theta$.This implies that in the present case when wavelength associated with electrons is equal to ($2d\ Sin\theta/n$) electrons cannot proceed further in the same direction but will be diffracted. Thus electrons moving in a specific directions with certain energies will be prevented from moving in the same direction of its original movement. This implies that certain energies are not allowed (forbidden) due to internal diffraction (reflection). The momentum of the electrons is given by $p= (nh\ /2dSin\theta)$. And the wave number associated with the electron is given by $k = (n\pi\ /d\ Sin\ (\theta))$ k is a vector. It has the same direction as the direction of movement of the electron.

k (Sin θ) is the

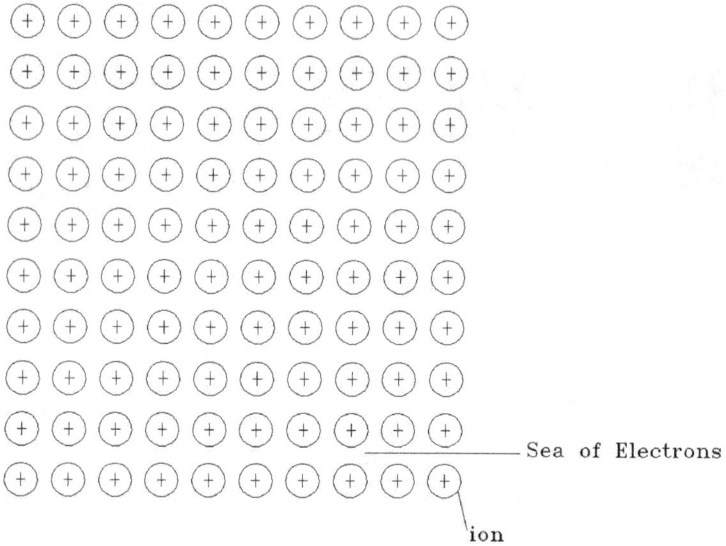

Fig.3.1 Arrangement of ions and sea of electrons in 2D Metals

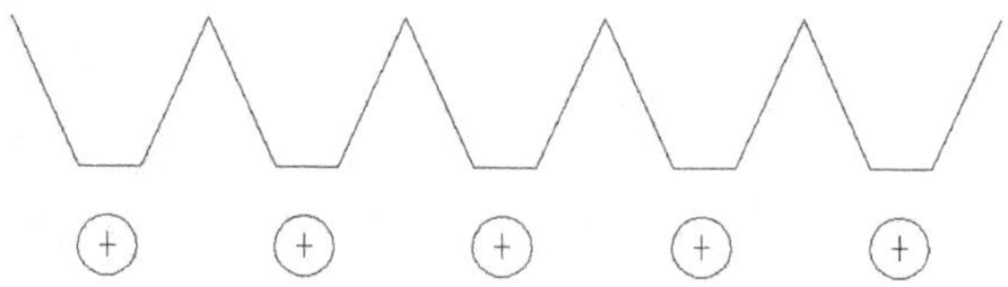

Fig.3.2 Variation of electro static potential along a row of ions in a metal

X-component of the k vectors shown in Fig 3.3(a) and θ is the angle of inclination of the diffracting atom plane of a crystal as shown by various possibilities of diffraction in Fig 3.3(b). k_x is the X component and is normal to the plane AB and k varies inversely with the inter planar spacing d. First crystallographic planes to diffract electrons will have large d values and therefore the lowest Miller indices (hkl).

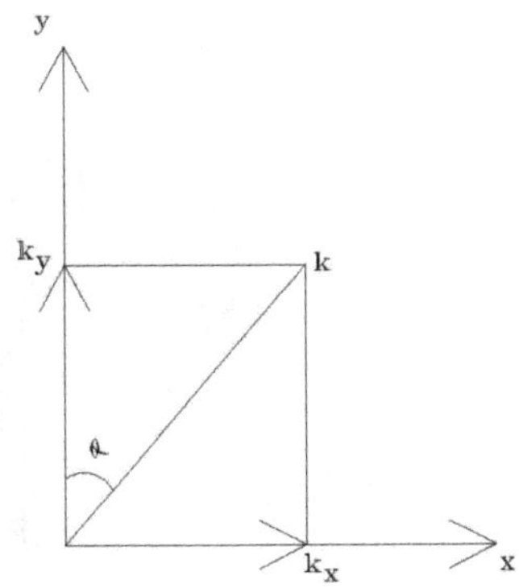

$$k = \sqrt{k_x^2 + k_y^2}$$

$$k_x = k \sin\theta$$

$$k_y = k \cos\theta$$

Fig.3.3(a) Vector 'k'

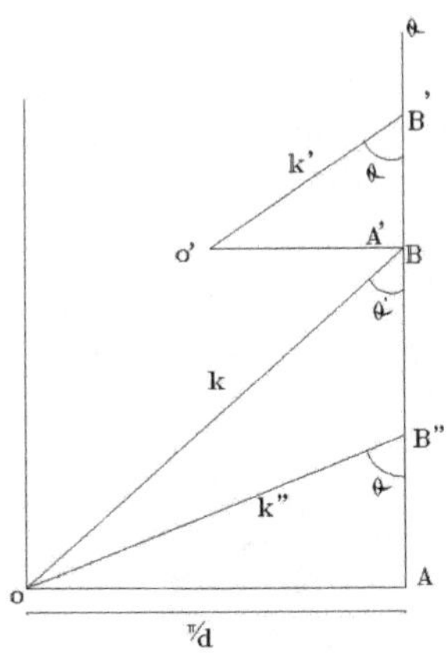

(i) $OB = K \sin\theta = \pi/d$ Diffraction occurs

(ii) $O'B' = k' \sin\theta' \neq \pi/d$ No Diffraction occurs

(iii) $OB'' = k'' \sin\theta'' = \pi/d$ Diffraction occurs

Fig.3.3(b) DIffraction Condition

3.2 THEORY

Consider a square lattice in 2D as shown in Fig 3.4(a). Diffraction will occur first from (100) planes. Electrons with very low energy will have very small values of k and can go unhindered in the lattice over long distances as the energy of electron becomes higher and higher. At some value k will be sufficiently high to make the electrons undergo diffraction.

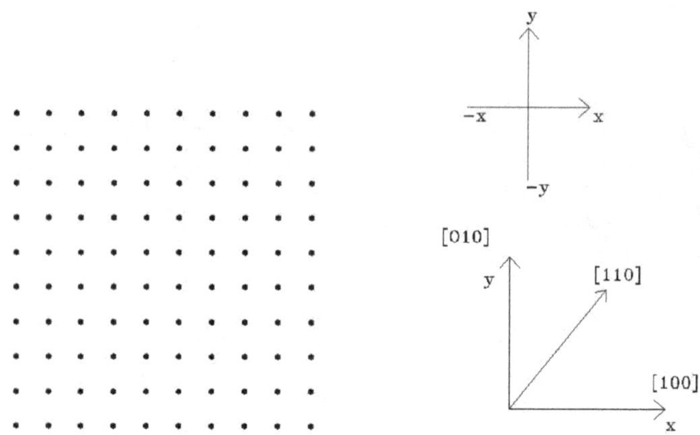

Fig.3.4(a) 2D Square lattice

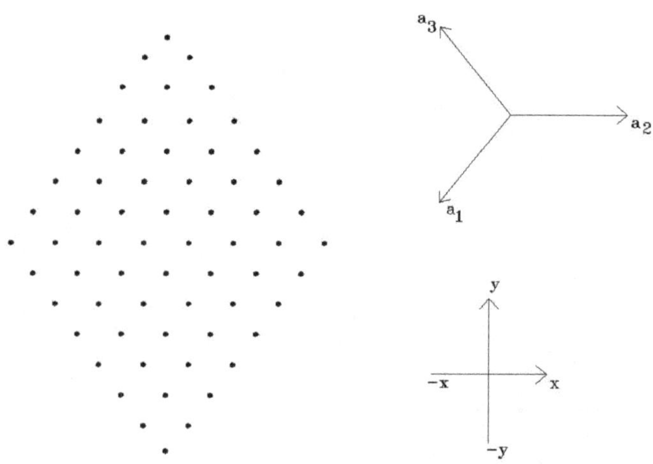

Fig.3.4(b) 2D Hexagonal lattice

3.2.1 SQUARE LATTICE

Consider a 2D k space with the axes as k_x and k_y. A wave vector k in this space will have two components. In the 2 Dlattice, vertical planes have (100), horizontal planes (010) and planes inclined at 45^0 to the two (110) as Miller indices. Consider an electron moving in the horizontal direction. It will be inclined at 90⁰ to (100).The condition for diffraction is as follows:

$$k= (\pi)/(d_{100})$$

When an electron moving in X direction possesses a wave vector value k_x=(π)/(d) diffraction will occur and will be pushed back. Therefore energy corresponding to this wave vector will be forbidden. Similarly for the negative horizontal direction k_x= - (π)/(d) is not allowed. Similarly in the positive and negative Y direction k_y= k= (π)/(d_{010}). d for(100) and (010) planes is nothing but the lattice parameter a. Therefore in k space one gets a square as shown in Fig 3.5(a) as the boundary delineating the allowed from the disallowed energy values. The region inside this boundary is called First Brillouin zone. All wave vectors falling inside the square and their corresponding energies can be possessed by electrons and they will move freely in the square lattice of Fig3.4 without any obstruction whatsoever. The corner points of the region in k space can be obtained by considering electron movement at 45^0 to k_x and k_y direction. Consider an electron moving in X direction. It will be inclined at 45^0 to the (110) plane. The condition for diffraction will be kSin(45)= (π)/(d_{110}).

d_{100} is equal to 'a' and d_{110} is equal to (a)($\sqrt{2}$). Therefore k becomes equal to2(π)/(a).

Similarly an electron moving at equal angles to horizontal and vertical directions will be inclined at 90 degrees to (110) plane and the condition for diffraction is as follows:

$$k= (\sqrt{2})\ (\pi)/(d_{100})= (\sqrt{2})\ (\pi)/(a)$$

This can be extended to all the other directions and quadrants. The forbidden boundary will be as shown in Fig 3.5(b). The region inside this boundary and outside the I zone is called the Second

Brilluoin zone. Fig 3.5(c) shows the third Brillouin zone for a square lattice. In Fig 3.5(d) the I, II & III zones are shown superposed.

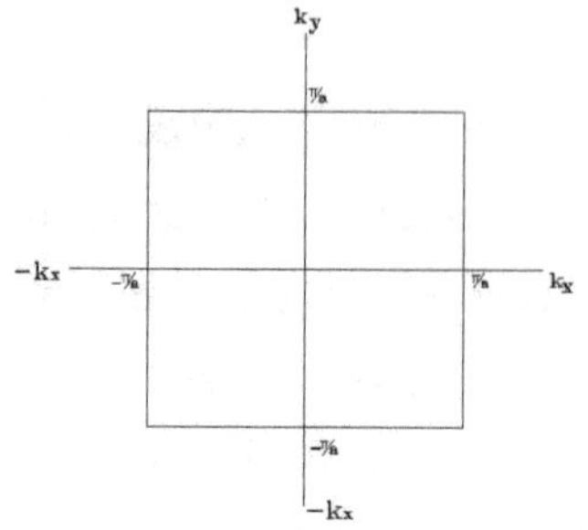

Fig.3.5(a) First Brillouin Zone Boundary

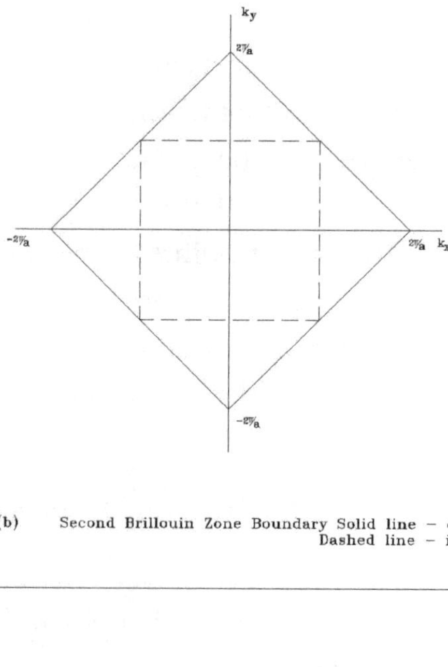

Fig.3.5(b) Second Brillouin Zone Boundary Solid line – outer Boundary
Dashed line – inner Boundary

3.2.2 HEXAGONAL LATTICE

A 2D hexagonal lattice is shown in Fig 3.4(b). In the type I diagonal direction diffraction will occur at k=(π)/(a) and in type II diagonal direction at k = (2π)/(√3a). The forbidden boundary will be a hexagon in k space but will be rotated by 30 degrees to the 2Dhexagonal lattice in normal space. Figs 3.6 (a) (b) & (c) show the I, II& III

Brillouin zones for the above lattice and in Fig3.6(d) all the three are shown superposed . The 2D lattice in normal Cartesian coordinate space and the I Brillouin zone in wave number space are shown for the square and hexagonal cases in Figs 3.7(a)&(b)and3.8(a)&(b) respectively.

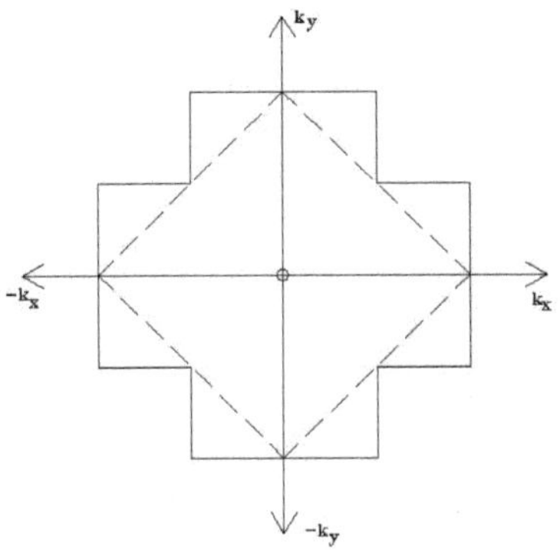

Fig.3.5(c) Third Brillouin Zone Boundary
Solid line – outer Boundary
Dashed line – inner Boundary

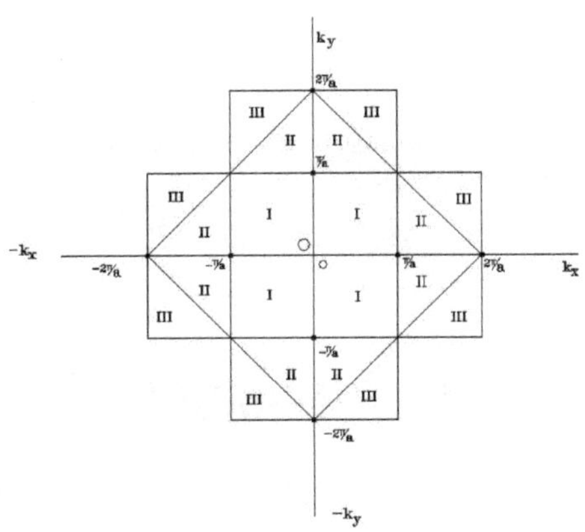

Fig.3.5(d) First Three Brillouin Zones
for a square lattice of side 'a'

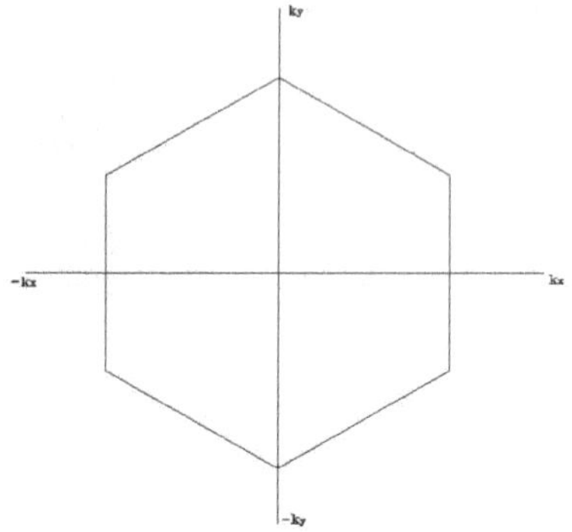

Fig.3.6(a) First Brillouin Zone boundary for 2D Hexagonal lattice

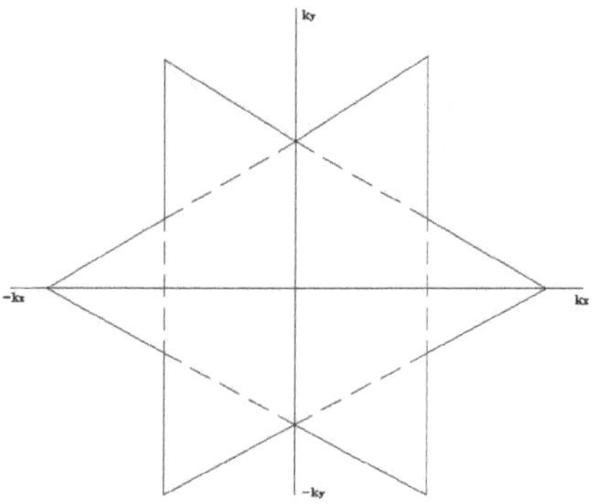

Fig.3.6(b) Second Brillouin Zone boundary for 2D Hexagonal lattice
Solid line – outer Boundary
Dashed line – inner Boundary

3.3 ENERGY AND WAVENUMBER

The allowed and forbidden energy bands can be best understood by plotting energy against wave number. Assume that electrons are moving in the X- direction in a square lattice. k_x will be increasing and k_y will remain zero. As k_x increases, energy will increase but it will not be continuous. At $k_x = (\pi)/(a), (2\pi)/(a),(3\pi)/(a)$...there will be breaks in the curve. Similarly in the negative X-direction also breaks will occur. At the wavelengths corresponding to these points electrons get diffracted and energy values are given by the following equation:

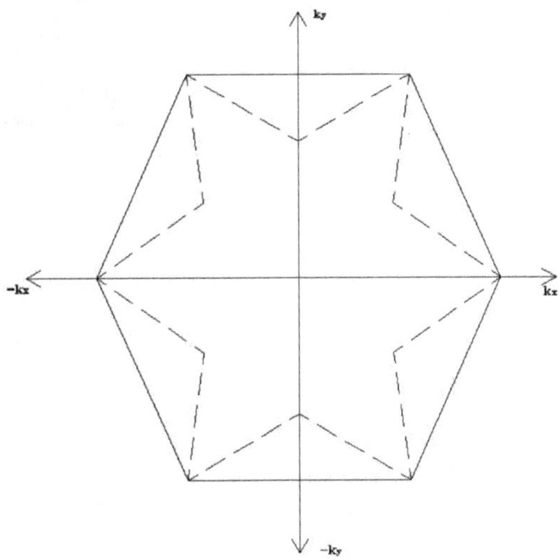

Fig.3.6(c) Third Brillouin Zone boundary for 2D Hexagonal lattice

Solid line – outer Boundary
Dashed line – inner Boundary

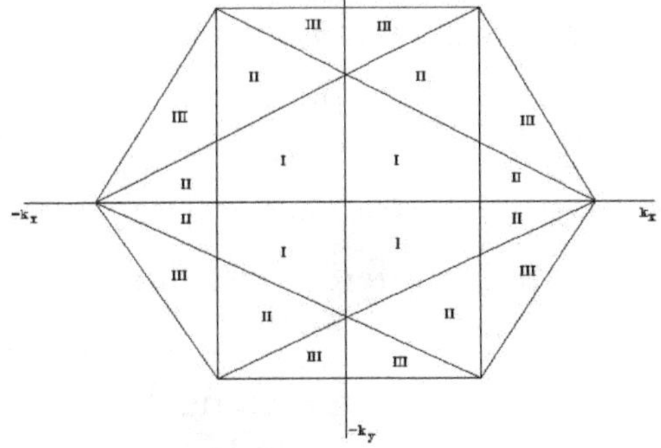

Fig.3.6(d) First Three Brillouin Zone boundaries of a 2D Hexagonal lattice

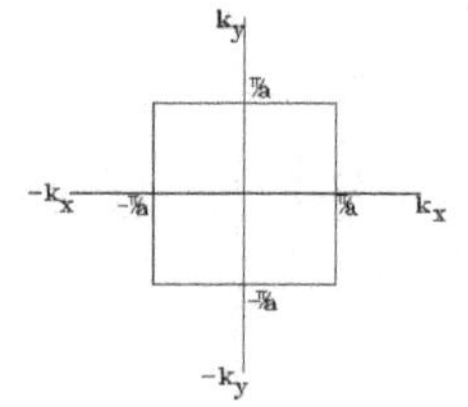

Fig.3.7(a) Brillouin Zone in 'k' space for square lattice of side 'a'

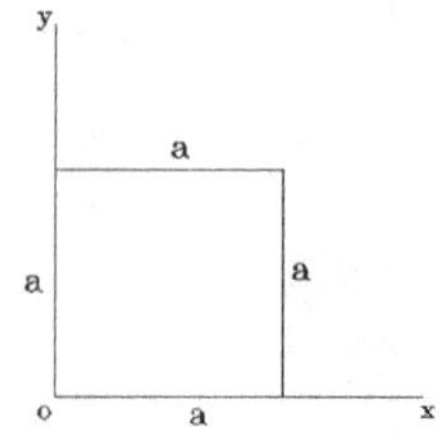

Fig.3.7(b) Square lattica of side 'a' in cartesian co-ordinate real space.

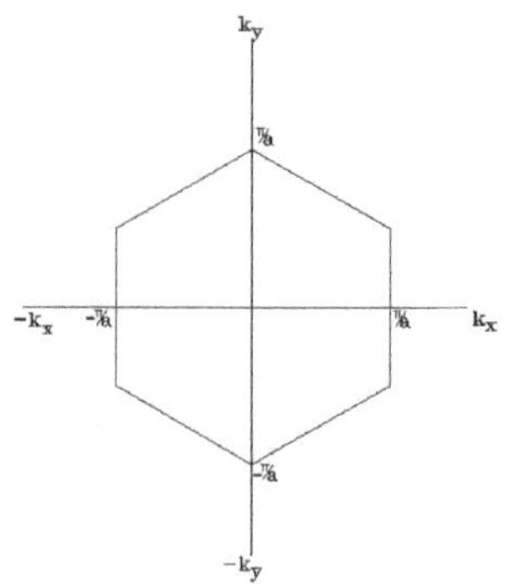

Fig.3.8(a) Brillouin Zone in 'k' space of a hexagonal lattice of side 'a'

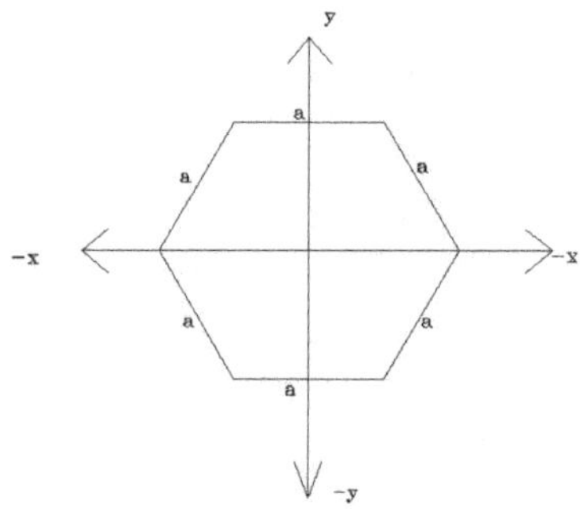

Fig.3.8(b) Hexagonal lattica of side 'a' in cartesian co-ordinate real space

$$\mathbf{E=(n)(h^2)(\pm k_x)^2/\ 8(\pi^2)(m)}$$

and are forbidden where n is an integer This is unlike the QFET where the curve is continuous. The curves for QFET & BZT are shown schematically in figs 3.9 (a) & (b). In the I zone itself depending on the direction of movement of electron even though k_x may be same, k can be different. Assume that one electron is moving ina direction inclined at 22.5^0, a second one in a direction inclined at 45^0 and a third electron along X-axis direction as seen from Fig3.10(a).The energy in the three cases will be different. At $k_x=(\pi)/(a)$ $k_{45}{}^0 > k_{22.5}{}^0 > k_0$and $E_{45} > E_{22.5} > E_0$. This gives rise to a Evs k_x curve as shown in Fig 3.10(b). This gives rise to several interesting situations as discussed below: CASE1: The highest energy in Izone may be less than the lowest energy in the II zone. Therefore an energy gap is present. CASE2: The highest energy in I zone is more than the lowest energy in II zone .i.e. An overlap occurs and no gap in energy value is present. It is continuous. In the first case three possibilities exist namely that the energy gap is large and insurmountable for the electrons, small and surmountable by thermal means and medium and bridgeable with dopant energy levels. All these are illustrated in Figs 3.11 (a) (b) & (c).

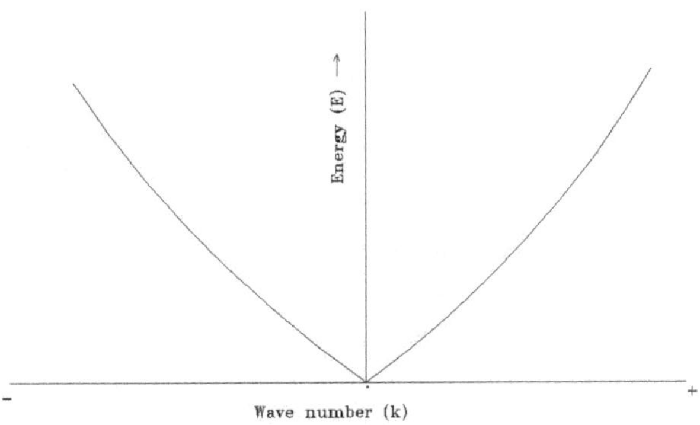

Fig.3.9(a) Plot of Energy against wavenumber according to QFET

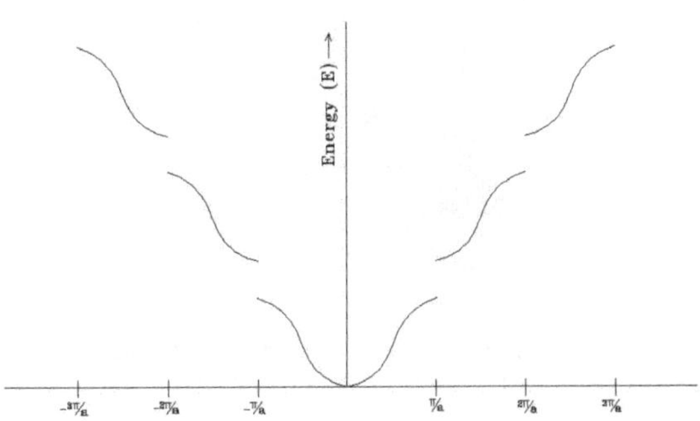

Fig.3.9(b) Plot of Energy against wavenumber according to BZT

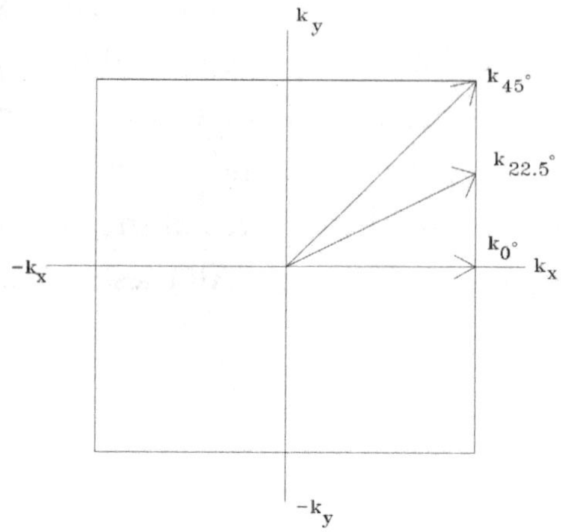

Fig.3.10(a) Maximum Wave number vector in three different directions in the first Brillouin zone of a square lattice

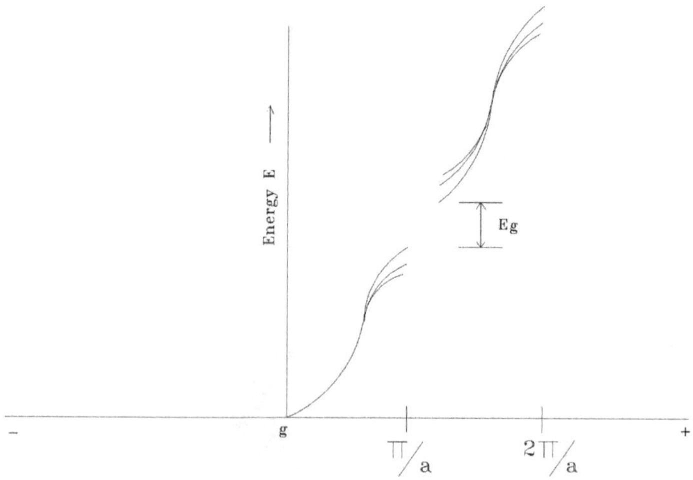

Fig.3.10(b) Variation of Energy with Wave number vector resolved in x direction (k_x)

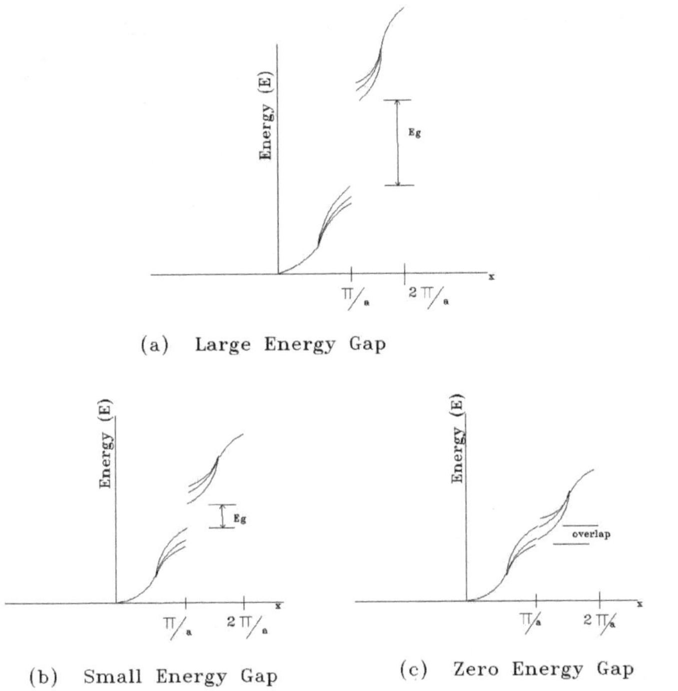

Fig.3.11 Plot of Energy against resolved Wave number vector k_x in x direction with different energy gaps.

3.4 FERMI CIRCLE AND BRILLUOIN ZONE

In k space the first Brilluoin zone of a square lattice of side 'a' in cartesian space is a square of side = (2π)/(a). One can superpose Femi circles of different diameter corresponding to maximum energy on this. As shown in Figs 3.12(a) (b) (c) & (d). It is possible because momentum (p) and wave number (k) are directly proportional and energy is proportional directly to the square of momentum. Additional situations are shown in Fig 3.13 (a) & (b) considering the II zone also. Fig 3.13 (c) shows the II zone hatched and all possible wave number vectors that start from the origin fall within this region comprising the permitted energies in the II zone. It is a rhombus of side = (4π)/(a) in k space. The largest Fermi circle inscribing this rhombus has a radius =(√2π)/(a).The biggest Fermi circle circumscribes and touches the four corners of the rhombus has a radius= (2π)/(a).

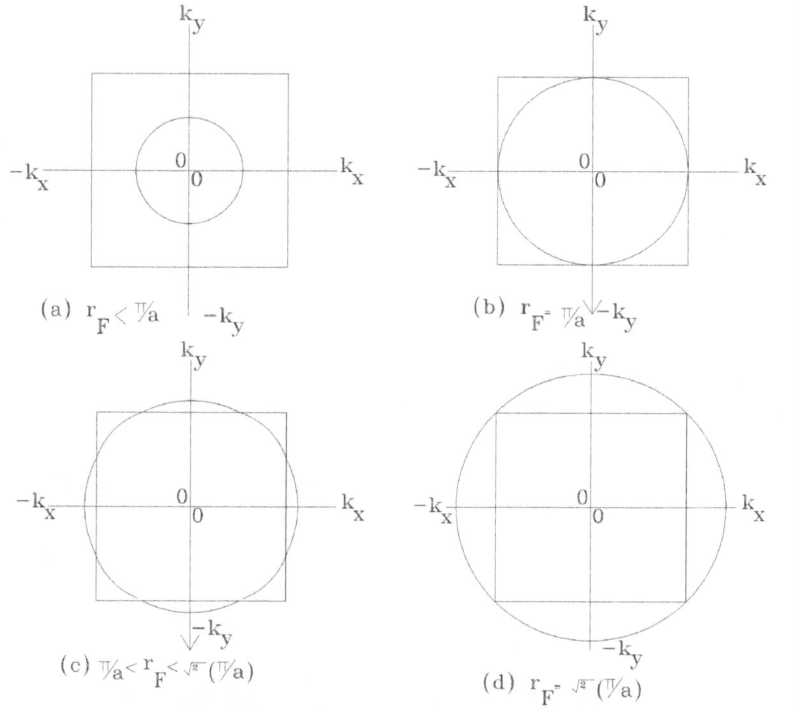

Fig.3.12 I Brillouin Zone of a square lattice and Fermi cicle of different radi r_F superimposed on it.

3.5 DENSITY OF STATES FOR 2D SQUARE LATTICE

In BZT the density of states when plotted against energy does not continuously increase .It increases steadily in the beginning, reaches a peak and then drops down drastically to zero. This can be explained with Fig 3.14(a) in which bigger and bigger Fermi circles are drawn

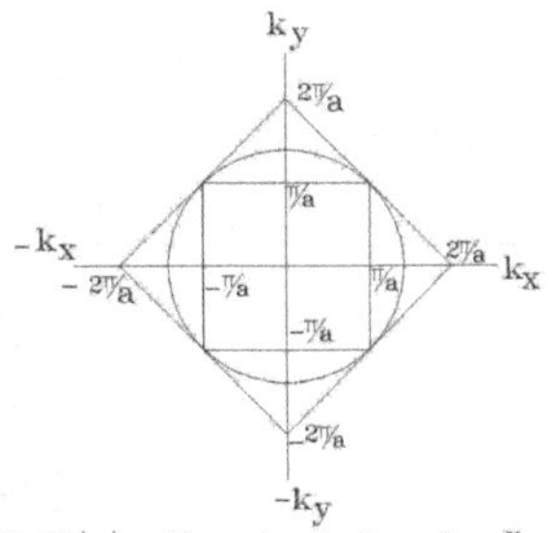

Fig.3.13(a) Fermi circle of $r_F = \sqrt{2}(\pi/a)$ inscribed in II BZ and circumscribed in I BZ

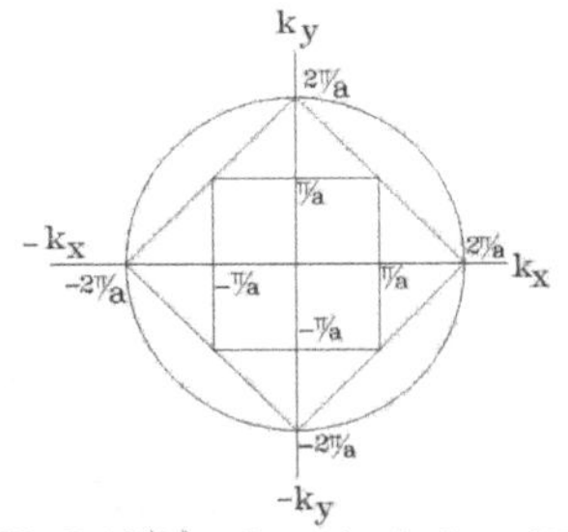

Fig.3.13(b) Fermi circle of $r_F = 2\pi/a$ circumscribing II BZ

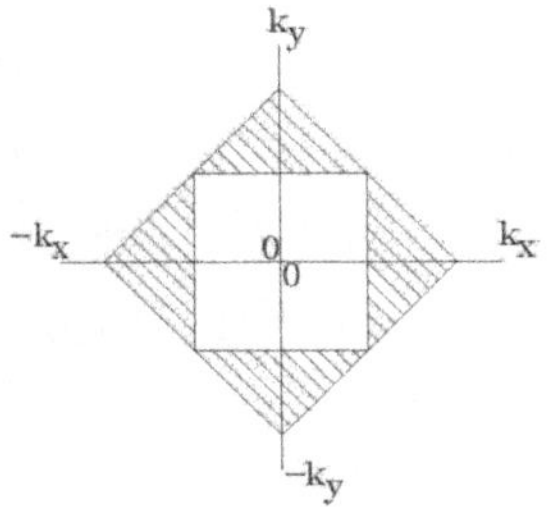

Fig.3.13(c) Allowed wave number vectors in II BZ shown hatched

over the I Brillouin zone. Obviously as the radius of the circle increases the number of electrons inside increases and the energy also increases. This is so only up to the Fermi circle inscribing the I zone. Afterwards even though circles become bigger large part of them lie outside the I zone. The available states increase and reach a maximum number when the Fermi circle just touches the zone boundary tangentially and afterwards decrease rapidly. Just when the Fermi circle touches only the four corners of the I zone the density of states reach their minimum number and drops to zero immediately thereafter. Fig 3.14(a) shows the ideal case. Actually as the Fermi circles reach the zone boundary they get distorted and develop curvatures as shown in Fig 3.14(b). Fig 3.14(c) shows a schematic density of states curve (Y-axis) plotted against energy (X-axis).Figs

3.15(a)(b)(c)&(d)show the geometric points of density of curve and Fermi circle corresponding to the filling of the I Brillouin zone with electrons of higher and higher energies schematically. The peak (A) in the curve of Fig 3.15(a) corresponds to the Fermi circle just touching the zone boundary. The region OACO corresponds to the filling up of the I zone up to the peak as hatched in Fig 3.15(b) and the region ACBA corresponds to the filling of I zone as shown hatched in Fig 3.15(c)The end point (B)in the curve corresponds to the maximum energy of electron in I zone the four corners of the square zone. The region OABO corresponds to the complete filling of the I zone as seen hatched in Fig 3.15(d). The point O in the curve corresponds to the central point of the square zone which is the origin of the k space. The maximum energy in the first zone is the energy corresponding to the peak in the second zone for the square lattice in 2D.

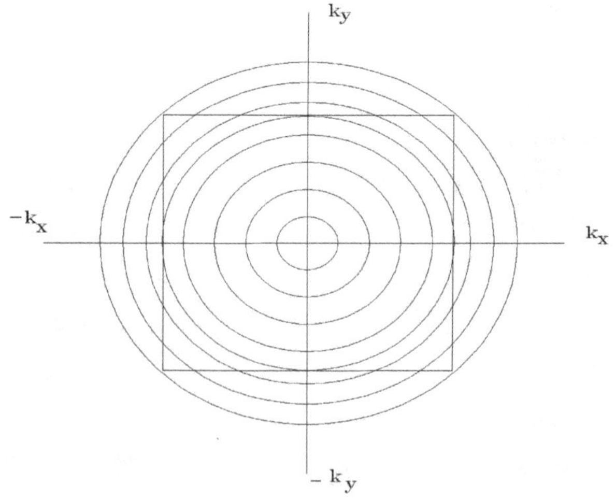

Fig.3.14 (a) Fermi circle of increasing radius r_F superposed on I BZ in 'k' space – Ideal case

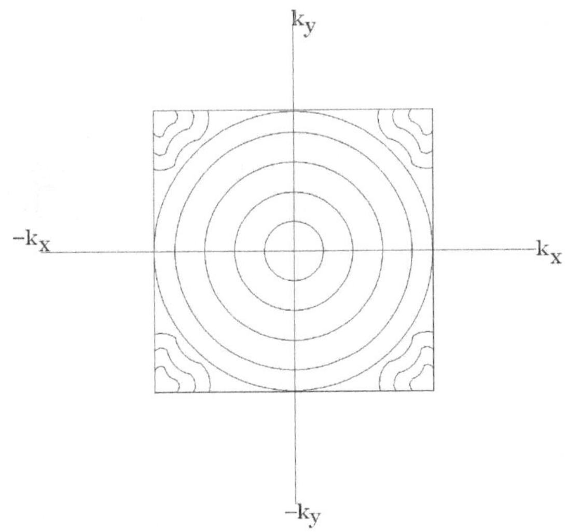

Fig.3.14 (b) Fermi circle of increasing radius superposed on I BZ in k space – Actual case [observe the distortions near zone boundary]

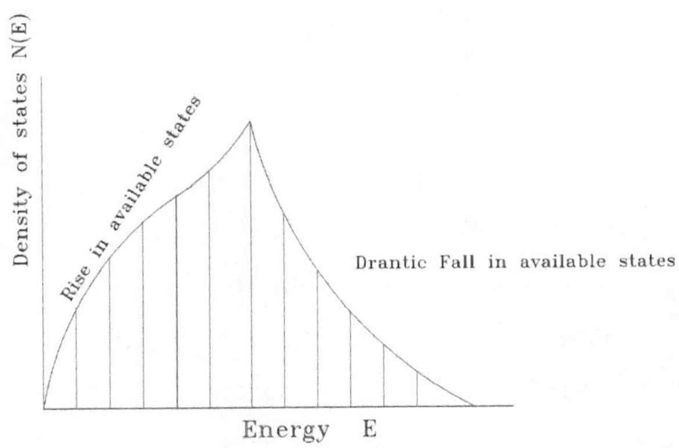

Fig.3.14 (c) The shape of Density of states curve against Energy corresponding to Fig.3.14(b)

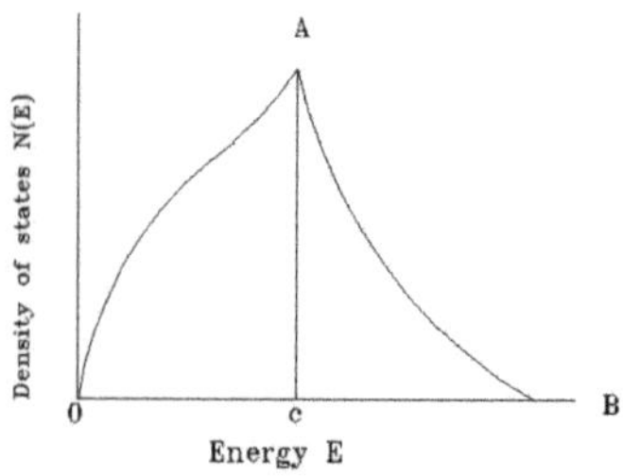

Fig.3.15 (a) Density of states against energy as given by BZT

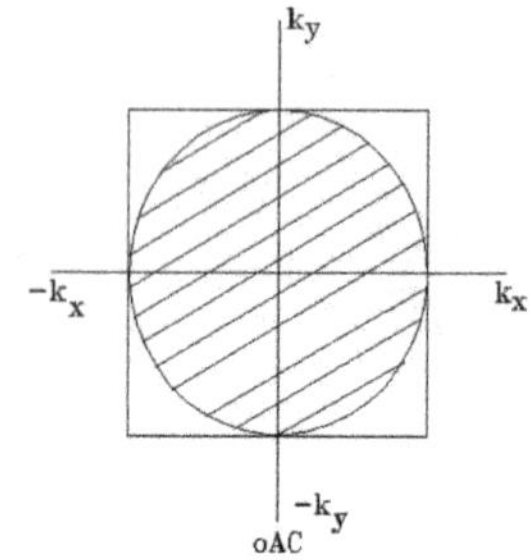

Fig.3.15 (b) Area of OACO corresponds to Fermi Circle just touching BZ boundary shown hatched.

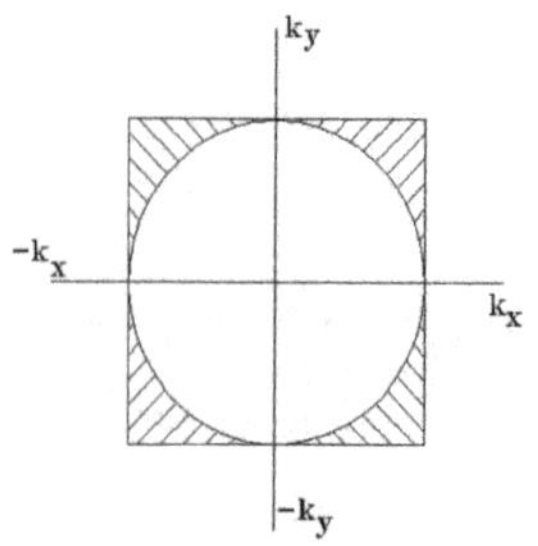

Fig.3.15 (c) Area of ABCA corresponding Fermi Circle first touching BZ Boundary shown hatched.

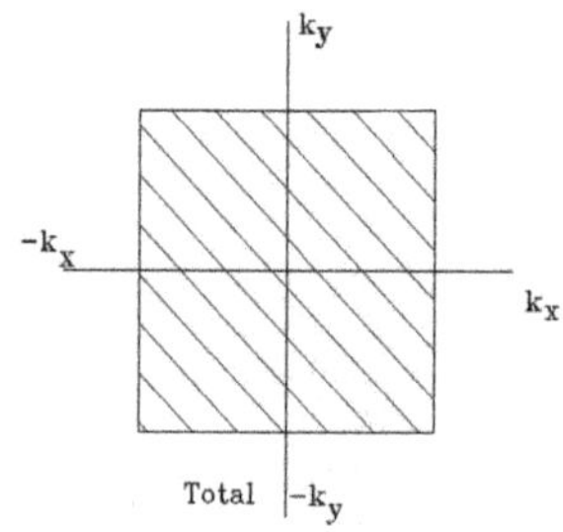

Fig.3.15 (d) Area of OABO corresponding to complete filling of BZ (shown hatched)

The various possibilities of densities of curve are shown in Figs 3.16(a)(b)(c)(d)(e)and(f).If there are two types of faces in the Brillouin zone there will be two peaks in the density of states vs. energy curve and if there are two types of corners in the former there will be two kinks in the later. There are as many peaks in the curve as there are types of faces in the zone and as many kinks in the curve as there are types of corners in the zone.

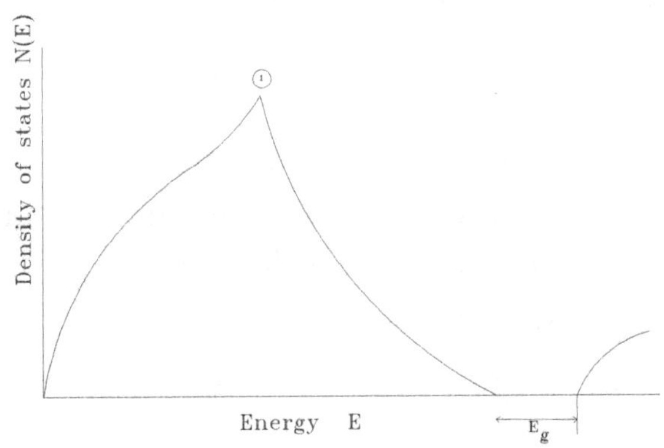

Fig3.16(a) I Brillouin Zone has one type of face only in k space

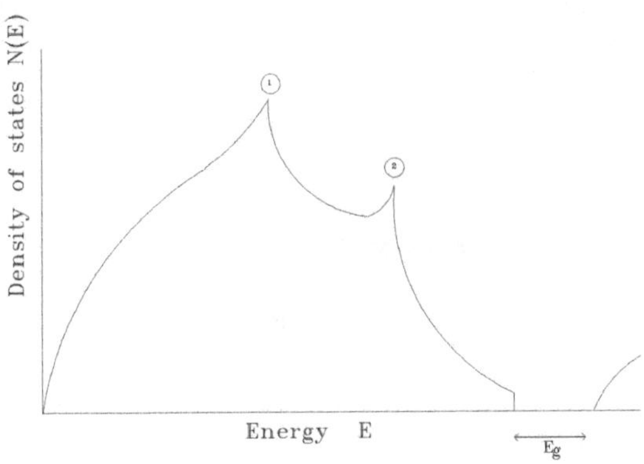

Fig3.16 (b) I Brillouin Zone has two types of faces in k space

3.6 BRILLUOIN ZONE IN 3D LATTICE

3.6.1 CUBIC METALS AND SOLID CRYSTALS

The boundary of the Brillouin zones can be established quickly and elegantly using diffraction conditions for electrons which is the same as that for X-rays. In a simple cubic crystal all planes will give rise to diffraction. The sum of the squares of the indices should be 1,2,3,4,5,6,7,8,9…etc In a face centered cubic crystal all the indices should be odd or even. The sum of the square of the indices should be 3,4,8,11,12…..etc. In body centered cubic crystal the sum of the squares of the indices should be even..2,4,6,8,10,12,14,16,18…..In diamond cubic crystal the sum of the squares of the indices should be 3,8,11,16… etc. (i.e. the (hkl) values should all be odd or if all even should be divisible by four)

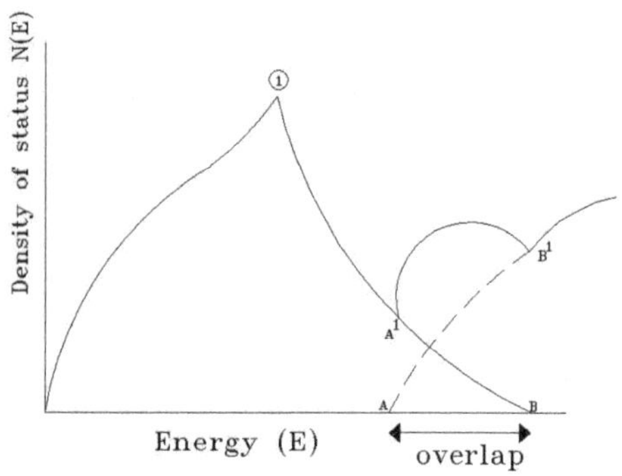

Fig.3.16 (c) One type of face in I Brillouin Zone in k space and a overlap of I & II zones in energy values

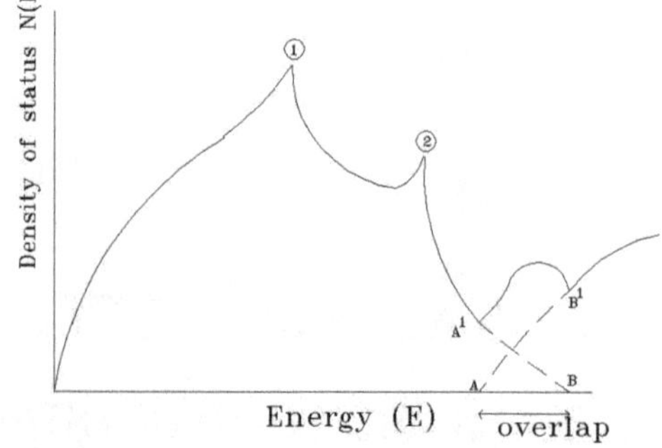

Fig.3.16 (d) Two types of faces in I Brillouin Zone in k space and a overlap of I & II zones in energy values

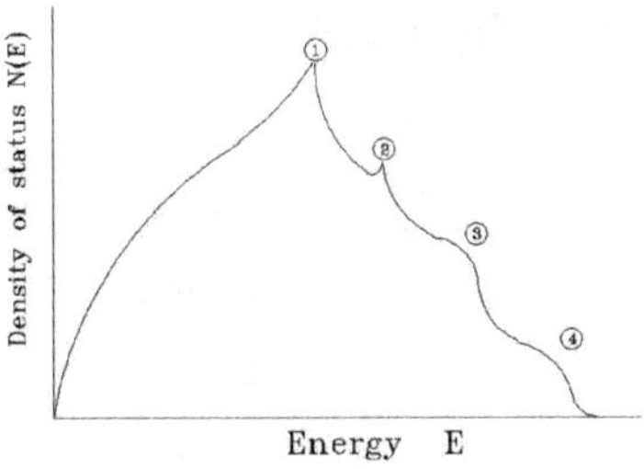

Fig.3.16(e) Two types of faces ① & ② and two types of corners ③ & ④ in I Brillouin Zone in k space

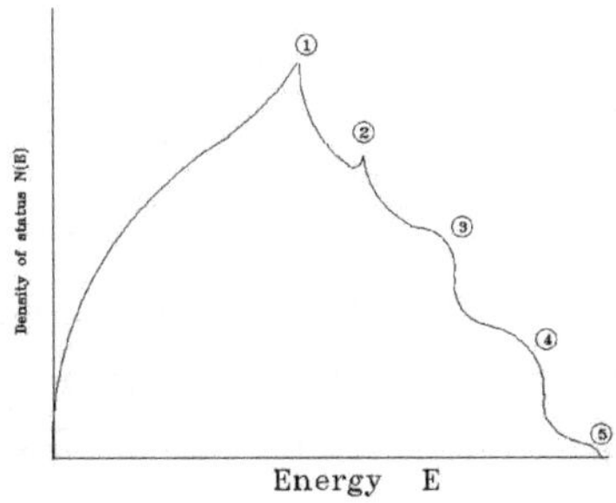

Fig.3.16(f) Two types of faces ① & ② and three types of corners ③ , ④ & ⑤ in I Brillouin Zone in k space

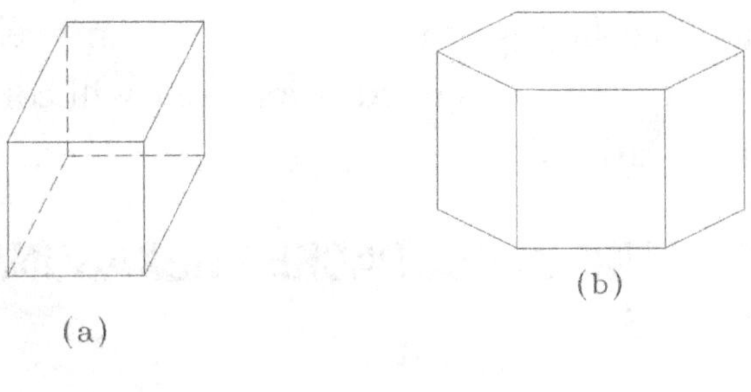

Fig.3.17 Brillouin Zone for (a) Simple Cubic & (b) Simple Hexagonal lattices

Therefore in a simple cubic crystal six (100) planes will diffract the electrons first and the first zone will be a cube of side 2 (π /a) and equidistant from the origin in k-space. The peak in the density of state curve will occur at an electron to atom ratio of 1.05.In a body centered cubic crystal twelve (110) planes will first diffract electrons and the first zone will be a Dodecahedron with all its 12 faces equidistant from the origin in k-space. The peak in the density of states curve will occur at an electron to atom ratio of 1.48.In face centered cubic crystal first the eight (111) planes will diffract the electrons and the Fermi sphere will touch first these zone boundaries corresponding to these planes. They will form the eight hexagonal faces of the zone. Then the six (200) planes will diffract and this will give rise to the six square faces of the first zone.The first zone will contain fourteen faces as its boundary and the shape will be a truncated octahedron. There will be two peaks in the density of states curve one at an electron to atom ratio of 1.36 and another at a ratio of 1.88. The shapes of the zone for the three types of cubic crystals are shown in Figs 3.17(a),3.18 (A) &(B).In all these cases when the I zone is completely filled electron to atom ratio will be 2.0.The I zone is called the valence zone and the next zone is called the conduction zone.In diamond cubic crystals the I zone will be truncated octahedron like FCC as it is considered as rwo interpenetrating FCC lattices. Silicon and Gallium Arsenide are two important materials falling in this class. In the unit cell there will be 8 atoms and the I zone when filled completely will correspond to an electron to atom ratio of 4.0.

3.6.2 SIMPLE AND CLOSE PACKED HEXAGONAL CRYSTALS

Applying the same reasoning as above for a simple hexagonal lattice in 3D one can say that the electrons will be diffracted by the prism planes first and the basal planes next. The first zone in k-space will

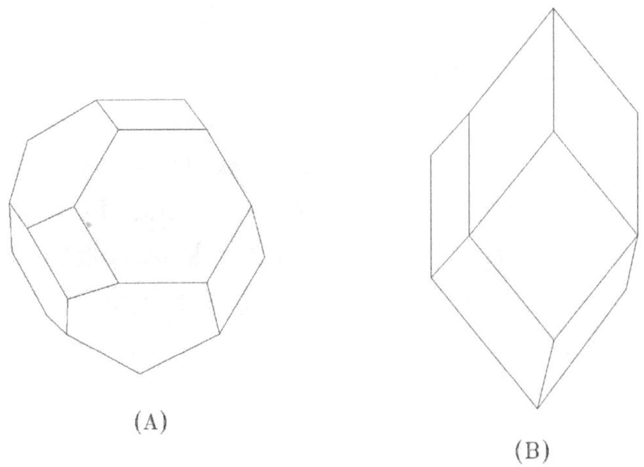

Fig.3.18 Brillouin Zone for (A) FCC & (B) BCC lattices

be a hexagon with $k_x = (4/3)(\pi /a)$ and $k_c = (2 (\pi /c))$ where 'a' and 'c' are the unit cell constants. The shape of the zone is shown in Fig 3.17(b). In hexagonal close packed crystal the first zone is a simple hexagon(arising from diffraction from six prism planes and two basal planes) which can accommodate one electron per atom and the second zone is a polyhedron (arising from diffraction from two basal planes and twelve pyramidal planes) which can accommodate one electron per atom are put together for convenience as a single zone that can accommodate two electrons per atom as is the case with simple body centered and face centered cubic metals. The relationship between lengths and directions in the unit cell in real space (Cartesian coordinates) and in the brillouin zone in 'k' space are given in Table 3.1 The shape of this zone is shown in Fig 3.19. This is called the valence zone and the next zone is called the conduction zone. The dimensions of the zone depend on the (c/a) ratio of the hexagonal crystals. It is indicated in Table 3.2 Considering the ideal aspect ratio of 1.633, metals like zinc and cadmium have a higher ratio and their I zone is slim and slender(longer)in k-space whereas magnesium and beryllium having a lower aspect ratio than the ideal possess short and squat I zone in k space. In the former two metals E_c/E_a is less than one and in the later two it is greater than one. If $(c/a)>1.633$ $E_c<E_a$ and vice versa One can consider two diagonal directions on the basal plane 'a' and 'b' such that a>b Then in k-space $k_a<k_b$ where the former is equal to (π /a) and the later is equal to$(2/\sqrt{3})(\pi /a)$.The vertical axis is 'c' and in k-space k_c will be equal to (π /c).If c<b< a then $k_c> k_b> k_a$ and $E_c > E_b > E_a$. If c>a>b then $k_c<k_a<k_b$ and $Ec <Ea <E_b$.

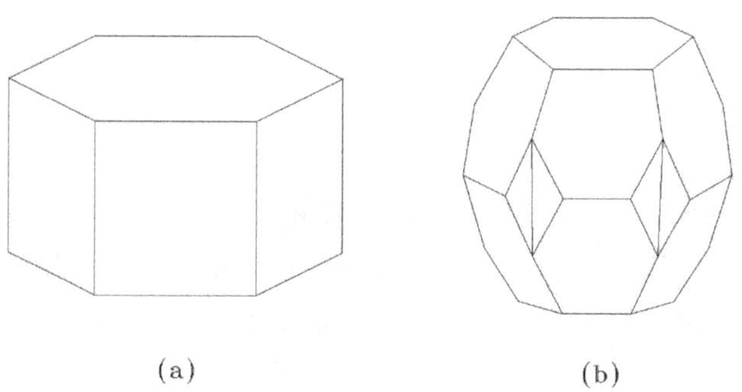

Fig.3.19 I Brillouin Zone for (a) HCP lattice when(a) (Ne/Na)=1 & (b) (Ne/Na)=2

Table 3.1 Wavenumber vector in HCP metals along different directions

Axis type	Miller-Bravis indices	Wavenumber vector	Length of axis
Vertical	[0001]	(π/c)	c
Diagonal Type I	$[2\bar{1}\bar{1}0]$	(π/a)	a
Diagonal Type II	$[10\,\bar{1}0]$	(π/b)	b

Table 3.2 Nature of Brilluoin zone with aspect ratio of HCPmetals

(c/a)	HCP metal	Ec/Ea	Brilluoin zone nature
1.585	Be	1.196	Slender(long)&Slim
1.625	Mg	1.137	" " "
1.866	Zn	0.863	Short &Squat
1.890	Cd	0.851	" " "

3.6.3 SUPERLATTICES (ORDERED LATTICES)

For superlattices the zone of the main lattice is retained but are crossed by new faces of energy discontinuity at wave numbers corresponding to additional reflections of the electrons in the superlattice.The density of states curve will have a peak before the peak of the main lattice making the superlattice more stable than the later. Strain energy of a superlattice is lower than the main lattice due to the ordered arrangement of the atoms in the former but lowering of Fermi energy in a superlattice is important in stabilizing the crystal structure. For a BCC superlattice such as CuZn intermetallic compound in addition to (110) reflections which give rise to Dodecahedral Brillouin zone additional (100) reflections occur giving a Cube inside the Dodecahedron as part of the Brillouin zone. One such zone is schematically shown in Fig 3.20.

3.7 MODELLING AND SIMULATION OF DENSITY OF STATES CURVE

The shape of the density of states curve can developed using moments of density of states distribution over energy. As follows:

$$\mu_n = \int_{E_i}^{E_f} N(E)[E-E_m]^n dE$$

where n is the order of the moment.

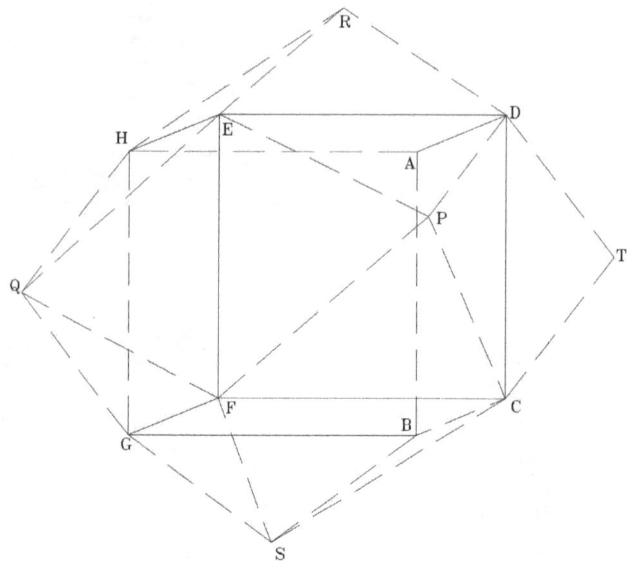

Fig.3.20 Brillouin Zone for BCC ordered lattice

$$\mu_0 = \int N(E)dE \text{ and } \mu_1 = 0$$

Mean energy=E_m=∫N(E)(E)dE / N(E)dE and

$$\mu_2 = \int N(E)[E-E_m]^2 dE$$

andμ3&μ4 give detailed shape of the zones.

The third moment is given by

$$\mu_3 = \int N(E)[E-E_m]^3 dE$$

and the fourth moment is give by

$$\mu_4 = \int N(E)[E-E_m]^4 dE$$

The distribution can be skewed, bimodal or unimodal as shown in Fig 3.21(a)(b)&(c).

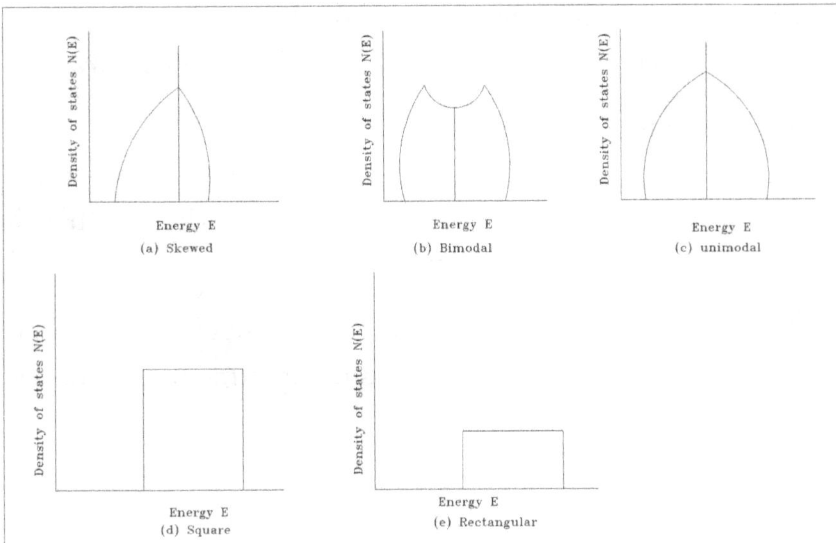

Fig. 3.21 Different types of N(E) Vs E curve for modelling & simulation.

One needs simple information to calculate the N(E)distribution over E for different crystal structure of the same metal or alloy. One can also consider a square or rectangular distribution of density of states as shown in Fig 3.21(d) & (e).

$$\mu_3=0 \text{and } \beta=(\mu_4/[\mu_2]^2)$$

When1< β < 1.8 it will be bimodal, when β= 1.8 it will be rectangular and when it is 3.0 unimodal Gaussian distributions

3.8 SUCCESSES, LIMITATIONS AND FAILURES OF BZT

It can explain electrical thermal optical and magnetic phenomena in metals admirably well. It can explain the occurrence of electron compounds at electron to atom ratios of (3/2)(21/13)&(7/4) in an alloy of two metals.

It cannot explain super conduction in ceramics or for that matter in polymers. It is applicable to crystalline solids only.

The zones are in imaginary k-space and not in actual crystals. It is only a geometric construction for a particular crystal structure but not a part of it. Its form and size depend on the structure but not upon the numbers in the sample material.

The peak in density of curves can occur even before the Fermi sphere touches the zone boundary as found experimentally in copper..

4

DENSITY FUNCTIONAL THEORY

4.1 INTRODUCTION

From the year 1957 onwards it was known that everything about BZT was not in agreement with experimental findings. By studying the variation of Magnetic susceptibility with field strength it was found that in Copper, the peak in the density of states curve does not correspond to the just touching of the zone boundary by Fermi sphere. This gave a fatal blow to the theory of electron phases in general and Cu-Zn system in particular. Secondly the zones are not in real crystal but in geometrically constructed k-space. This led to a situation that a crystal with any arbitrary lattice parameter like 10 mm, 100 mm, 1000 mm etc. can be a metal and an electrical conductor. It is to say that inter atomic spacing plays no role in determining the electrical properties. This led to lot of intense activity among material scientists .With powerful computing facilities to their aid, developments and refinements were made by them. Energy bands were theoretically calculated. Thirdly the concepts were suitably modified to include amorphous materials such as metallic glasses obtained by Rapid Solidification techniques. All these gave rise to what is called the Density Functional Theory (DFT).

4.2 THEORY

The single electron potential in a solid is uniquely determined by the multi electron density in the solid. The electron density plays the fundamental role, not the wave functions as thought till now. The single electron local equations are to be solved self consistently as there are many electrons in a primitive unit cell of a solid. The so called Local Density Approximation (LDA) is used to calculate the exchange correlation energy. Combining DFT & LDA, the energy bands can be computed *ab initio* with powerful computational facilities that are available now. It is found to be reliable and more accurate than in the past.

The local density of electrons can be further refined to Local Spin Density (LSD) so that electrons spinning in clockwise and anticlockwise directions can be taken into account separately. This leads to better accuracy. For alloy design this will be precise enough. For understanding magnetic phenomenon gradients in exchange correlation energy has to be considered. It leads to a better calculation of the energies of atoms & molecules and their chemical interactions.

Total energy of an electron consists of potential, exchange correlation and kinetic energies as given below:

$$\mathbf{E}_T=\mathbf{E}_P\,(=\mathbf{E}_{ep})+\mathbf{E}_{XC}(=\mathbf{E}_{ee}+\mathbf{E}_{pp})+\mathbf{E}_K$$

The Schrodinger equation can never be solved for a real metal. Suitable and relevant assumptions have to be made to arrive at a solution which is a compromise made with the actual case on hand. Nearly Free electron Approximation and Tight Binding Approximation are two such compromises. The former is good for monovalent alkali metals and the later for 3d transition metals. The so called Chemical theories using resonance of electrons also are inaccurate in as much as they arbitrarily choose numerical values for parameters to obtain results that are in good agreement with measured values of physical properties.

In DFT-LDA method the Schrodinger equation to be solved is not for a multi electron element. (many electron wave equation) which is insurmountable but a one electron problem moving in a fixed effective potential. Later is arrived at by taking into account the kinetic, potential and exchange correlation energies and calculating the density of the non interacting electrons as a function of its position in the real solid. In an actual metal or solid electrons are interacting in a potential field of the solid. This situation is replaced by a group of non interacting electrons moving in a fictitious potential field (V_{eff}) which is determined by the total energy E_T of the system which is itself a function of the charge density. This charge density is to be iteratively obtained by plugging in the Schrodinger Equation, improved values at every step. Initially a charge density n_0 is used and with every iteration an improved value n_1, n_2, n_3.....up to n_f are used to get a very high accuracy. This is done till the energy $E(n_f)$ becomes minimum.

The local density of electrons at a distance `r' from an atom is taken as an approximation to be the average uniform electron density in the solid.ie Local Density is a function of position of electrons in a solid. The energy and potential of a single electron in a solid at a position 'r' are a function of the local density of electrons at that position which itself is a function of the position 'r'. Function of Function is called Functional i.e. F[f(x)]. The electron (charge) density is a unique function of wave function but wave function is not a unique function of charge density.

4.3 FERMI SURFACE AND ENERGY BANDS

Energy bands in a material can be calculated and shape of Fermi surface predicted ab initio by computational methods based on DFT & LDA. There are three approaches to this namely Orthogonal Plane Wave Method(OPWM), Pseudo Potential Method(PPM) and Augmented Plane Wave Method (APWM). The first method uses the tight binding model which assumes that the valence electrons are strongly attached to the ion cores. The second method assumes that the valency electrons move in an electrostatic potential field which is weak and uniform. This field arises from the interaction of ion cores and other electrons with valence electrons . The third method calculates the potential around each ion called the `the muffin tin potential `. This potential looks like an inverted cylindrical tin box around an ion.

There are several experimental methods available to calculate the band structures and the nature of the Fermi surface. The latter is very essential because the electronic properties of a material like electrical conductivity, magnetism etc depend not on the total number of valence electrons but on only a fraction of them which are on and near the Fermi surface and the corresponding number of the density states. This is given by the following equation.

$$N(E_F)=(N_V)/2(E_F)$$

where the symbols have their usual meanings. Knowing the Fermi surface will greatly help in predicting and understanding the electronic properties.

Following experimental methods are available and are well developed and fine tuned.

1. de Haan-vans Alphington effect method
2. Magnetoacostic effect method

3. Ultrasonic attenuation method
4. Anamolous skin effect method
5. Magnetoresistance method
6. Cyclotron resistance method
7. Positron annihilation method
8. Modulation spectroscopy method.

The first method helps in estimating the area of the Fermi surface. The second method gives the largest diameter of the Fermi sphere. The third method is similar to the second method but interpretation of the result is difficult. The fourth method gives the curvature of Fermi surface. The fifth method indicates the contact point of the surface with the Brillouin zone boundary. The sixth method estimates the velocity of the electrons on the Fermi surface. The seventh method gives an idea about the number of electrons in the cross sectional area of a planar slice of the Fermi sphere. The eighth method is an optical method and has taken a preeminent position. It has several advantages over other methods. It is precise and accurate. It is simple in principle but involved in practice. Optical spectra of metals, alloys, semiconductors and insulators can be recorded easily at ambient temperatures. No vacuum is required. Most materials are opaque. Light penetrates only the surface upto about 10 nm. Therefore measurements are made on the surface.One can measure Reflectance (R), Absorption (A), or Polarisation (P) at different energies. Over and above the background one gets sharp features (peaks or troughs) at certain energies corresponding to interband transitions in metals and semiconductors. The background is due to intra band transition in metals. In semiconductors and insulators no interband transition will occur as the valency band is completely filled. In insulators no interband transition will occur as the energy gap is large. The sharp features can be enhanced to enable easy recognition and identification if one plots dR/R, dA/A and dP/P against energy. These techniques are called modulation spectroscopy techniques. Additionally by these techniques one can identify direct and indirect transitions in semiconductors. Interband and intra band transition in metals can be studied.

4.3.1 METALS

Theoretical calculations and experimental observations agree well for simple metals and crystals in band energy calculations. For alkali metals having BCC crystal structure like Sodium ab initio calculations vary from experimental observations near the surface of the first Brilluoin zone. The band gap also differs but the shape of the Fermi surface is a sphere in both cases.

For the FCC noble metals like Copper, Gold, Silver etc both the approaches give similar results. The Fermi surface is a sphere with eight holes coaxial with <111> direction and parallel to the {111} planes. For the alkaline earth metals like BCC Barium, FCC Calcium, HCP Manganese etc both the approaches result in a spherical Fermi surface with a total of fourteen holes eight in<111> and six in <100>directions in the lower energy 4s band. In the higher energy 3d band eight round coin shaped disks appear. In trivalent metals like FCC Aluminium the shape of the Fermi surface is more complicated. It is broken into pieces. In aluminium the largest piece is continuous while the smaller pieces are disjointed. Transition metals like the ferromagnetic BCC Fe ,HCP Co and FCC Ni are very complex and large discrepancies occur between the two methods. Due to ferromagnetism an additional energy term has to be considered. It is called exchange correlation energy. In metals the Fermi energy level falls within the band while in insulators and semiconductors it falls in between the bands in the energy gap. Therefore no Fermi surface appears for the latter.

The discrepancies between theoretical calculations and experimental observations are a welcome feature as it helps in understanding clearly the electronic properties of real Solids compared to ideal formulations and assumptions one makes in ab initio computational methods. The variations and similarities between free electron bands in FCC, BBC and HCP crystals & actual bands in real Solids can help us understand the behaviour of electrons in the later.The energy of a free Electron will be continuous while in a solid it will have gaps. For aluminium the conduction electron behaves like a free electron.

4.3.2 SEMICONDUCTING COMPOUNDS

Band structure calculation can be done for semiconducting compounds also like elemental semiconductors. For example it has been calculated using DFT & LDA for Ga As with a valence four and with a diamond cubic crystal structure like Si .True to its nature the calculation shows a small bandgap.

E vs. k for energy bands are shown in the reduced zone scheme whereas the diagram shown in chapter 3 figure 3.9 (b) is in the extended zone scheme. There is also a method called the periodic zone scheme. In this scheme E vs k is shown for every zone in the whole range of $-n\pi/a$ to$+n\pi/a$. In the reduced zone scheme E vs K for all the zones are shown in the range of$-\pi/a$ to $+\pi/a$.In the extended zone scheme E vs k for the first zone is shown between $-\pi/a$ to $+\pi/a$ the second zone between$-\pi/a$ to$-2\pi/a$ and$+\pi/a$ to$+2\pi/a$ and so on. Bands are shown as E vs. k curves. Zones are shown as N(E) vs E curves. k is inversely related to atomic spacing `a`as shown in chapter 1.

5

ELECTRONIC PROPERTIES

5.1. ELECTRICAL PROPERTIES

5.1.1 CRYSTALLINE METALS

Solids can be divided into conductors, insulators semiconductors and superconductors. Why a solid behaves in a particular manner electrically can be nicely explained with BZT. For example conduction is explained with the help of zones and Fermi circle in k-space in 2D and can be extended to 3Dlattices.It is illustrated in Fig 5.1(a) (b) & (c) for a partially filled valence zone and completely empty conduction zone for a square lattice. The first picture shows the situation when no external electric field is applied. The distribution of electrons is symmetrical about the origin in k-space. The Fermi circle is centered on the origin indicating that the maximum value of k vector in all directions is the same. The area inside the Fermi circle represents the energy states filled by valence electrons and the region outside the circle but inside the square boundary of the I zone represents the empty unfilled states. No flow of electrons will occur as the electric field is zero. The second picture shows the situation when an electric field `E' is applied in the $-k_x$ direction. The points A&B in Fig 5.1(a) have shifted to A'&B' in Fig 5.1(b). Some energy states are vacated while some states are freshly filled.

The former is represented by the left hand crescent and the later by the right hand crescent in Fig 5.1(c) The electrons will be accelerated in the $+k_x$ direction (that is towards the right) and the distribution is unsymmetrical. This is shown in Fig 5.2 in the form of E vs. k_x curve with and without electric field applied. This contributes to a net charge movement towards the right leading to a current flow towards the left in the direction of the electric field. The velocity of electron at time 't' is given by

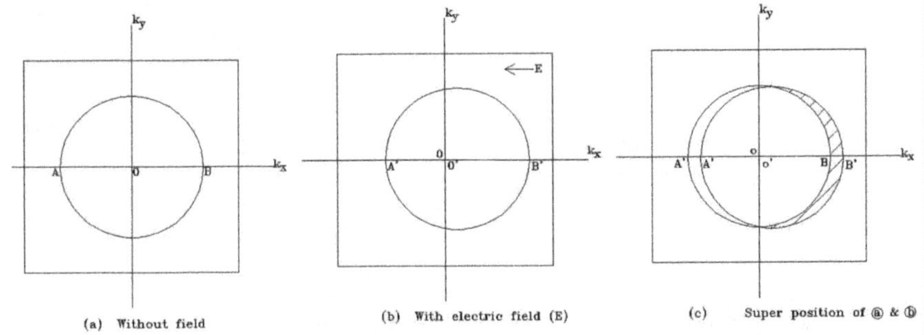

Fig.5.1 Movement of Fermi Circle under the influence of electric field

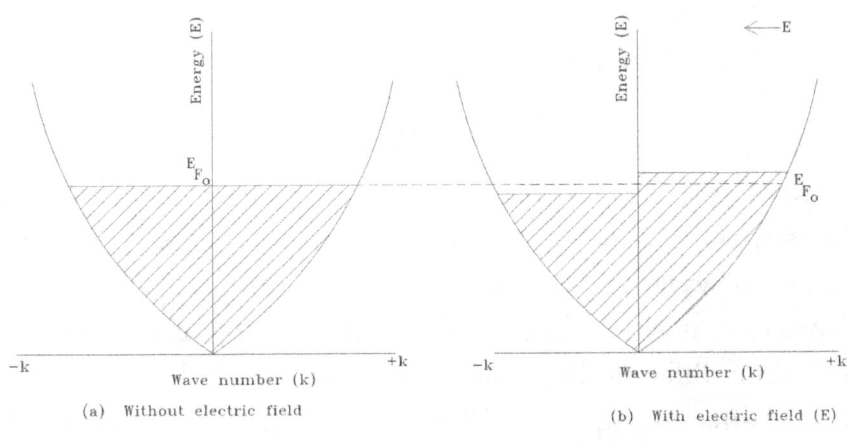

Fig.5.2 Energy against wavenumber in the absence and presence of electric field.

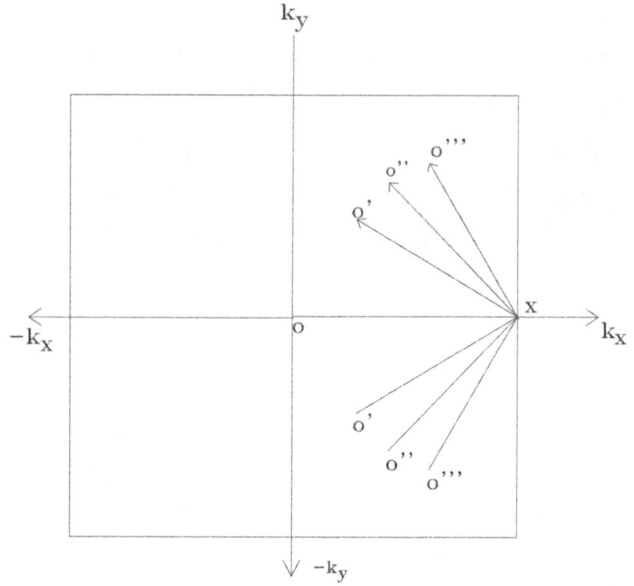

Fig.5.3 Various possible directions of diffrection for an electron at the Brillouin Zone Boundary

$$v=v_0+at$$

and acceleration is given by

$$a= [(e)x(E)]/(m)$$

where E and a are constant and with time of passage velocity increases. But it can not increase indefinitely as it will lead to an increase in wave number vector for which there is a limit in the valence zone at which electrons will be diffracted by the boundary of the zone in different directions. This limit is oo' in k_x direction and oo" in a direction equally inclined (45°) to k_x & k_y directions. No part of the Fermi circle can fall outside the zone. That is, it can not cross the boundary. Assuming that the electron initially was moving in k_x direction it may be diffracted such that it has a wave number

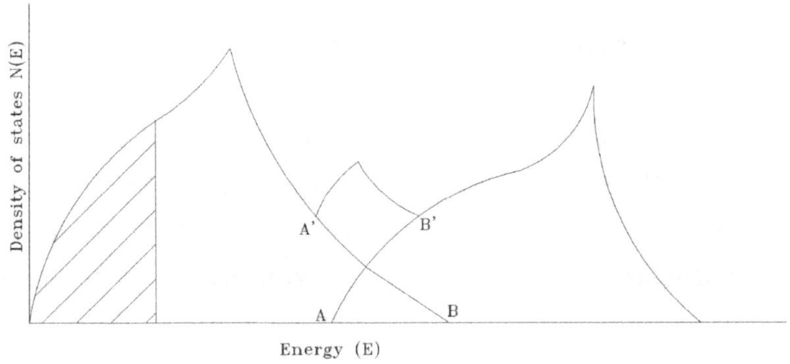

Fig.5.4 Partially filled conduction zone (eg.: Copper) for metals with (Ne/Na)=1

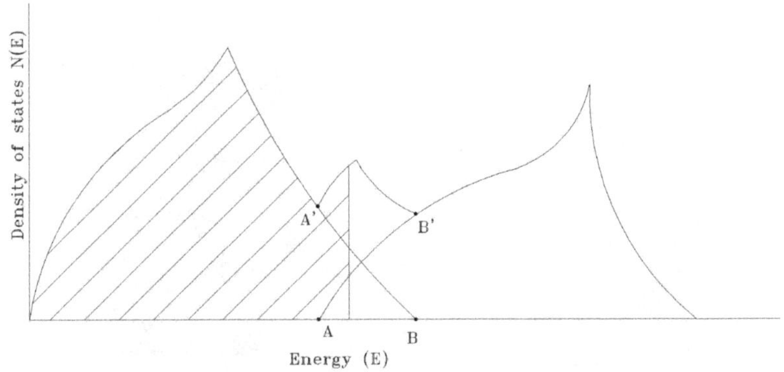

Fig.5.5 Partially filled valence zone with overlapping conduction zone. (eg.: Magnesium) for matal with (Ne/Na)=2

vector having a $-k_x$ component on resolution. Such diffraction will occur even at a temperature of 0K These reflections are different from collisions with the lattice. After diffraction the electron may have any wavenumber corresponding to wave vectors xo', xo'', xo''', xo'''', xo''''', xo'''''' etc assuming that before diffraction it was ox. It is illustrated in Fig5.3 It is assumed that electrons are freely moving without collisions which is not true. It may undergo collisions with lattice ions which is the real situation. In that case the electrons will possess a wave number vector that will fall in the left hand crescent which represents nothing but unfilled states. Originally the electrons will have wave number vectors which fall in the right hand crescent shown hatched in Fig 5.1(c).It can have collisions in which energy is not lost or lost. Both are allowed and possible. That means collisions can be elastic(ENERGY CONSERVED) or inelastic(ENERGY LOST). This gives rise to resistance in metals. An electric field of normal voltage will not enable an electron to pass from one zone to another zone.

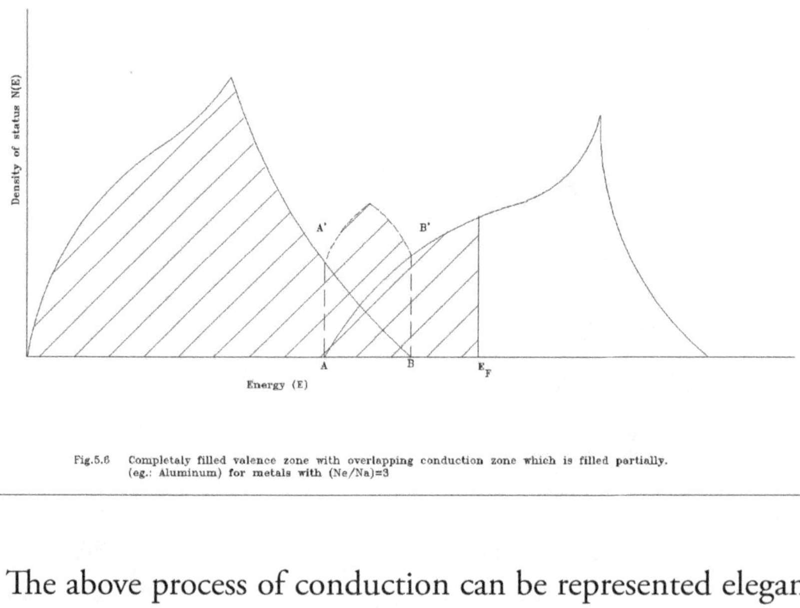

Fig.5.6 Completaly filled valence zone with overlapping conduction zone which is filled partially. (eg.: Aluminum) for metals with (Ne/Na)=3

The above process of conduction can be represented elegantly with the density of states N(E) vs. energy E curves, as shown in Figs 5.4for copper[valence is one],5.5 for magnesium [valence is 2] and 5.6 for aluminium [valence is3]. The valence zone is partially filled in copper and electrons can move to higher states of energy easily as these are unfilled. In magnesium [HCP] the conduction zone overlaps the valence zone and even though the valence zone is completely filled [$(N_e/ N_a)=2$] unfilled states are available immediately above the filled states due to the continuity provided by the overlap of the zones. In aluminium [FCC] the valence zone has to accommodate

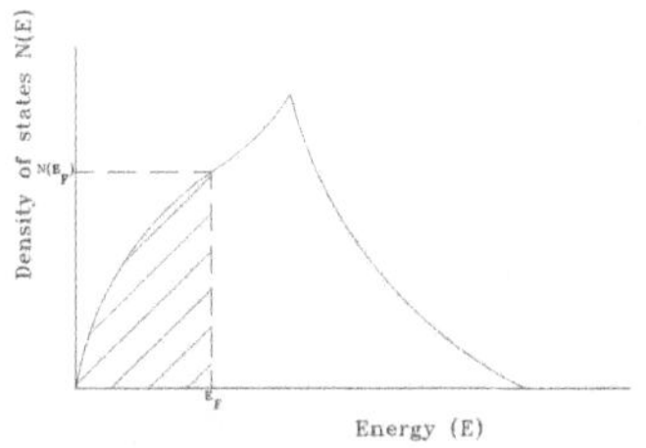

Fig.5.7 Monovalent Metal (Ne/Na=1) Fermi electrons are more but E_F is Less.

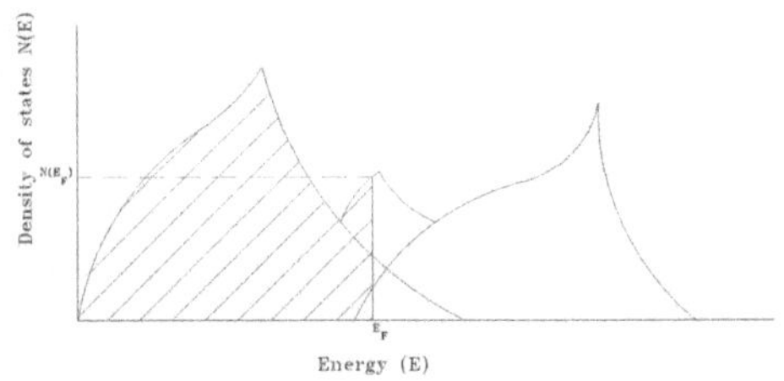

Fig.5.8 Bivalent Metal (Ne/Na=2) Fermi electrons are less but E_F is high

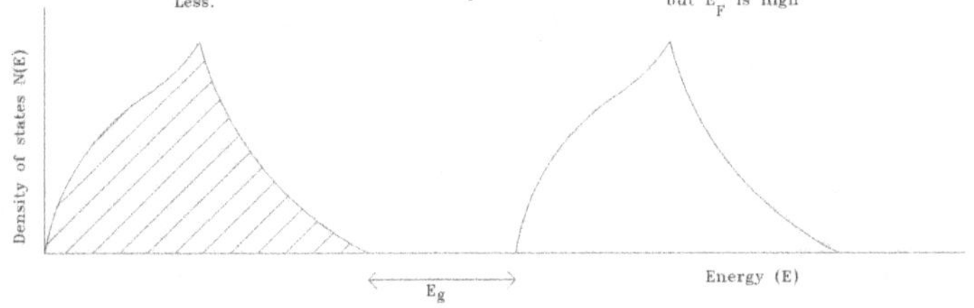

Fig.5.9 Valence and Conduction zones in an insulator – Large Energy Gap

$[(N_e/N_a)=3]$ and it overflows and partially fills the conduction zone resulting in conduction. Mono valence conductors have higher conductivity due to higher number of Fermi electrons compared to bivalent conductors as shown in Fig 5.7 & 5.8. For insulators such as diamond[DC] the valence zone is completely filled and the conduction zone is separated from it by a large energy gap [>2eV] which can not be surmounted thermally. It has no free electrons as all the valence electrons are used up for bonding covalently with other carbon atoms. It is illustrated in Fig 5.9. On the other hand graphite [HCP] is a conductor. Its first zone is partially filled. It has one free electron while three are used up for bonding with other carbon atoms it its own plane. It is illustrated in Fig 5.10 (a) (b) & (c). Intrinsic semiconductors like silicon and germanium have their valence bands completely filled but their conduction zones are separated by narrow energy gaps[<2 eV] which can be overcome thermally. At a room temperature of 303K thermal energy available is [1/40] eV and at 1273K [1/10] eV. It is illustrated in Fig5.11.The conductivity of such materials increase with increase in temperature

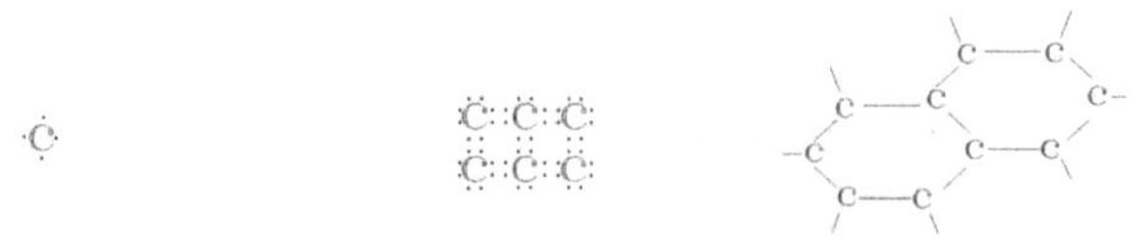

(a) CARBON ATOM (b) DIAMOND (c) GRAPHITE

Fig.5.10 Bonding in Diamond & Graphite

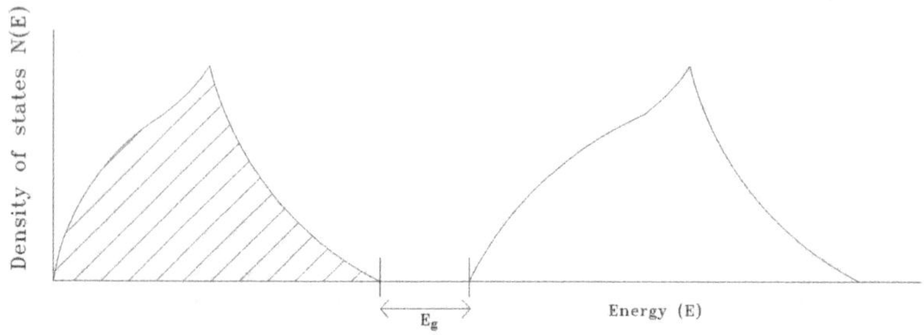

Fig.5.11 Valence & Conduction zones in a semi conductor (small E_g)

as more and more electrons go to the conduction band and are able to move freely in an electric field. Figs 5.12(a) & (b) illustrate the process of conduction in impurity semiconductors (n-type & p-type). If an atom with valence 5(dopant) replaces a silicon atom with valence 4 then one electron will be available for free movement in an electric field . The conduction is due to excess electron. It is called n-type semiconduction. On the other hand if an atom with valence 3 (dopant) replaces a silicon atom a hole (an electron deficiency) is created and conduction will take place by its movement in an electric field. It is called p-type semiconduction. The dopant energy levels will fall in the forbidden zone. If the dopant has valence higher than the semiconductor the energy level will be near the conduction zone and electrons from the so called donor levels will jump into the conduction zone and give rise to conduction. The majority carriers are electrons in the conduction zone. Such a process is called n-type conduction. On the other hand if the dopant atom has a valence less than the semiconductor the energy level of the dopant atoms will fall just above the valence zone and electrons will jump into the so called acceptor levels leaving behind holes in the valence zone. In such cases the conduction will be by holes in the valence zone. These holes are the majority carriers and such a process is called p-type conduction. The desirable impurity or dopant concentration will be 100-1000ppm. The undesirable impurities will be less than ppb.

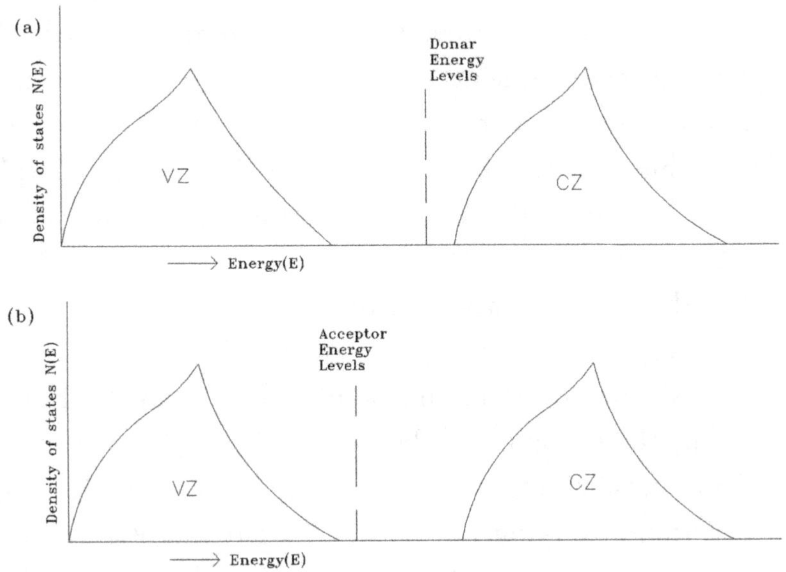

Fig.5.12 N(E) Vs E for (a) n type & (b) p type semi conductors.

5.1.2 AMORPHOUS METALS

For amorphous materials no long range order or periodicity exists in the arrangement of its atoms. Therefore Brillouin zones cannot be constructed since Bloch theorem is not valid for them. Still density of states exists and N (E) vs. E can be constructed. But here one should understand the terms localized and delocalized (extended) states defined by Anderson Model. When the potential inside a material at different positions of atoms is more or less similar then the electron states are said to be de localized and the broadening of energy states will occur. On the other hand the potential inside a material at different positions of atoms are widely different and varying over a wide range, the energy states will not broaden. The electron states are localized as it is varying according to the position of electrons in the material. There may occur a wide gap in energy for an amorphous material from filled to unfilled states and this gap in energy can be bridged by the existence of several localized states falling in the gap. Sometimes there can be an overlap over filled and unfilled energy levels. In the latter case one will come across amorphous conductors. Metallic glasses come under this group. Amorphous semiconductors also fall in this category. But the conductivity in the amorphous condition will be less if the semiconductor is doped unlike intrinsic semiconductor. In silicon this can be seen from Figs 5.13, 5.14, 5.15 (a) & (b) which indicate the nature of bonding in crystalline intrinsic, amorphous intrinsic and crystalline impurity silicon. The amorphous silicon has dangling bonds which provide more free electrons but these bonds will be saturated by tying with dopant atoms. To increase conductivity the dopant atoms should be freed and this is done by tying up the dangling bonds with hydrogen before doping. Thus amorphous hydrogenated silicon will have higher conductivity.

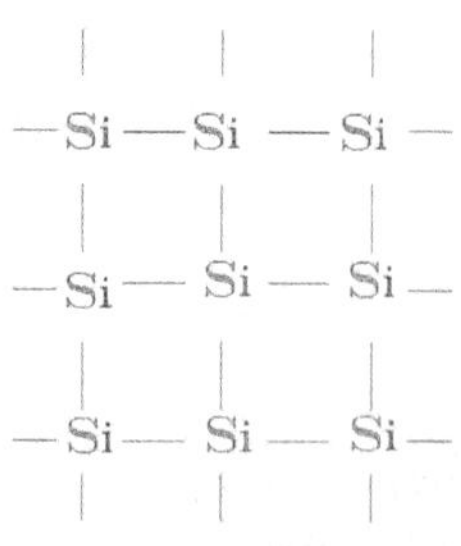

Fig.5.13 Crystalline silicon

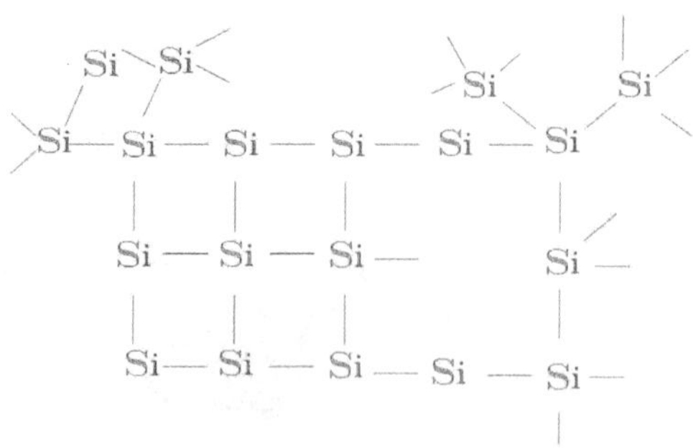

Fig.5.14 Amorphous silicon with dangling bonds

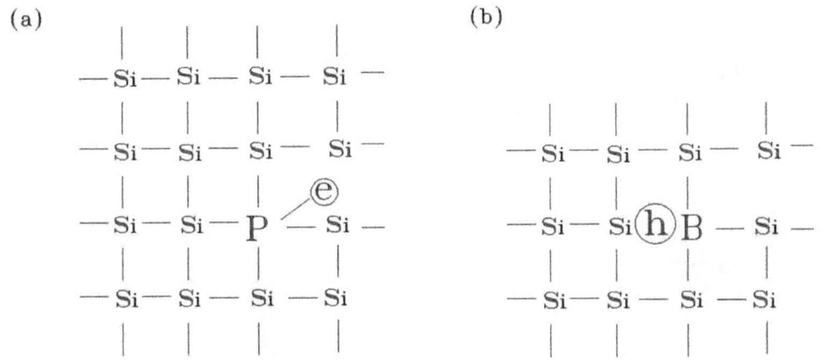

Fig.5.15 Bonding in (a) n type & (b) p type silicon semi conductors

5.1.3 CRYSTALLINE POLYMERS

Crystalline polymers can conduct electricity. The phenomenon is explained on the basis of unbonded electrons. Let it be assumed that a double bond is broken into a single bond leaving one free electron in a carbon atom as shown in Fig 5.16 (a) for trans poly acetylene. It brings two single bonds in to adjacent positions. Electrons from an adjacent carbon atom can break itself free and occupy the poison in this atom to restore the double bond under the action of an electric field as seen in Fig 5.16 (b). This flow of electrons breaking bond at one atom and restoring bond at another atom under the influence of an electric field is called ***soliton*** conduction. The BZT is applicable here since the polymers considered are crystalline. The free electron is in the valence zone and can move into the conduction zone as it is loosely bound to the atom due to broken bonds.

5.1.4 CRYSTALLINE CERAMICS

In crystalline ceramics conduction is by movement of ions. They are ionic conductors. In oxides of metals with variable valence such

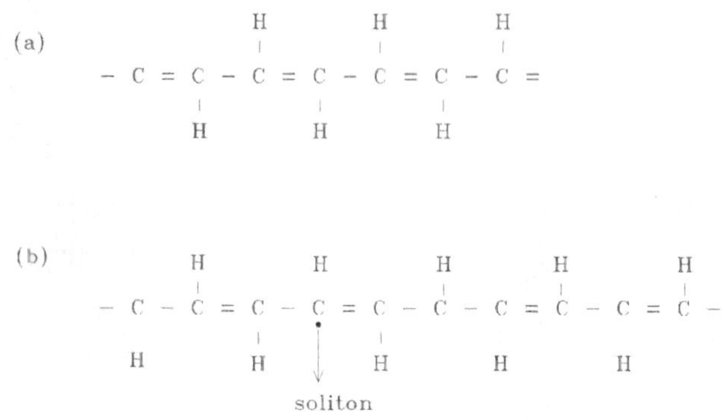

Fig.5.16 Condection in polymer by soliton movement.

(a) Trans polyacetylene (non Condecting)

(b) Trans polyacetylene (Condecting) with a broken double bond.

as titanium, the dioxide is an insulator as it has no free electrons while the mono oxide is a conductor as it has free electrons that are not used up in bonding. Nonstoichiometric zinc oxide is a n type semiconductor while stoichiometric zinc oxide is an insulator. Stoichiometric cuprous oxide is an insulator while nonstoichiometric cuprous oxide is a semiconductor. Nickel oxide is an insulator but nonstoichiometric nickel oxide is a p type semiconductor. $Sn_3In_2O_9$ is a conductor i.e. $(SnO_2+In_2O_3)$

5.1.5 SUPER CONDUCTION

Superconducting state is an ordered state .The ordering is that Fermi electrons exist in pairs called cooper pairs. The two electrons constituting the pair have opposite and equal momentum and opposite spin as shown in Fig 5.17(a). The superconducting state has lower energy than the normal state as shown in Fig 5.17(b). The Cooper pair drifts cooperatively through the crystal without resistance. There is a critical temperature below which this pair is stable and super conductivity is destroyed above this temperature due to the instability of this pair of electrons. Phonons are not required in normal conduction but they are a must for super conduction. Phonons are Bosons and have to be treated mathematically with Bose-Einstein statistics. Number of phonons need not be conserved. As temperature increases their number increases and vice versa. In a super conductor a Cooper pair of electrons and a phonon undergo an interaction called the exchange process. (This is called BCS theory of superconductivity) Hence good conductors are not good superconductors as the later requires phonons while the former does not need them. Poor conductors (due to electron-phonon collisions) like ceramics and polymers are better candidate materials for super conduction. The BCS theory of superconductivity is excellent for metals and intermetallic compounds. However it is inadequate for ceramics and polymers.

5.1.6 DIELECTRIC PROPERTIES

Polarization in a material causes the centre of gravity of the positive and negative charge to be separated giving rise to dipoles and their associated moments. An ideal dielectric material cannot be polarized. It will be a perfect insulator. Such a material does not exist in reality. Normally materials undergo polarization to different levels depending on the electric field. Without an external field no polarization will be possible. The frequency of the alternating field and the temperature are also important in determining the extent of polarization in materials. In a dielectric material the resistance to passage of current will be high.

In a covalent solid like diamond only electronic polarization takes place. The electron cloud will be centered at a different place compared to the nucleus. In an ionic solid like sodium chloride the

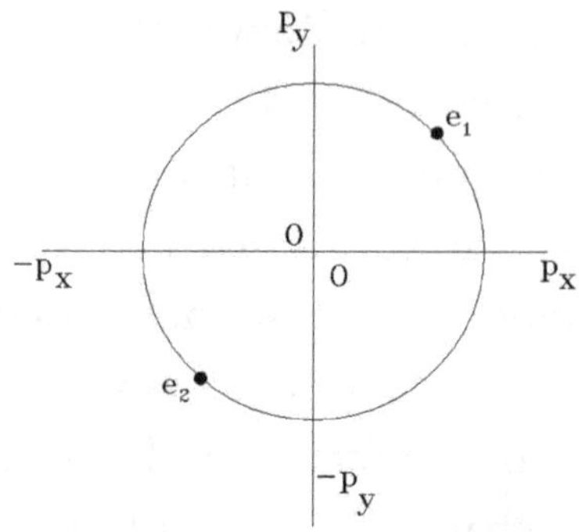

Fig.5.17 (a) Cooper pair of electrons (e_1 & e_2)

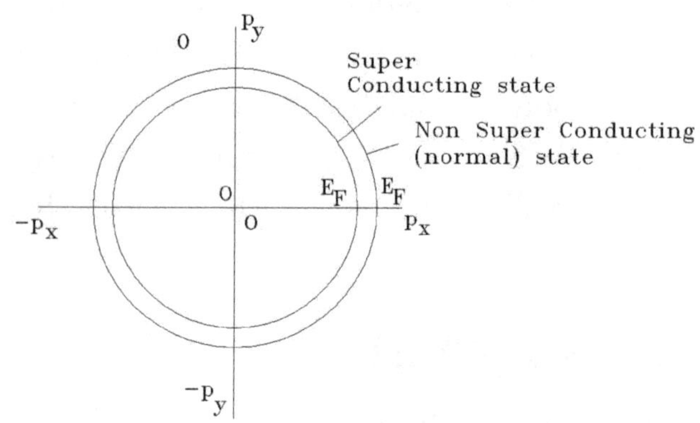

Fig.5.17 (b) Fermi circle & Energy for normal & superconducting states

positive and negative ions will be separated and ionic polarization takes place. In gas such as nitrobenzene the dipolar molecules will acquire a dipole moment in an electric field and molecular polarization takes place apart from electronic and ionic polarization. The fourth type of polarization called space charge polarization will take place in multiphase (different electrical properties) crystalline solids wherein a buildup of charges can take place at grain boundaries under the action of an electric field.

$$\mathbf{P=(\varepsilon_r)\,(E)}$$

Where P is polarization, E is electric field and ε_r is relative permittivity. In a static electric field (under the influence of Direct Current) orientation of electric field and therefore the dipoles will be same and constant under a given field strength. But in an electric field of an alternating current the direction of field changes twice within every cycle and therefore polarization will follow this changing direction. If the frequency is very high it cannot keep pace with the field and the polarization lags behind the field. It is illustrated in Fig 5.18. For example with very small wavelength x-rays & γ-rays no polarization takes place and the rays simply pass through the matter. With long wavelength rays such as UV ,visible & IR radiation only electronic polarization is possible. With longer wavelength radiation such as micro and radio waves both electronic and ionic polarization can take place. At still longer wavelengths and very low frequency, say power and audio frequencies molecular, ionic and electronic polarization can take place since time available

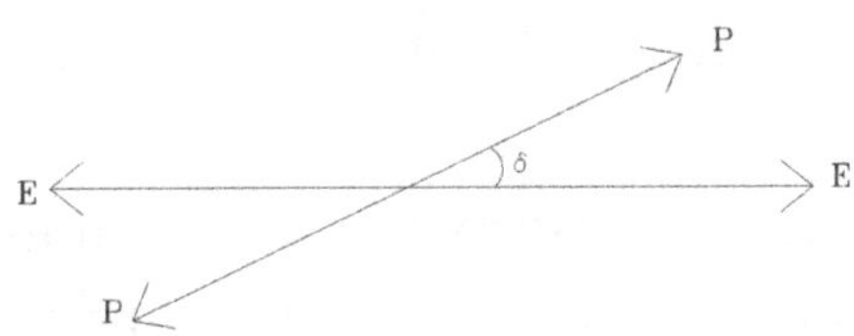

Fig.5.18 Polarization legs behind A.C Electric Field

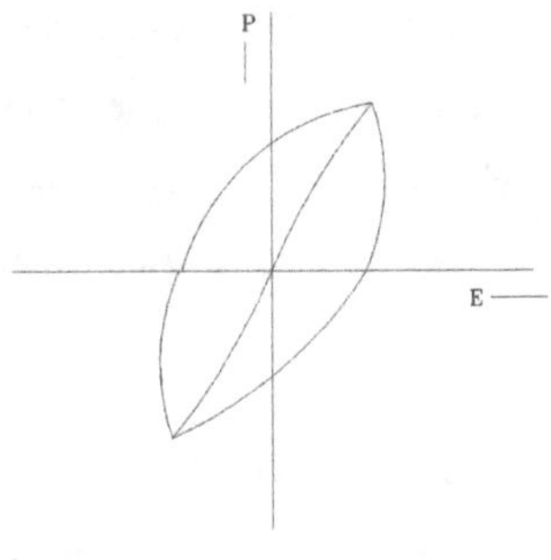

Fig.5.19 Ferroelectric Hysteresis Loop

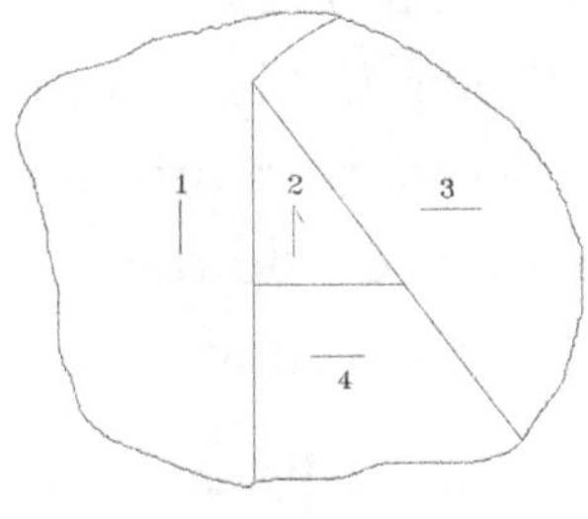

Fig.5.20 Domains in a Ferroelectric material (Four are shown).

is large for polarization to keep pace with the field. Also at audio and power frequencies space charge polarization takes place in multiphase alloys and solids. As temperature increases polarization increases and remains constant and finally falls at high temperatures. At large electric fields polarization may be very high and dielectric breakdown occurs and an insulator becomes a conductor

5.1.7 PIEZOELECTRICITY

Some solids without crystal symmetry undergo polarization in the presence of stresses that are applied. This phenomenon is called piezoelectricity. Quartz is a good example for this. PZT [Lead zirconium titanate] is a widely used material in this category.

5.1.8 FERROELECTRICITY

Even when no external field is applied some solids are polarized. It is called spontaneous polarization. Each unit cell of the crystalline solid develops a dipole moment. All these dipoles are aligned in a particular direction even in the absence of an external electric field. There is a spontaneous interaction among the dipoles of adjacent unit cells. The relative permittivity ε_r is very high. It is of the order of 1000. Such a material when subjected to an electric field whose direction is reversed from positive to negative shows a hysteresis loop. It is shown in Fig5.19. A ferroelectric material has a domain structure as shown in Fig 5.20. In each domain the dipole moment is pointing in a different direction so that the net moment is zero. By applying an electric field the domains can be aligned. Ferroelectric domain walls do not move easily.

The domain walls are very thin [wall thickness is 0.2nm], narrow and have high energy. No rotation of domains is necessary as new domains can nucleate and grow easily. This is in contrast to ferromagnetic domains [several of them exist in a single grain and will not cross grain boundaries in a polycrystalline material] which are thick [10 to 100 nm] and spread out over large regions resulting in low energy [0.001J/m2].They have high mobility. Moreover, the ferroelectric hysteresis [P vs. E] loop is more square than ferromagnetic hysteresis [B vs. H] loop. Barium titanate is a very widely used ferroelectric material.

5.1.9 PHOTOCONDUCTION

Electrons can be excited into the conduction zone from the valence zone by photons [***optically***]. The process is governed by the laws of Einstein's photoelectric effect. This leads to conduction in materials. It is called photoconduction. For supplying energy of 2eV a field of 160 MV/m is required.

5.2 MAGNETIC PROPERTIES

5.2.1 CLASSIFICATION OF TYPES OF MAGNETISM

The magnetic property of a material is studied using its magnetic moment. The magnetic moment of an atom arises due to (a) Orbital motion of an electron and (b) the spinning motion of an electron. The nucleus also contributes to the magnetic moment due its angular momentum but it is negligible because of its very large mass compared to the electron mass. The angular velocity of the nucleus is lower compared to that of electrons. The orbit of an electron precesses about the direction of an externally applied magnetic field resulting in a change in angular momentum. A free electron of the n electrogas in a metal can undergo a circular motion when subjected to an external magnetic field. Angular momentum contributions from core and valence electrons due to their orbital and spinning motion give rise to dia and para magnetism

Diamagnetism is due to the circular orbital motion of the electrons. Para magnetism is due to the spinning motion of the electrons. These are exhibited by materials only when an external magnetic field acts on them. A diamagnetic material[copper, gold, siver, zinc, lead, silicon etc] will arrange itself in such a way that it counters the applied field whereas a paramagnetic solid [potassium, sodium, magnesium, aluminium, chromium, vanadium, manganese, titanium molybdenum etc]will arrange itself in alignment with external field to aid & add to it.

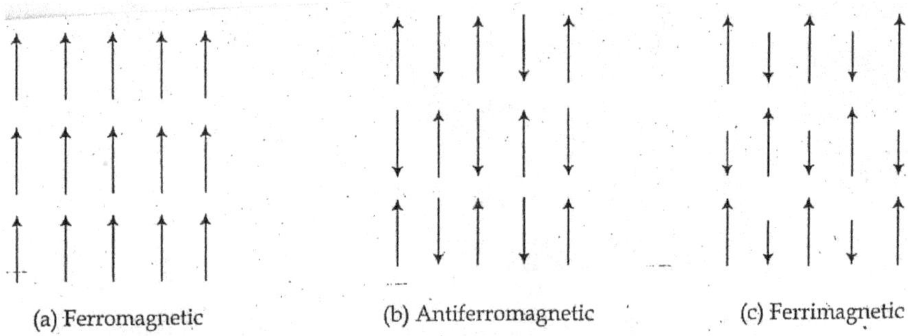

Fig.5.21 Magnetic Moments in Adjacent atoms in Solids

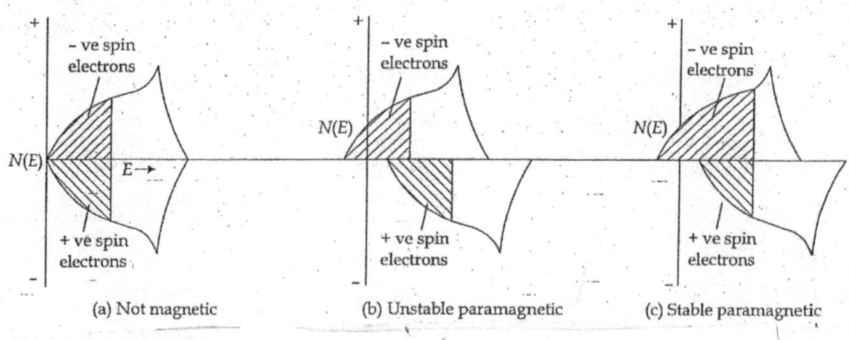

Fig.5.22 Explanation of Paramagnetism by BZT

A third type of magnetic phenomenon occurs even in the absence of an external magnetic field. In this there are three types namely Ferro, Antiferro and Ferrimagnetism.In a ferromagnetic material [iron,nickel,cobalt,gadolinium etc] each atom is a magnetic dipole with a dipole moment and all of them are aligned in the same direction Therefore the total moment of the solid is high and strong magnetism is exhibited by the solid. It is shown in Fig 5.21(a). In Fig 5.21(b) each atom has a dipole momeunt but the adjacent atoms have opposing moments which results in cancellation and the solid exhibits no net magnetism. It is said to be antiferromagnetic. [α-Manganese, Manganese oxide etc.] In Fig 5.21(c) a solid with two different atoms and atomic dipole moments are shown. All the moments of one type of atom are pointing in one direction and the other type of atom in the opposite direction. Therefore there is a net magnetic moment and the solid exhibits magnetism even in the absence of an external field. It is said to be ferrimagnetic [Eg:Ferrospinels. In one unit cell 8 molecules will be present. Each molecule will be a dipole and have a net dipole moment.]

5.2.2 ZONE THEORY AND MAGNETIC PHENOMENON

BZT can satisfactorily explain the magnetic phenomenon in crystalline materials with the help of density of states variation with energy curve.

Para magnetism is explained by considering the spin of the valence electrons in an atom. When there is no field a paramagnetic solid will not show any net magnetic dipole moment. Consider a metal with N_e electrons in an electron gas. Half of them will have positive [anti parallel] spin and the other half negative [parallel] spin. It is depicted by a partially filled valence zone with two regions one above and one below the X-axis on which energy is marked in Fig 5.22(a).When an external field of strength H is applied the energy of electrons with negative spin is decreased by μ_B (H) and positive spins increased by μ_B(H) where μ_B is the magnetic dipole moment of a single electron called Bohr Magneton. It is illustrated by the shift in Fig 5.22(b) of the top half to the left and the bottom half to the right of the Y-axis. This shows a net magnetic moment but is a high energy state and is unstable. Electrons in positive spin state below the X-axis can lower the energy by going to negative spin state above the X-axis. Fig 5.22(c) shows a lower energy and more stable state than what is found in the previous figure. The overall energy is decreased by $2\mu_B H$ and the change in dipole moment of a Fermi electron will be $2\mu_B$.The total number of Fermi electrons is $2N(E_F)$. The paramagnetic susceptibility is given by

$$\chi_{para} = (\mu_B)^2 \mu_0 N(E_F)$$

Similarly one can obtain the diamagnetic susceptibility of a material. It is given by

$$\chi_{diaa} = [(\mu_0)(N_e)(e)^2 (r)^2]/(6m)$$

where `r' is the radius of the outermost electron orbit and N_e is the number of outermost electrons and e is the charge of the electron. Insulators and semiconductors have a completely filled valence band and therefore have equal number of positive and negative spin electrons and their spin moment will cancel and they will exhibit only diamagnetism In any metal both para and diamagnetic contributions will be there from electrons. A metal will have a small positive susceptibility if paramagnetic or will show small negative susceptibility if diamagnetic depending on which of the two is dominant. For copper `r' and `N_e' are large but N (E_F) is small. So it will be diamagnetic showing a small but negative susceptibility.

BZT can explain the phenomenon of ferromagnetism in iron, nickel cobalt etc adequately on the basis of electronic structure and energy. The outer most electrons are considered for this purpose and are distinguished as 4sand 3d electrons which is not the accurate picture. Still it is simple enough for quantitative and qualitative

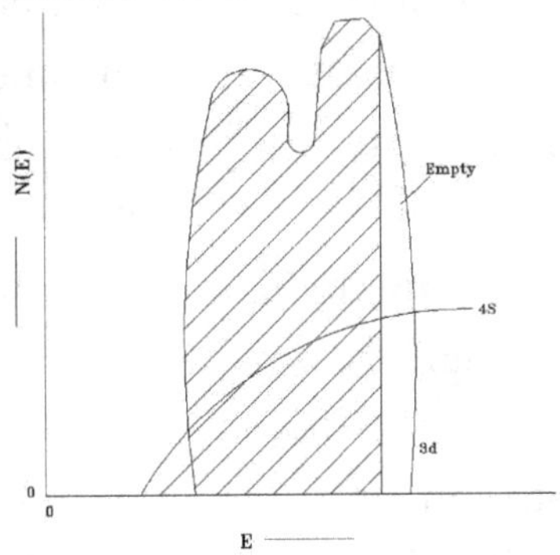

Metal	3d	4s	Total
Iron	7.8	0.2	8
Cobalt	8.3	0.7	9
Nickel	9.4	0.6	10

Fig.5.23 Actual distribution of electrons in 4s & 3d orbitals (Figure is schematic)

understanding of the phenomenon. Fig 5.23 gives the distribution of valence electrons in 4s&3d orbitals or shells..The contribution of the electrons in 4s orbital or shell to dipole moment is negligible and therefore not included. Only 3d electrons are considered.

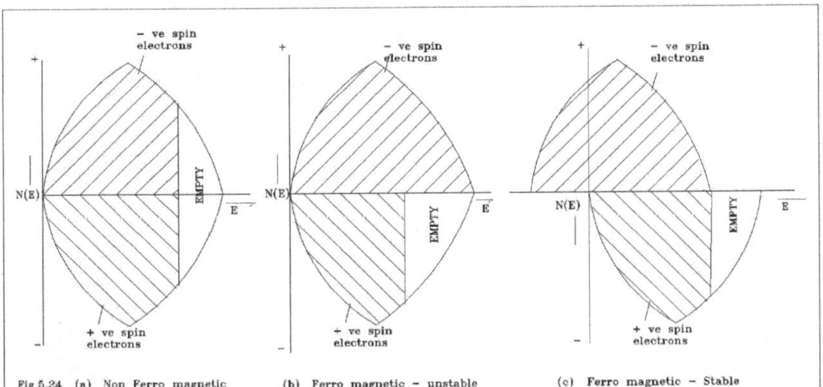

Fig.5.24 (a) Non Ferro magnetic (b) Ferro magnetic - unstable (c) Ferro magnetic - Stable

Nickel is considered for detailed explanation. Fig 5.24(a) shows the valence zone of nickel in two halves one above and another below the energy axis. The 9.4 electrons of the d shell is split equally as 4.7 with – spin and +spin. But this gives no net magnetic moment for the metal. Now if the electros are divided as 5 with – spin and 4.4 with +spin one will get net magnetic moment but this configuration does not give minimum energy. So it won't be stable. Electron from the upper half having – spin can come to the lower half by changing its spin, resulting in instability. It is shown in Fig 5.24(b).

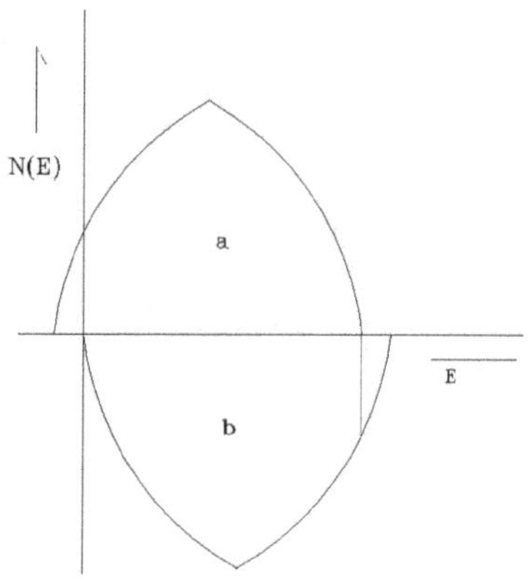

Metal	– ve spin (a)	+ ve spin (b)	Magnetisation (BM)
Fe	5	2.8	2.2
Co	5	3.3	1.7
Ni	5	4.4	0.6

Fig.5.25 Ferro magnetism in Fe, Ni & Co

Fig 5.24(c) shows a stable ferromagnetic nickel. The completely filled half zone has a lower energy and therefore the upper half is shifted towards left. No electron can go from lower to upper half which is completely filled or from upper to lower half as it will lead to higher energy. Fig 5.25 shows the net moment for iron, nickel and cobalt. The ferromagnetic state of iron on one hand and that of nickel and cobalt on the other hand requires a modification of the above explanation for iron. The distribution of electrons in iron is considered as follows: Instead of 5 -&2.8 + one should take4.65 - and 2.45+ spin. This leaves empty states in both the halves of the valence zone. The net moment is not altered. But this explains the reason for the ferromagnetic stability of iron being lower than that of ferromagnetic nickel and cobalt and also the increase of saturation moment in iron in contrast to nickel and cobalt on alloying with aluminium

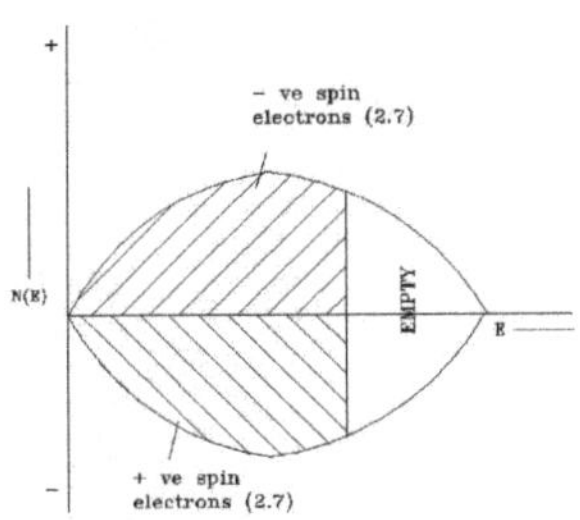

Fig.5.26(a) Non Ferro magnetic

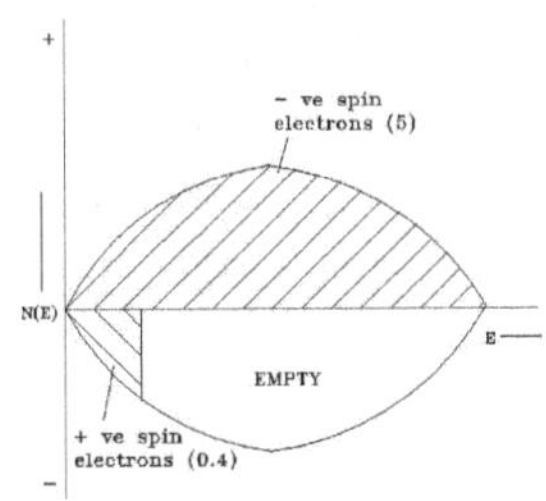

Fig.5.26(b) Unstable Ferro magnetic

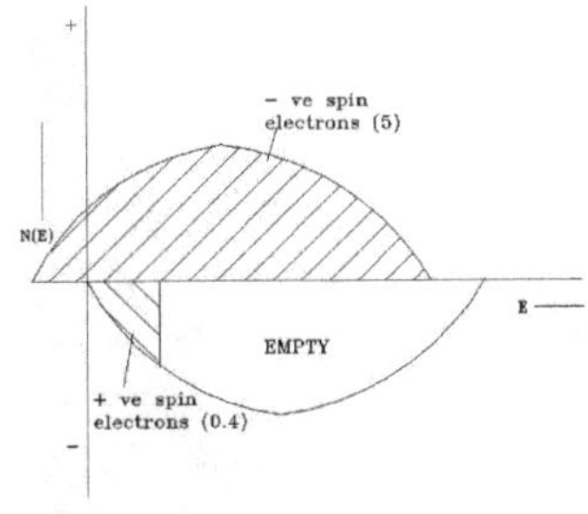

Fig.5.26(c) Unstable Ferro magnetic

The above explanation raises a question as to why chromium or manganese is not ferromagnetic, after all, since these have unbalanced spins. It is explained with the spread of energy and the electronic structure quantified by the radius ratio of the outermost orbit of the atom and the 3d orbital. Consider Fig 5.26(a) showing the distribution of electrons (2.7 with- spin and2.7 with + spin.) and the large breath of the valence zone. No net magnetism as expected. Consider Fig 5.26(b) in which the distribution is 5 with – spin and 0.4 with +spin. Net magnetism is present but energy is high and stability is absent. Consider Fig 5.26(c).The completely filled half band has lower energy and therefore shifts to the left but the breath of energy is so large that still the system has unstable configuration as electrons from upper half can come to lower half. This explains why chromium is not ferromagnetic. Similarly one can explain manganese. The breath of energy spread depends on the electron cloud extension in ion space and for ferromagnetism to

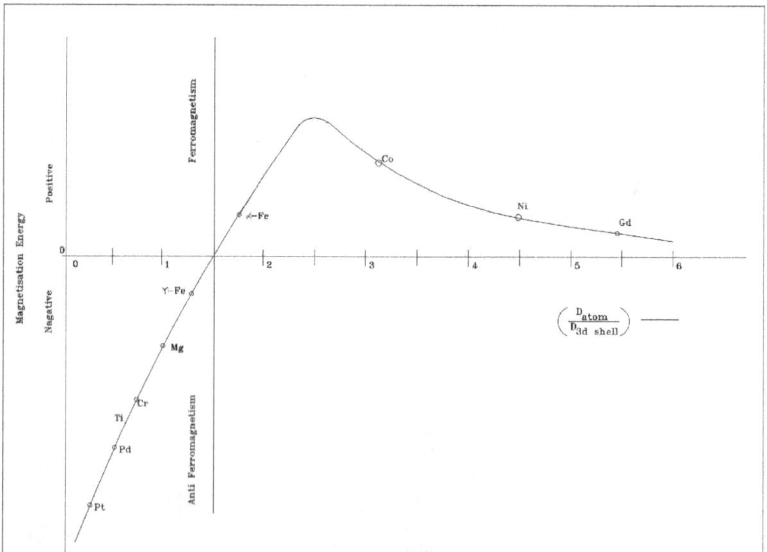

Fig.5.27 Slatter Curve

exist the radius ratio of 3d shell to the atom has to be considered. If this ratio is below 1.5 no ferromagnetism will be exhibited as is the case with FCC iron, chromium, manganese etc. and above 1.5, ferromagnetism is exhibited as is the case with BCC iron, cobalt, nickel, gadolinium etc. It is shown by the plot of Magnetic energy [Eunmagnetised-Emagnetised] against the radius ratio shown in Fig 5.27. The above explanation is too much of a simplification. One cannot justify the splitting of electrons in outermost orbitals as 3d and 4s electrons as in reality spd hybridization takes place. Still the theory is useful in alloy design. Heusler Alloys are synthesized based on it.

5.2.3 PIEZOMAGNETISM

Under the action of applied stresses a material can become magnetic. It is called piezomagnetism. As compressive stress increases, M & μ increase for nickel and decrease for iron. The effect of tensile stress is just the opposite. The inverse phenomenon is called magnetostriction. Dimensions of a material change when subjected to a magnetic field. A ternary alloy of terbium-disprosium-iron exhibits very large magnetostriction compared to iron or iron alloys.

5.3 THERMAL PROPERTIES

Thermal expansion, thermal conductivity, thermal heat capacity, thermionic emission and thermo-electric potential are considered in this section. Explanations based on quantum theory and phonons are a considerable improvement over the classical approach. It leads to better accuracy and predictions of properties

5.3.1 THERMAL EXPANSION

In a solid such as a metal, atoms vibrate over their mean position. Fig 5.28(a) shows a curve of potential energy against inter atomic spacing

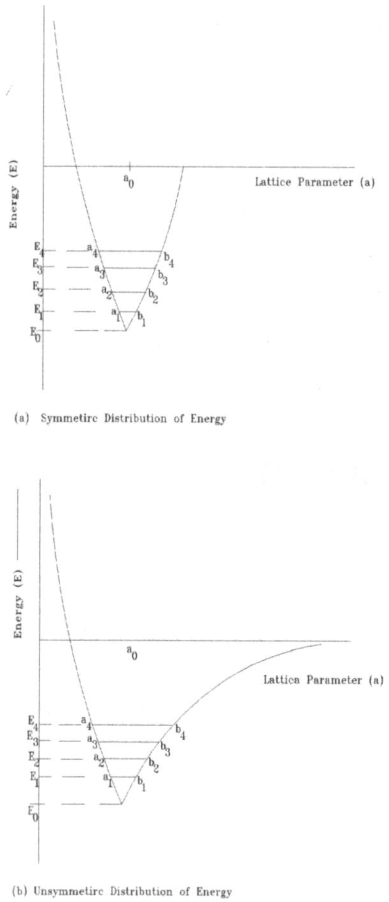

Fig5.28 Explanation for thermal expansion

The curve is symmetrical about the atomic spacing at absolute zero (0K) and the energy is minimum at 0K. Suppose the temperature is increased to different values. Correspondingly the energy increases and the atom vibrate about their mean position as shown but the curve is still symmetrical and average spacing is still a. Therefore no thermal expansion occurs. The above situation does not exist in real solids as the potential energy curve is asymmetrical as shown in

Fig 5.28(b).In this case as temperature increase vibration about mean position is not equal and therefore there is a net increase in length of the metal, the so called thermal expansion of metals. The interatomic spacing follows the path PQ in the figure as the asymmetry of the energy distribution increases the expansion will also increase. Different solids have different distribution and therefore expansion will take place to a different extent in different solids. Ceramics show the least expansion, metals come in the middle followed by polymers with highest expansion. Thermoplastics show higher expansion than thermosetting polymers. Alloys and composite materials can be designed to have desired values of linear expansion. INVAR an alloy of iron and nickel has zero expansion and carbon- carbon composites can have minimum expansion and good dimensional stability.

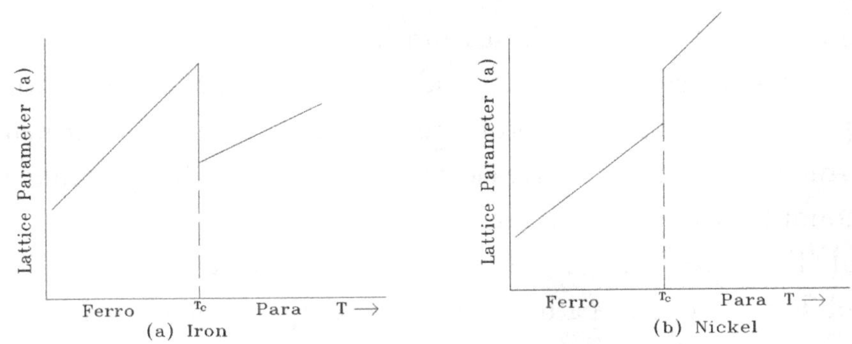

Fig.5.29 Lattice Parameter of Fe & Ni against temperature.

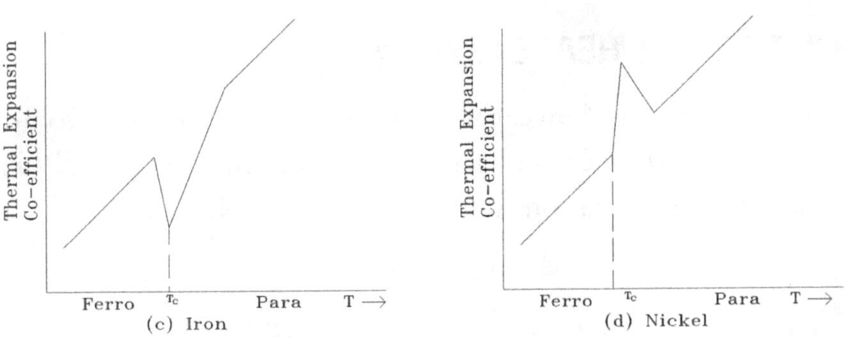

Fig.5.30 Thermal Expansion of Iron & Nickel against temperature

Anomalous expansion occurs in ferromagnetic iron and nickel due to ferro to para transition at Curie temperature as shown in Fig 5.29 and 5.30 showing the variation of lattice parameter and linear thermal expansion coefficient with temperature schematically for iron and nickel.

5.3.2 THERMAL CONDUCTIVITY

In solids such as metals which have excellent thermal conductivity the phenomenon is explained on the basis of conduction by electrons, being dominant rather than conduction by phonons. Unlike phonons electrons are Fermions and their number has to be conserved. One cannot create or destroy electrons. They have to be mathematically handled with Fermi-Dirac statistics. Metals have a high number of Fermi electrons (i.e. those near the Fermi surface) and free electrons also. These can conduct heat from hot place to cold place due to their small mass, high velocity and high mobility. Mean free path is high. Collisions are few and far in between. In ceramics not many Fermi or for that matter free electrons are present. These conduct by phonons. At the hot end there are more phonons than at the cold end. Their mass is large and so move at low velocity. They have low mobility. Mean free path is less and undergoes collisions with the ions in the lattice frequently.

5.3.3 THERMAL HEAT CAPACITY

There are two types of heat capacity one measured at constant volume (dE/dT) denoted as C_v and another at constant pressure(dP/dT) denoted as C_p.The relationship between the two is given by

$$C_p=C_v+R$$

Classical approach of Dulong and Petit gave a constant heat capacity for solids which is independent of temperature which was not accurate. Actually it varied from 0.0 to6.2 asymptotically. Einstein gave a quantum mechanical treatment to the phenomenon. He made several assumptions for this. Improving upon the assumptions of Einstein, Debye has given an excellent theoretical model & explanation of heat capacity of solids. Since phonons have to be considered Bose-Einstein statistics has been used for the purpose. He was able to give very nearly accurate theoretical values of heat capacity in agreement with experimental values.

The following assumptions are central to the general explanation of heat capacity of solids. Vibrating atoms are to be considered as oscillators in 3-D.The energy of vibration is quantized and the basic quanta is phonon. These phonons are particles corresponding to elastic waves propagating through a crystal with the speed of sound. These are not electromagnetic waves but mechanical ones. Phonons like electrons (valence and conduction zones) have two zones called the acoustic and the optical. Density of vibrational modes

D(ω) can be plotted against ω for phonons similar to N(E) vs. E for electrons.The energy of an oscillator is quantized as given below:

$$\mathbf{E_n=(nh\omega)/(2\pi)}$$

Number of phonons are not conserved. As temperature increases their number increases and decreases as the temperature is decreased unlike electrons whose number is independent of temperature. The oscillators are coupled and not independent unlike Einstein's model. The frequency of vibration of 3N oscillators vary in a frequency interval of 0 to ω unlike the single frequency of vibration assumed for all 3N oscillatorsin the earlier model. The results are shown in Fig 5.31(a). In a solid heat capacity at constant volume arises due to two factors namely electrons and phonons. The total heat capacity is the sum of the two.

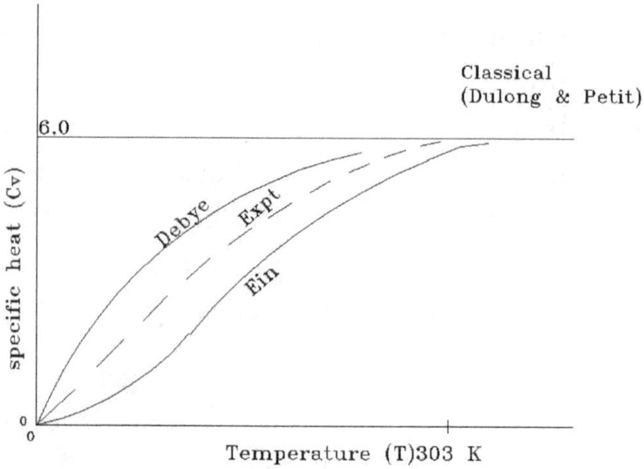

Fig.5.31(a) Specific heat against temperature below R.T and above absolute zero

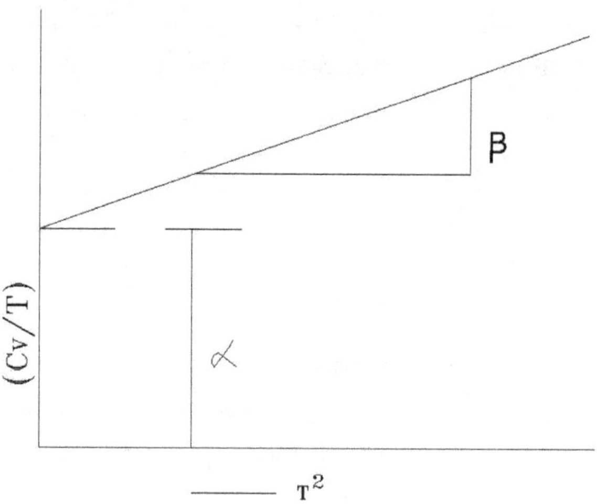

Fig.5.31(b) Relationship between heat capacity and temperature.

$$C_{vtot} = C_{vel} + C_{vph}$$

$$= \alpha T + \beta T^3$$

where α and β are constants.

Electronic contribution is very small, only 1% of that of phonons at 303K(RT). Fig 5.31 (b) shows a plot of (C_v/T)vs T^2 which is a straight line. It can be used to estimate the two constants α and β.

5.3.4 THERMIONIC EMISSION

In a metal with a Fermi of E_F and work function of Φ an electron can be excited into free state by supplying energy. It is illustrated in Fig 5.32 The energy supplied is by thermal means i.e. by raising the temperature. It is called thermionic emission. Richardson's equation governs the process and is given below:

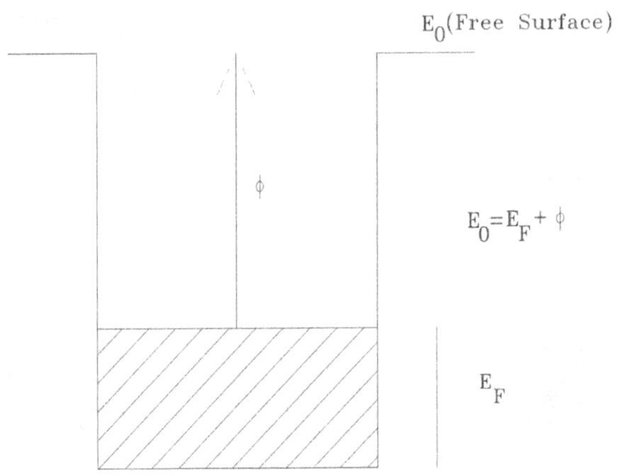

Fig.5.32 Work function of a Metal

$$\mathbf{J=AT^2EXP(-\Phi/kT)}$$

where J is current density in the filament, T is temperature in Kelvin, and A is a constant, k is Boltzman constant and Φ is the work function of the filament material. The dominant factor is not T^2 but $(-\Phi/kT)$ for the temperature dependence of electron emission.

For tungsten even though the work function is large the factor (Φ/kT) is sufficiently low for adequate electron emission.

5.3.5 THERMOELECTRIC POTENTIAL

If two compositionally different materials are joined together at ends and a temperature difference is maintained between the two ends of the junction an electric potential difference is created and electric current flows. It is called the Seeback effect. (ΔV) /(ΔT) is called Seeback coefficient of thermoelectric power. For semiconductors it will be of the order of millivolts and for metals it will be of the order of micro volts per degree Kelvin. There are two other thermoelectric coefficients. All three are positive for p-type semiconductors and metals. For n-type semiconductors all three are negative.

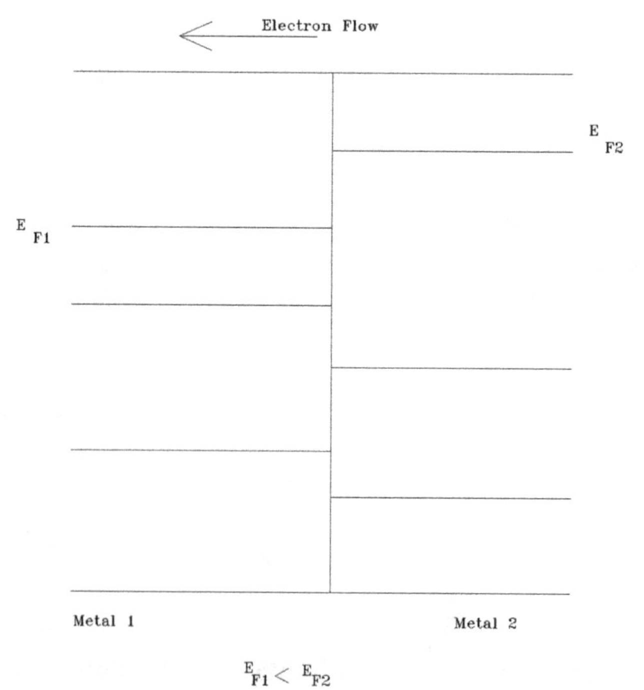

Fig.5.33 Principle of Metal – Metal Junction

There are different types of junctions such as metal –metal junction as shown in Figs 5.33&5.34, impurity semiconductor p-n junction as in Figs 5.35&5.36 and metal intrinsic semiconductor junction as in Fig 5.37 &5.38. The contact potential developed across such junctions is shown in Fig5.39. The diffusion potential (V_o) developed across an impurity semiconductor junction of p-n type is shown in Fig 5.40. The above diagrams are schematic.

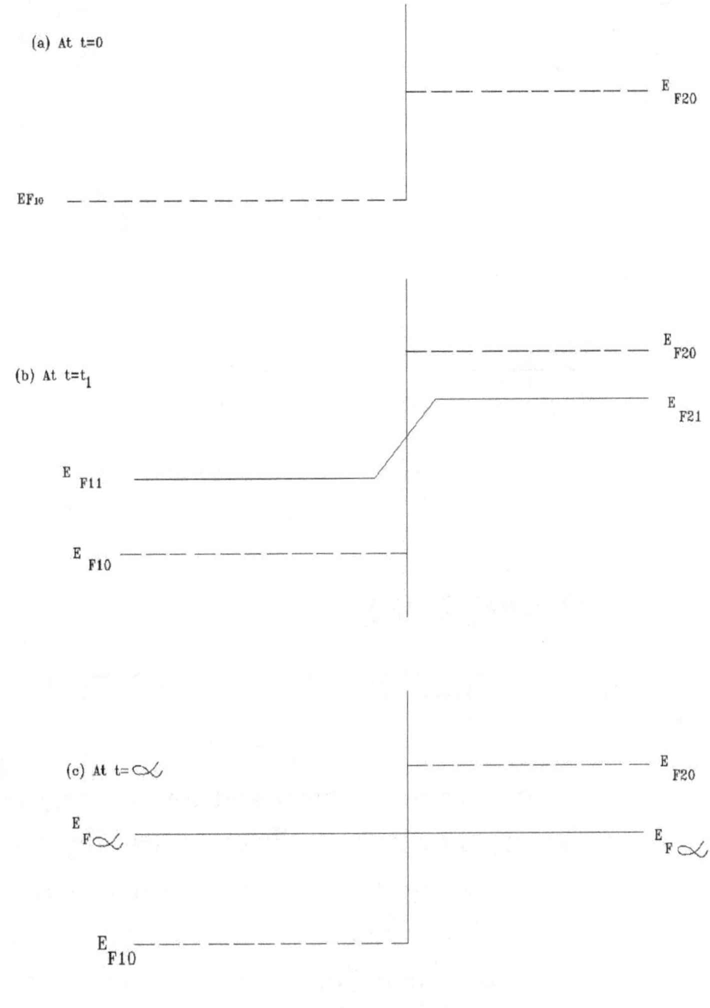

Fig.5.34 Three stages in M-M Junction(schematic)

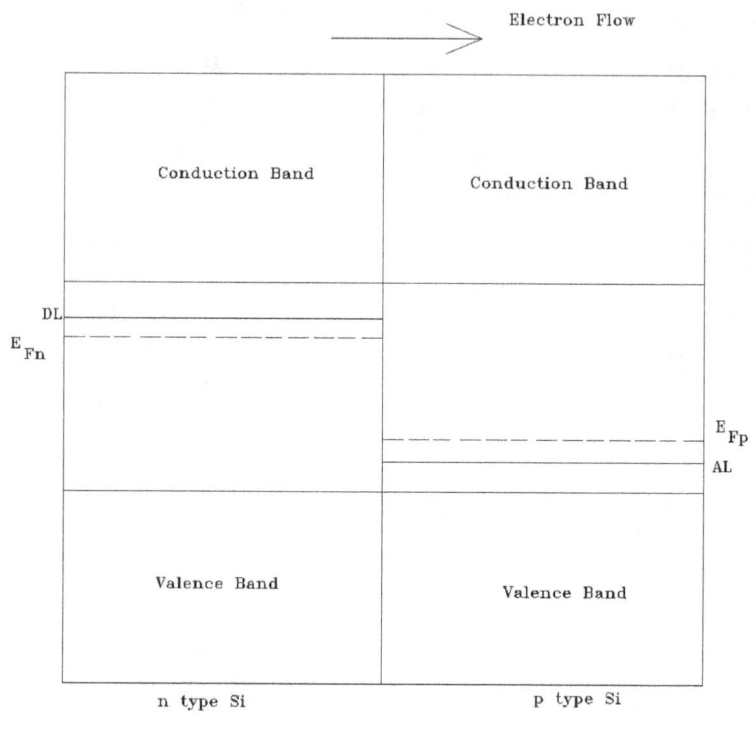

Fig.5.35 Principle of inpurity Semi Conductor Junction

5.4 OPTICAL PROPERTIES

5.4.1 OPAQUE, TRANSLUCENT AND TRANSPARENT SOLIDS

When visible light (of long wavelength and low energy) falls on solids, the photons may not have sufficient capability to excite electrons to higher energy levels in the solid. There may not be much absorption of light. But it may be refracted or transmitted. The fraction of initial intensity of light Io, that is absorbed IA, reflected IR and transmitted IT depends on the solid. This can be represented as follows mathematically:

A=(IA/I0)

T=(IT/I0)

R=(IR/I0)

A+T=R=1

I0=IA+IT+IR

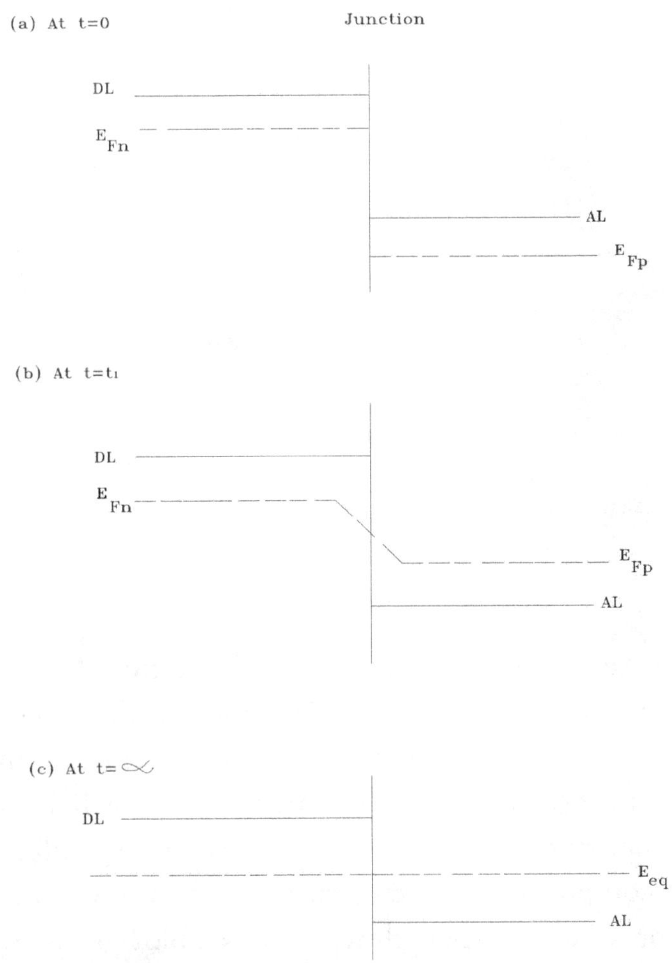

Fig.5.36 Three stages in a inpurity semi conductor junction (schematic)

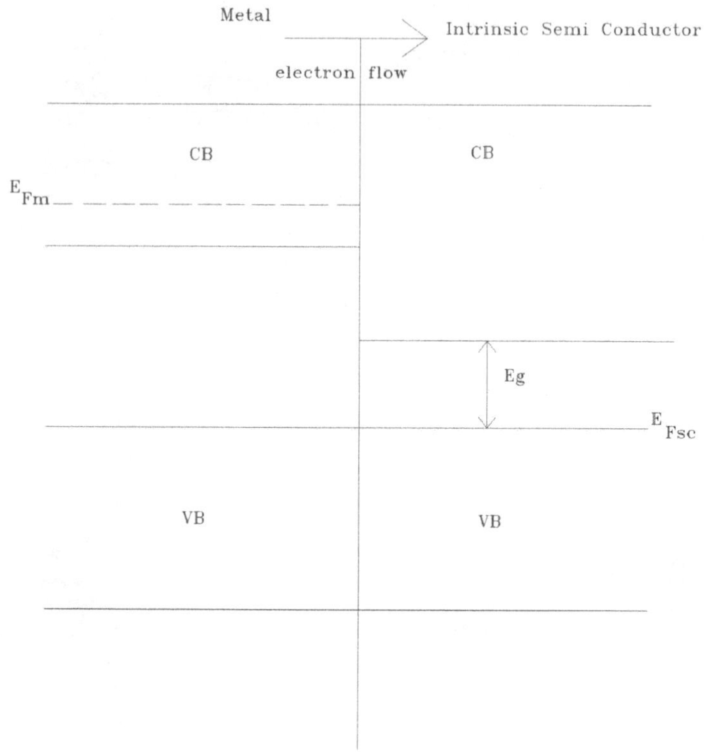

Fig.5.37 Principle of Metal – Instrinsic Semi Conductor Junction

In the case of metals R will be very high since they are opaque and A and T will be very less. This is used in the field of optical metallography to reveal the microstructure of metals and alloys. Most of the insulators are transparent and T will be very low. Semiconductors may be opaque or transparent depending on their chemical composition, crystal structure etc. The colour of solids depends on which wavelength region of visible light is reflected in the case of transparent solids. There is also a third kind of solid called translucent which is partially transmitting. Most insulating

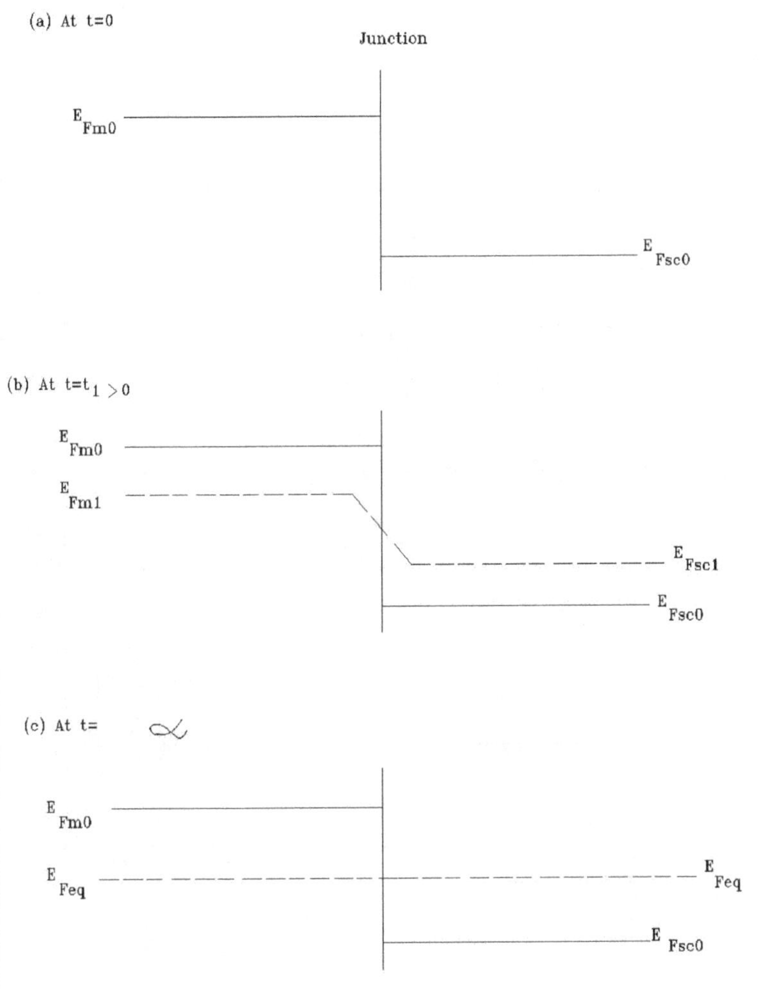

Fig.5.38 Three stages in Metal - Intrinsic semi conductor junction(schematic)

crystalline solids are transparent to visible light due to the large energy gap and the incident light photons being low in energy due to longer wavelengths. When light enters such a solid from air or vacuum it does not travel inside undeviated but is bent by an angle.

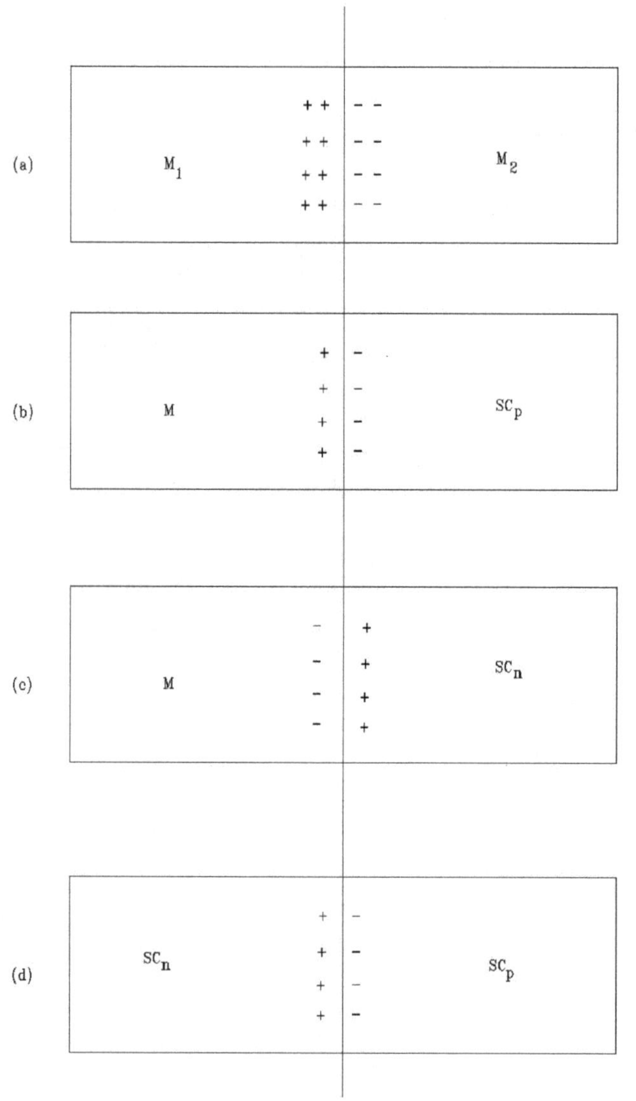

Fig.5.39 Contact Potential Developed Across different junctions(schematic)

The angle of bending depends on the angle of incidence of light and on the refractive index of the solid. According to Snell's law

$$\mathbf{n_s = sin(\alpha_I) / sin(\alpha_R)}$$

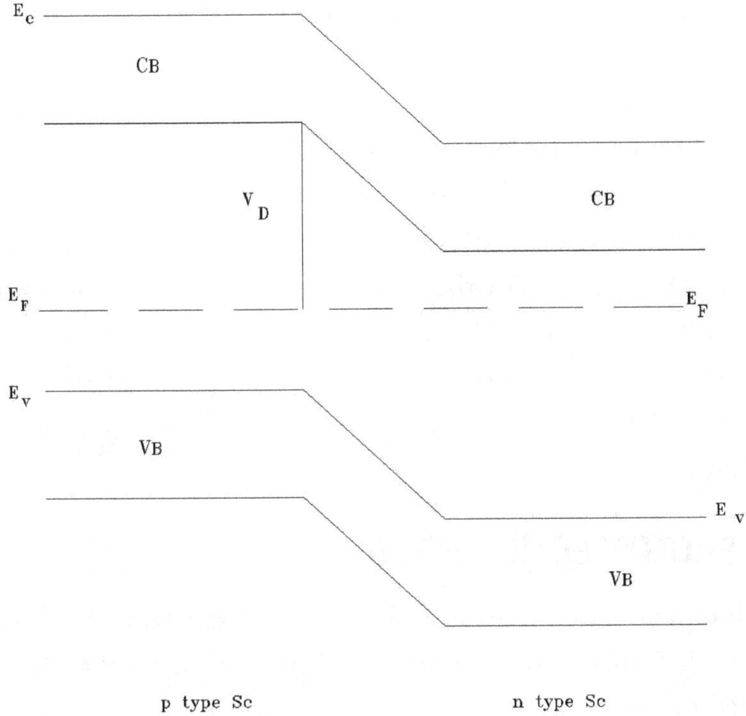

Fig.5.40 Diffasion Potential Acrom impurity semiconductor junction (schematic)

It is assumed that the refractive index for air and vacuum is one. Refractive index of a solid depends on the velocity of light in the solid. It is defined as the ratio of the velocity of light in vacuum to that in the solid. Fig 5.41 illustrates the refraction process. The refractive index of a solid depends on the permittivity and permeability of the solid as given below:

$$(\mathbf{n}_s)^2=(\mu_r)\ (\varepsilon_r)$$

Velocity of light in solid is less than velocity in vacuum.[$3x10^{10}$ m/s].Light travels slowly in solid. It is due to polarization of atoms in solid by light which is nothing but electromagnetic radiation. For cubic crystals which are isotropic, the refractive index is the same in all directions. For tetragonal and hexagonal crystals two values are specified. These crystals have one optic axis. When light travels parallel to this direction the structure is isotropic. In any other direction the structure is anisotropic. These are called uniaxial crystals. For orthorhombic, triclinic and monoclinic crystals there are two optic axes about which the structure is isotropic. These are called biaxial crystals. For them three values of the refractive index are given. Refractive index values are related to crystal structure and symmetry. It is a fingerprint so to say of a crystalline solid. It can be used for identification of crystalline solids. It is used as a routine analytical tool.

5.4.2 PHOTOELECTRIC EFFECT

The principle of interaction of photons with electrons is illustrated in Fig 5.42. Absorption or emission of photons can take place. It is described below

5.4.2.1 ABSORPTION OF PHOTONS

When light of sufficient energy falls on a solid having empty electron states above filled states, the photons may excite the electrons into these empty states. For metals the energy required by photons for this purpose may be very less as they are good electrical conductors and possess a large number of empty states above E_F. For semiconductors the energy required is high since all the states in the valence zone are filled and the conduction zone is separated by an energy gap albeit a small one. Incident photons should have a minimum frequency given by (E_g/h). For insulators the gap is large and the incident photons should have higher energy and have higher minimum frequency. Therefore ceramics which are insulators will have a higher minimum

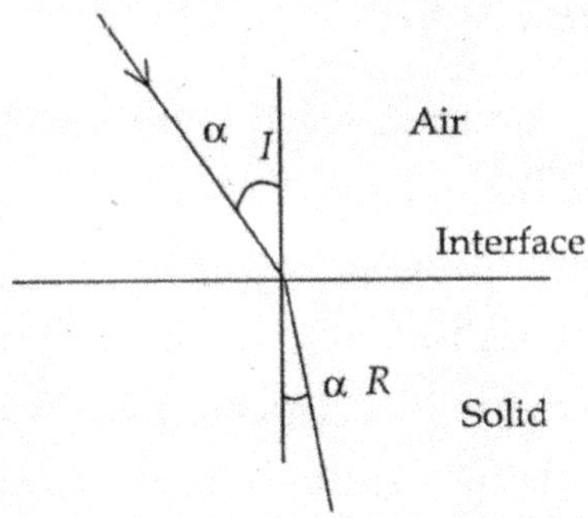

Fig. 5.41 Principle of refraction.

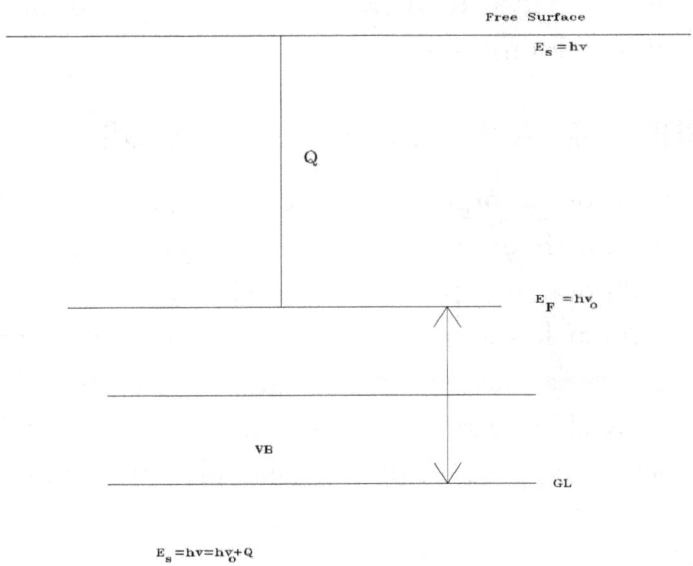

Fig.5.42 Principle of Photo electric Effect and Work function

frequency than semiconductors. Under an electric field these excited electrons can flow and cause current. The phenomenon is called photoconductivity.

5.4.2.2 EMISSION OF PHOTONS

There are two types namely unstimulated (spontaneous) and stimulated emission. The excited electrons discussed in the previous section can drop down to lower energy levels emitting photons. If this occurs on its own without any assistance from outside it is called spontaneous emission. Such emissions are of different types namely photoluminescence, electroluminescence, cathodeluminescence and thermoluminescence, depending on the type of initial excitation. The second kind of emission occurs when excited electrons are forced by incident radiation to emit photons which are phase coherent. This is the basis of **LASER**(Light Amplification by Stimulated Emission of Radiation) and **MASER**(Microwave Amplification by Stimulated Emission of Radiation).

5.4.3 DIRECT & INDIRECT BAND GAP SOLIDS

The emission or absorption of photons can take place in a semiconductor without involving phonons. Neither absorption nor emission of phonons take place. It is called Direct band gap material. The maximum at lower energy level and the minimum at higher energy level occur at the same wave number vector value. As shown in Fig 5.43(a).Gallium Arsenide is an excellent example for this kind of phenomenon.Suppose the process takes place with emission or

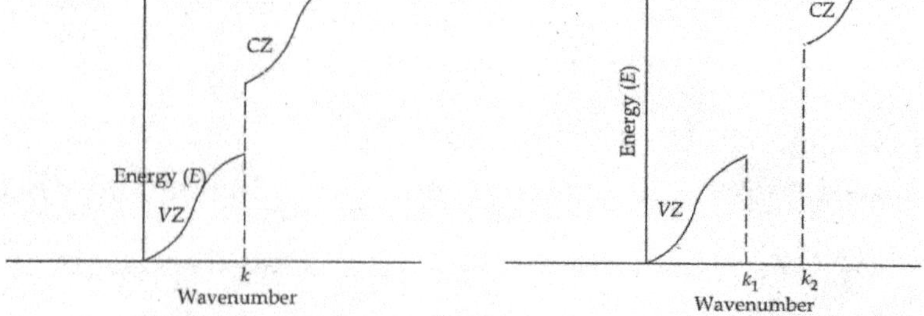

Fig. 5.43 Principle of direct and indirect bandgap transitions.

absorption of phonons as shown in Fig 5.43(b) in a material it is called indirect band gap material. Silicon is one such material. In the later type of materials quantum efficiency is very less and therefore they are not useful for Lasers.

5.4.4 OPTICAL SPECTRA OF SOLIDS

When electromagnetic radiation (invisible or visible light falls) on a material certain wavelengths are absorbed, some are partially

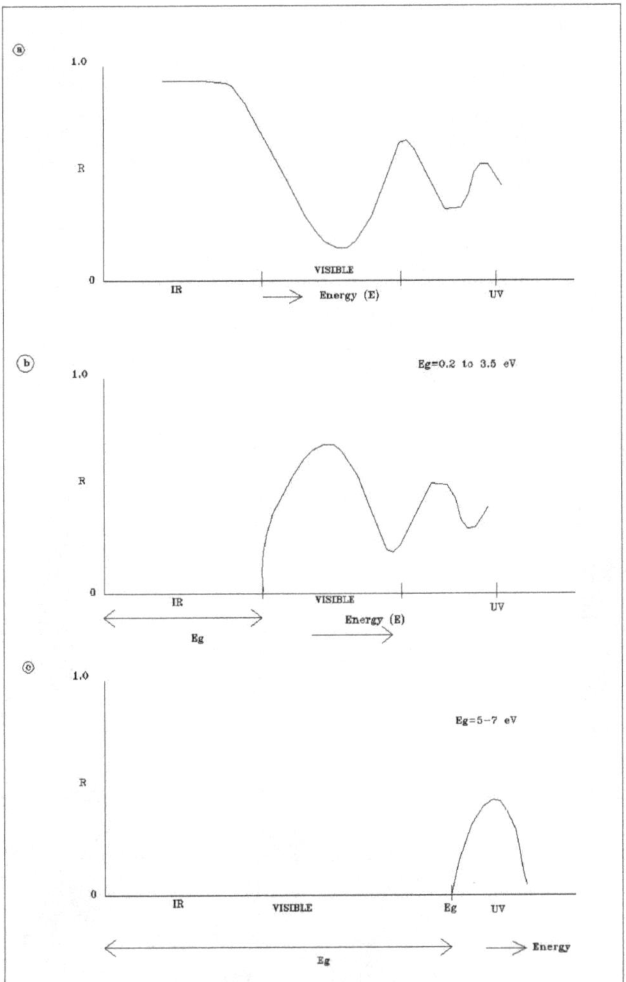

Fig.5.44 Optical Spectra (a) Metal (b) Semi Conductor (c) Ceramic

absorbed and some are transmitted. Based on this a plot of reflectivity against wavelength can be plotted. It is called the optical spectrum of that material. A typical plot is shown for a metal (opaque), intrinsic direct band gap semiconductor and a ceramic (transparent) in Figs 5.44 (a) (b) & (c).

5.4.5 INTERBAND AND INTRABAND TRANSITIONS OF ELECTRONS

The intraband transition can occur as shown in Fig 5.45 in metals and extrinsic semiconductors not in insulators (ceramics) or intrinsic semiconductors. The former two can absorb the longer wavelengths

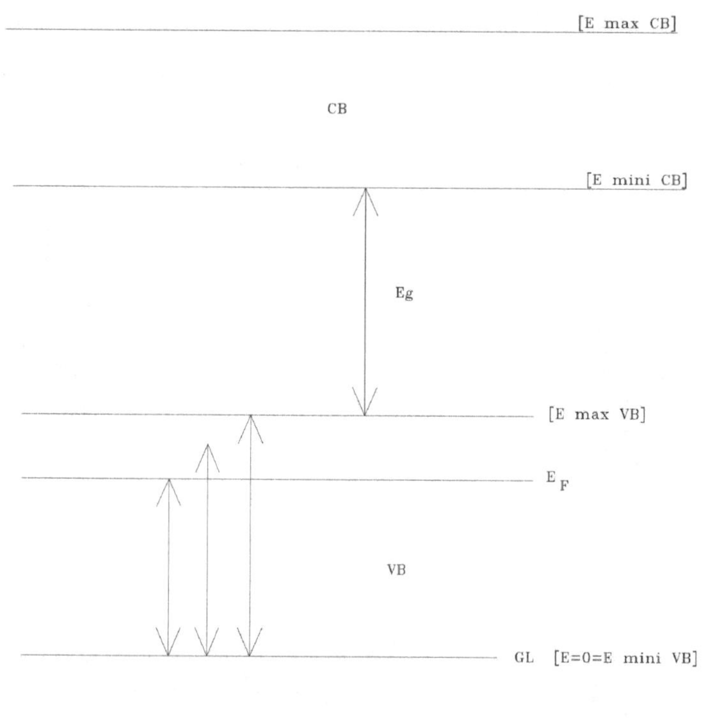

Fig.5.45 Intraband transitions

but the later two cannot. Transitions can occur within the valence band itself in metals as empty states are available above filled states. Such intraband transitions occur with participation of phonons. In all cases the momentum of electrons and photons must be conserved and the total energy must be conserved. The momentum of a photon is much smaller than that of an electron. Phonons have small energy and large momentum. In the electron-photon interaction phonons may be involved or not involved to conserve momentum and energy. In metals both inter and intra band transitions are possible. In semiconductors and insulators no intraband transition is possible. In metals intraband transitions are not quantized but continuous. The indirect interband transitions can be neglected due to its weak nature (2 or 3 orders of magnitude less) compared to direct interband transitions.The former occurs only when the later is absent. Interband transitions for all solids are quantized. Indirect interband transitions are important in semiconductors

5.5 ZONE THEORY AND ELECTRON PHASES IN ALLOYS

Consider an alloy of copper and zinc. In the phase diagram one sees phases of α (terminal FCC phase), β (ordered BCC intermediate phase), β'(disordered BCC intermediate high temperature phase), γ (intermediate defect BCC electron phase), δ(high temperature BCC intermediate phase), ε (HCP intermediate electron phase) and η (terminal HCP phase). Each one has a typical crystal structure and occurs over a range of composition. β occurs at a composition of 50 atomic % copper and 50 atomic %zinc. This corresponds to an electron atom ratio of 1.5(3/2).Similarly at a ratio of (21/13) and (7/4) new phases γ and ε appear. It is not only in this system but also in several others, such a phenomenon occurs. These phases are called electron phases or electron compounds. A change in crystal structure occurs, for example (FCC) α transforms to (BCC) β. And this is explained with the help of zone theory and density of states curve. In Fig 5.46 as the electron to atom ratio changes on adding (alloying) zinc to copper the density of states curve is filled to different extent. Consider the curves for FCC and BCC at a ratio of 1.5 as shown superposed in Fig 5.47.The highest energy in FCC

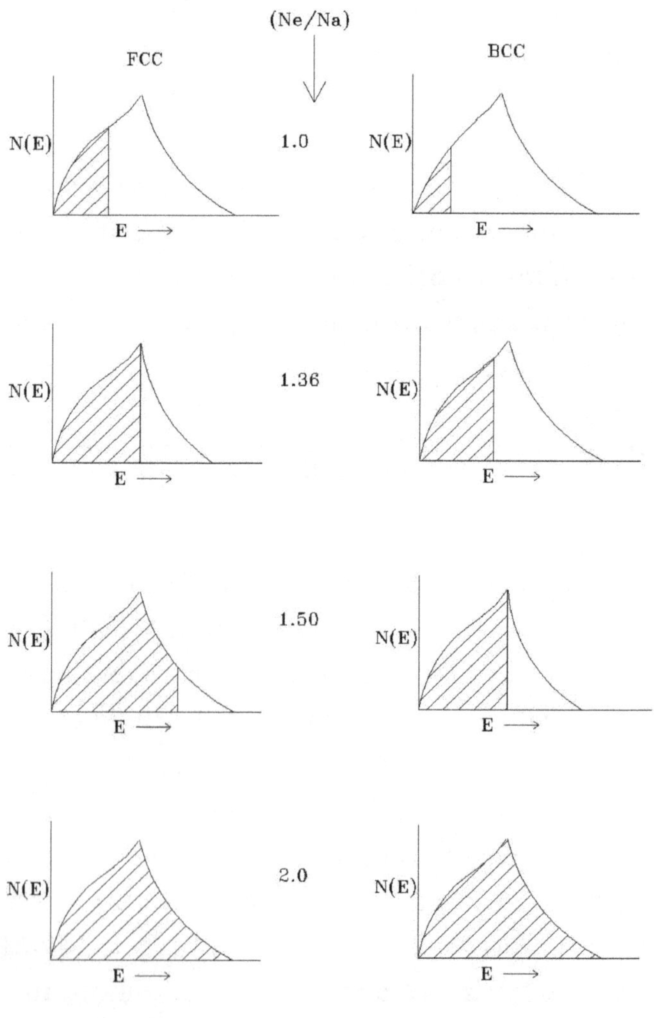

Fig.5.46 Filling of Energy levels in FCC & BCC Lattices

is greater than that in BCC. So energetically BCC is favourable and the alloy transforms from FCC to BCC crystal structure. This sort of simple and elegant explanation can be extended to other phases in various alloy systems.

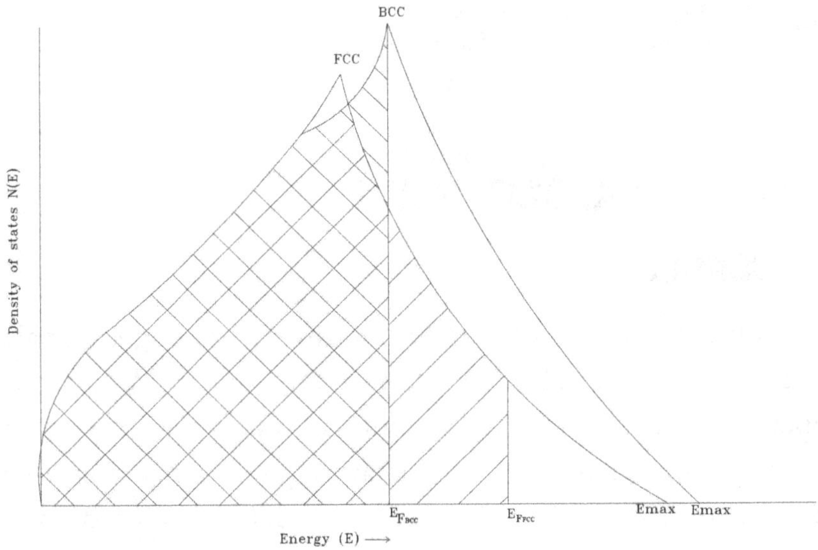

$E_{F_{BCC}}$ Corresponding to (Nc/Na)=1.5 is lower than $E_{F_{FCC}}$ Corresponding to the same Electron to AtomRatio.

Fig. 5.47 Illustration of Energy stability of BCC over FCC at (Ne/Na)=1.5 in Cu-Zn system

5.6 CRYSTAL STRUCTUR OF METALS/SOLIDS

The crystal structure depends on the electron to atom ratio.The electrons to be considered are the s&p electrons present in the outer orbit.The d electrons do not directly influence crystal structure. The following correlation developed by Engel and independently confirmed by Brewer(Ref. 18 Vol. II) holds good:

If Ne/Na ≤ 1.5 will give rise to BCC, ≥1.7 and≤ 2.1will give HCP and ≥2.5 and≤ 3will give FCC crystal structures.The above correlation is based on promotion and bonding energies of different types of crystals.

6

MATERIALS AND PRODUCTION

6.1 ELECTRICAL MATERIALS

6.1.1 CONDUCTORS

Copper and aluminium are two important conducting materials in everyday engineering. They are produced in appreciable quantities. Copper is expensive and heavy in contrast to aluminium. These two are used as wires predominantly in carrying electricity from power plants (nuclear, thermal, hydro etc.) to users over long distances. Aluminium-Zirconium alloy is used for overhead transmission as it can withstand higher temperature during service.Transmission and distribution losses due to I^2R heating take place and lead to drop in voltage. If care is not taken these may be high and result in inefficiency and monetary losses. Such wires can be produced by wire drawing. The process is shown in Fig6.1(a) and the carbide die is shown in Fig6.1 (b) Dies can also be made of maraging steels and diamond for critical applications where cost is not a consideration. High speed steels may be adequate and cost effective in certain situations.. Wire drawing is the dominant route of wire production. Wires have diameter <5.0 mm .Usually wires are pulled from the exit side of the die. One principal stress is tensile and the other two stresses are compressive. Generally multiple block drawing is used to produce longer lengths. Each block will have a die and reduction will be progressive. For ferrous wires a speed of 10m/s is the limit.

For nonferrous wires such as copper and aluminium the limit may go as high as 30 m/s. During the process a lot of heat is generated, but usually the wire drawing is done at room temperature. There is no problem of buckling. No container is used. Extrusion is also used. for making wires. There are several types of extrusion processes as shown in Fig 6.1 (c.) .Here the billet is pushed from the entry side of the die and wire comes out through the exit side. All the three principal stresses are compressive. Container is used in conventional and hydrostatic extrusion. Containerless extrusion is not suitable for producing wires. Hydrostatic extrusion has become the chosen method for producing long lengths. In this the forces are the least and friction is zero. Strips can also be used. They are produced by strip drawing. The cross section will be rectangular. One way to eliminate the power losses is to use super conducting wires. As of now there are technological problems in realizing this. Efforts are on in several countries to realize this dream as early as possible.

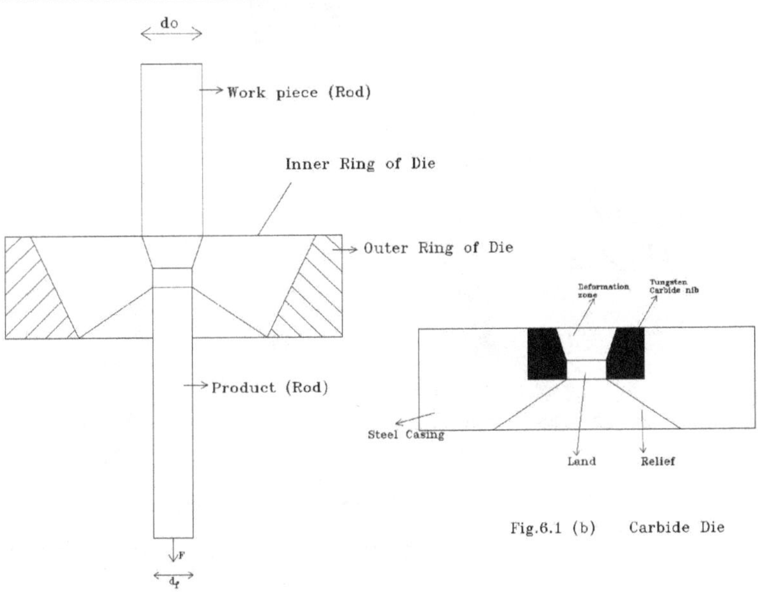

Fig.6.1 (b) Carbide Die

Fig.6.1 (a) Wire Drawing Process

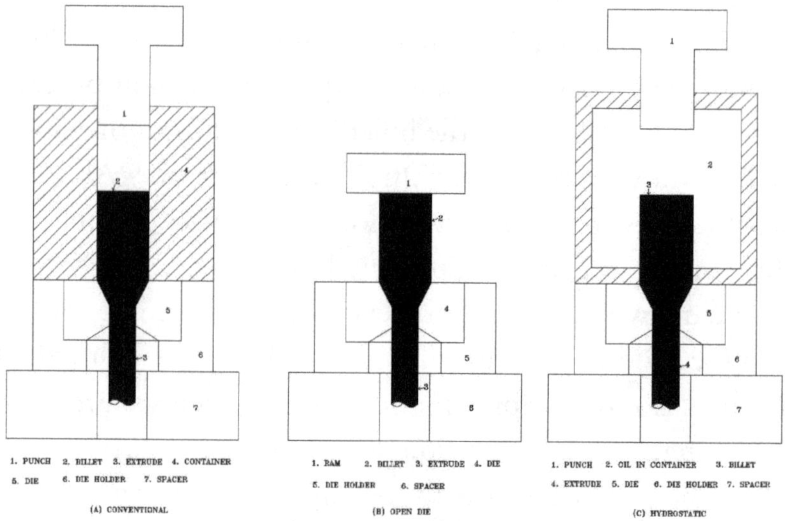

Fig.6.1 (c) Axysymmetric Rod Extrusion Processes

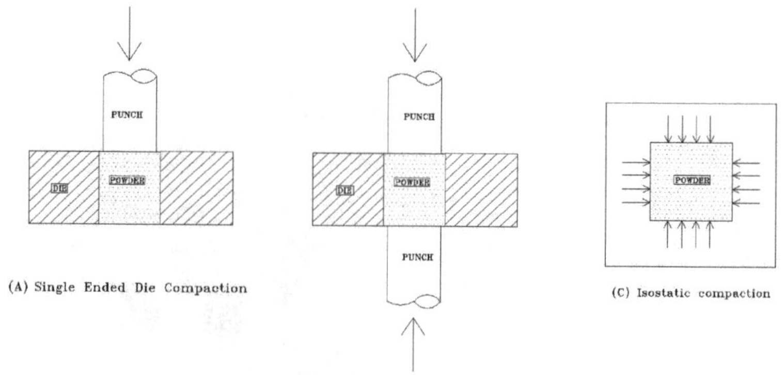

Fig.6.1 (d) Types of Powder Compaction Processes

6.1.2 RESISTORS

Resistors should possess both conductivity and resistivity in adequate measure. If resistance is either zero or very high(current is negligible) heat generated will be nil. In general alloys such as nichrome, kanthal, and manganin are used in wire or strip form as heating elements and standard resistors. Ceramic heating elements such as silicon carbide and molybdenum disilicide are used in furnaces.

6.1.3 INSULATORS

Ideal insulators should have infinite resistance. They cannot be polarized. Actual insulators with very high resistance help humans in handling safely electrical equipment and instruments. Also they prevent short circuiting and leakage of currents in unwanted regions in electrical & electronic circuits. Rubber is an important material under this category. Alumina, aluminium nitride, beryllium oxide and porcelain are very useful ceramic materials in this regard. Relative permittivity is very low for these materials and power losses are considerably lower. They possess good mechanical, thermal and chemical stability. These have excellent thermal shock resistance. Material and manufacturing costs are affordable. The electrical resistivity of some materials is given in Table 6.1(a)

Table 6.1(a) Electrical resistivity of materials

Material	Electrical resistivity(Ohm-m)x10^{-8}
Al	2.8
Cu	1.7
Ag	1.5
W	5.5
Mo	4.9
Pt	10.9

Ta	15.5
Nichrome	108
Manganin	48
Kanthal	135
Silicon carbide	$10x10^{10}$
Molybdenum silicide	$2.5x10^{10}$
Aluminium nitride	$10x10^{11}$
Silico dioxide	$10x10^{24}$
Silicon nitride	$10x10^{11}$
Barium titanate	$5x10^{11}$
Boron carbide	$5x10^{11}$
Wood	$4x10^{17}$
Rubber	$10x10^{18}$

6.1.4 DIELECCTRIC AND PIEZO ELECTRIC MATERIALS

The dielectric materials undergo polarization in an electric field. They also have high resistance. Relative permittivity is adequate and power losses are low.

The piezoelectric materials undergo polarization under stress.

Dielectric materials can be classified as those with relative permittivity < 12 and > 12.In the former category, cotton, silk, paper, polymer are used below 363K, organic binder filled asbestos and mica are used below 403K and silicone binder filled mica and asbestos are used below 453K. Above this temperature mica, asbestos and glass without fillers are used. Titania based ceramics are considered and used for permittivities >12 and <100.

PZT(lead zirconium titanate) and quartz are two such material which are widely exploited. Low permittivity ceramics are widely used for their electrically insulating properties. Clay and talc based ceramics called electrical porcelains come under this category. They are inexpensive. They have good thermal shock resistance..They possess mechanical, thermal and chemical stability over a wide range of environments.

6.1.5 FERROELECTRIC MATERIALS

These exist in polarized form even when no electric field is applied. Their relative permittivity is very high. Barium titanate is an excellent material in this category. If the material is in single crystal form a square loop as seen in Fig6.2(a) occurs and is useful for switching devices in computers. It is produced by P/M route as shown in Fig 6.1(d). It involves compaction and sintering .Compaction can be done at room temperature ,Sintering is done at high temperature[T_s=0.8T_m]. If no constituent powder melts it is called solid state sintering. If the lowest melting component only melts it is called liquid state sintering. In Hot Isostatic Pressing, compaction and sintering are done at high temperature and constant compressive stresses.

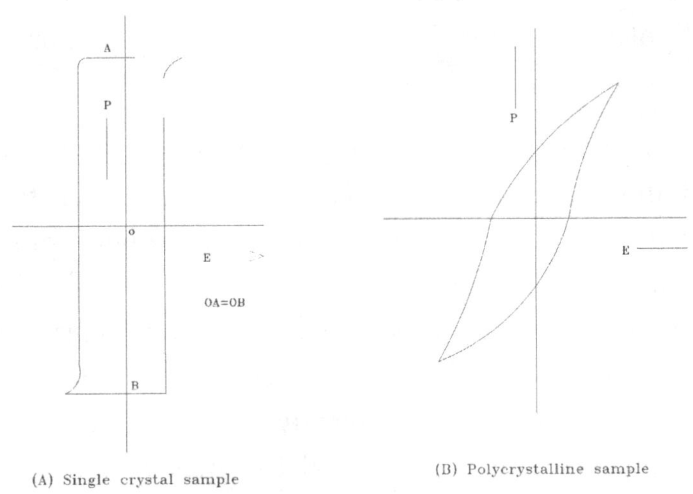

Fig.6.2 (a) Ferro Electric Hystresis Loop

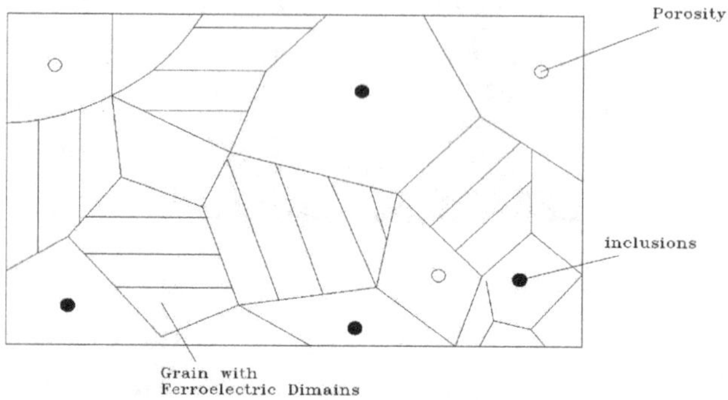

Fig.6.2 (b) Schematic Microstructure of polycrystalline single phase Barium Titanate ($BaTiO_3$) compound exhibiting domains

Barium carbonate and titanium dioxide with required additives and dopants are compacted into desired shape and sintering is done at 1673K to get it in polycrystalline form so as to get a small and narrow hysteresis loop as shown in Fig 6.2(a). The microstructure is shown schematically in 6.2(b). After sintering the material is annealed in an electric field between 278K and 393K to orient the electric dipoles in a particular direction to realize maximum dipole moment.

The relative permittivity changes with temperature as shown in Fig6.3 and peaks occur wherever there is phase transformation and crystal structure change. To suppress polymorphic phase transformations and to stabilize the tetragonal form of the material alloying is done. Strontium is added to partially replace barium. The relative permittivity shows no spikes in the temperature range of our concern and increases linearly with rise in temperature. Coarse grained (>15 μ m) material has smaller hysteresis losses than fine grained. Polycrystalline barium titanate has positive temperature coefficient(resistivity increases above curie temperature)

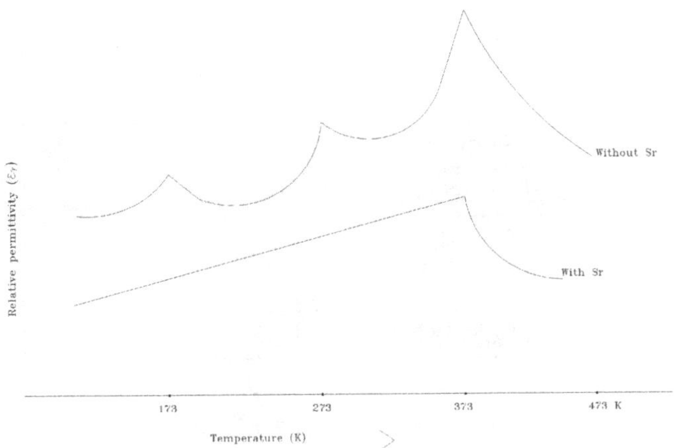

Fig.6.3 Varriation of relative permittivity of $BaTiO_3$ with temperature

while single crystal material has negative temperature coefficient. Relative permittivity of required value can be tailor made to suit the application by alloying barium titanate. Its sensitivity is less compared to other ferroelectric materials but is more durable and can withstand accidental mechanical abuse in handling and transportation.

Sol-Gel technique can be used to produce barium titanate. It can be produced in powder form through the precipitation process by reacting barium chloride and titanium chlorate in a suitable atmosphere. Then it can be sintered into required shapes and suitable annealing treatment in an electric field can be given. The relative permittivity of some materials is given in Table 6.1(b)

Table 6.1(b) Dielectric properties

Material	Permittivity
AlN	8.8
Al2O3	6.6

Si3N4	6.0
SiO2	3.8
SiC	8.5
Fused Silica	4.0
Rubber	3.8
Wood	5.5
Porcelain	6.0
PVC	3.5
Polyehylene	2.3
Paraffin	2.0
Lithium Niobate	78
Barium Titanate	4000
Silicon	11.5
Germanium	15.8
GaAs	10.9

6.1.6 SEMICONDUCTORS

These can be elemental or compound in nature. Silicon and germanium fall in the former category while Gallium Arsenide comes in the latter. Silicon is the most important among all the semiconductors and this age is called ***silicon age*** where information processing is the key to success wherever you are in, home or office or industry. The first transistor was developed with germanium. It can be easily refined to semiconductor grade than silicon as in the later impurity level has to be lower by four orders of magnitude than in germanium. In spite of this silicon has taken the centre stage due to its abundance on earth, easy availability and low cost. Extrinsic semiconductors are the workhorse of the industry. The mobility of electrons and holes are lower in silicon than in germanium. The effective mass of electrons is lower and the effective mass of hole is more in silicon than in germanium. Both have diamond cubic crystal structure, the bonding is covalent and coordination number is four. Intrinsic silicon has a band gap of 1.11eV.It is doped with pentavalent donor impurities (P,As,Sb etc) to get n-type and trivalent acceptor impurities (B,Al,Ga,In etc) to get p-type extrinsic silicon semiconductors. Silicon is an indirect band gap material. Quantum efficiency for emitting light is low due to dissipation of energy of excited electrons by emitted phonons. .Therefore it is not useful for LASERS or LEDs even though it has no rival or competitor in sight for solar panels and computers. Gallium Arsenide is a III-V compound semiconductor. It has a diamond cubic crystal structure and bonding is partially covalent and partially ionic. It is a direct band gap material. Its energy gap is 1.34 eV. Both n and p type semiconductors can be got by doping with germanium.If germanium substitutes for gallium excess electrons will be present to give n type semiconductor and if substitutes for arsenic p type semiconductor will occur. By subjecting gallium arsenide to a special heat treatment process this can be achieved. It is very useful for LASERs and other optoelectronic applications. Devices made of GaAs are faster (two and a half times) than that of Si. Noise is considerably less due to the high band gap. Vulnerability to cosmic radiation is less. It is more expensive than Si. It is heavier than Si. All said and done, Si is no competitor for GaAs. Each has its own sphere of activities and importance.

Semiconducting compounds formed between IV & IV and II & VI group elements apart from III&V are routinely used. Each such compound has a unique energy gap and properties may vary from each other. These are listed in Table 6.1(c). Ternary and quaternary compounds are widely used to ensure efficiency and stability during operation of devices.

Table 6.1(c) Semi conducting properties of materials

Material	Nature	Energy Gap(RT)	Conductivity(Ωm)$^{-1}$	Mobility (μ_e) (μ_h)
Carbon	IT	5.47	10^{-12}	(0.18) (0.12)
Germanium	IT	0.66	2.2	(0.39) (0.19)
Silicon	IT	1.12	$9x10^{-4}$	(0.15)(0.0450)
Grey Tin	DT	0.08	1o ^{6}	(0.14) (0.12)
GaAS	DT	1.42	-	(0.85)(0.04)
InAs	DT	0.36	-	(3.30)(0.046)
GaP	IT	2.26	-	(0.01)(0.007)
GaN	DT	3.36	-	(0.04)(0.01)
InSb	DT	0.17	-	(8.0)(0.125)
α -SiC	IT	2.99	-	(0.04)(0.005)
ZnO	DT	3.35	-	(0.02)(0.18)
CdSe	DT	1.70	-	(0.08) (-)
ZnS	DT	3.68	-	(0.02)(0.0005)
PbS	IT	0.41	-	(0.06)(0.07)

Hall coefficient is positive for p-type and negative for n type semiconductors. First one should obtain semiconductor grade material from metallurgical grade material that has been obtained from starting minerals. It means that a high degree of purity is required (impurity should be less than parts per billion.)Such a high purity material is then perfected so as to be free of dislocations and grain boundaries. Otherwise devices will not function efficiently. The purity is achieved by zone refining and perfection is achieved by single crystal growth.

6.1.7 ZONE REFINING

The semiconductor grade material is obtained from metallurgical grade material by effecting nonequilibrium solidification in which segregation of dissolved impurity atoms takes place. The required solidus and liquidus lines in a phase diagram are shown schematically in Fig 6.4 and the undesirable and desirable freezing range (narrow and wide) is shown schematically in Fig6.5(a)&(b).Following assumptions are made: Diffusion in solid is nil and diffusion in liquid(the melt) is very fast. The liquid remains homogeneous. The process is carried out as shown in Fig6.6(A).The rod to be purified is refined portion by portion called zone. Ten zones are shown in the figure. A heater is starting to move from the left and travels forward towards the right. It goes at a particular speed. Three stages are shown

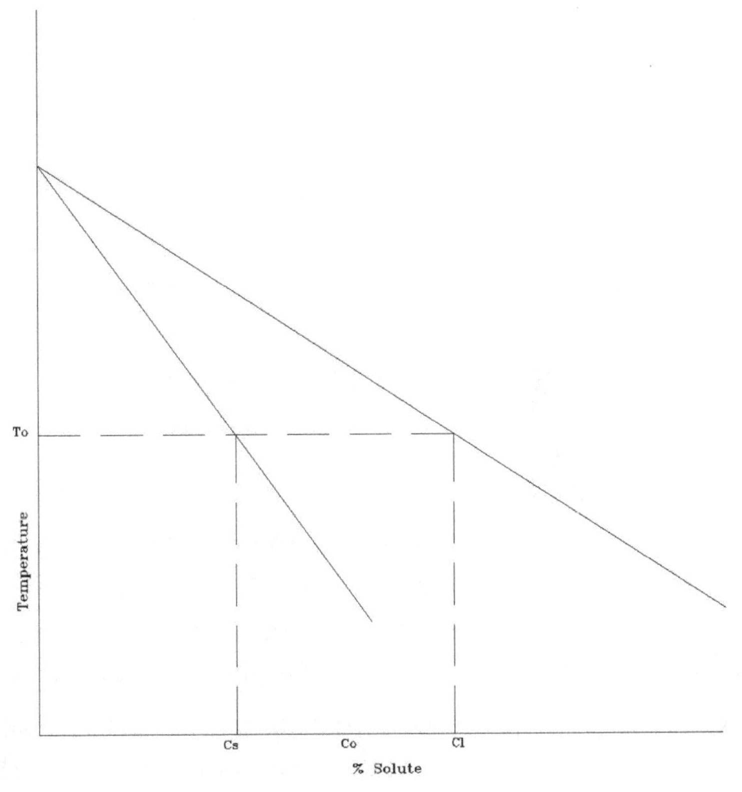

Fig.6.4 Principle of Zone Refining to achieve very high purity to get SCG material

in the figure. A single pass is finished when the heater is at the tenth zone on the right. Again the heater can be placed in the first zone and the process repeated. Fig 6.6 (B) shows a length dx of one zone getting solidified on the left and molten on the right. Using this one can mathematically treat the process and theoretically arrive at the concentration profile in the rod after one pass and also after a given number of passes. The governing equation is given below:

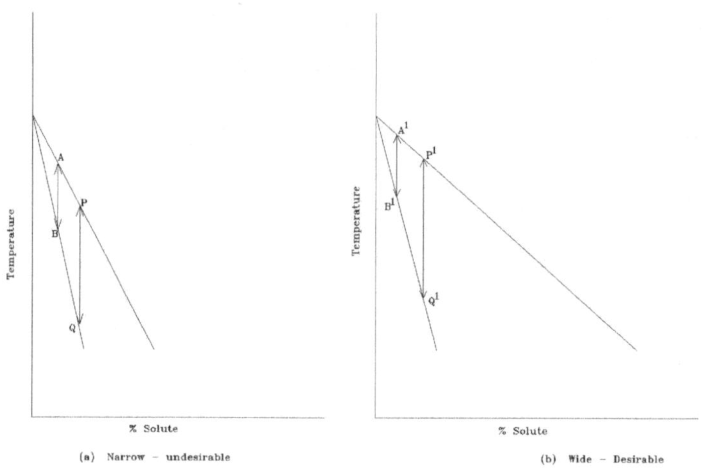

Fig.6.5 Freezing Range suitable for zone refining

$$C_s = C_0[1-\{(1-K)EXP(-K(x/l))\}]$$

Where l is zone length, L is rod length, $K=[C_s/C_l]$ is segregation constant, C_0 is initial concentration of impurity in solid. K is less than one. C_s is the impurity in the first solid to be formed and C_l in the first liquid to be formed in the first zone after the heater moves to the second zone. Solid is purer than liquid. K should be as small as possible (0.1,0.2,0.3 etc) implying the desirability of a wide freezing range. Several passes [multi pass zone refining] are given to achieve the required purity level. A typical concentration profile is shown after one pass in Fig 6.7

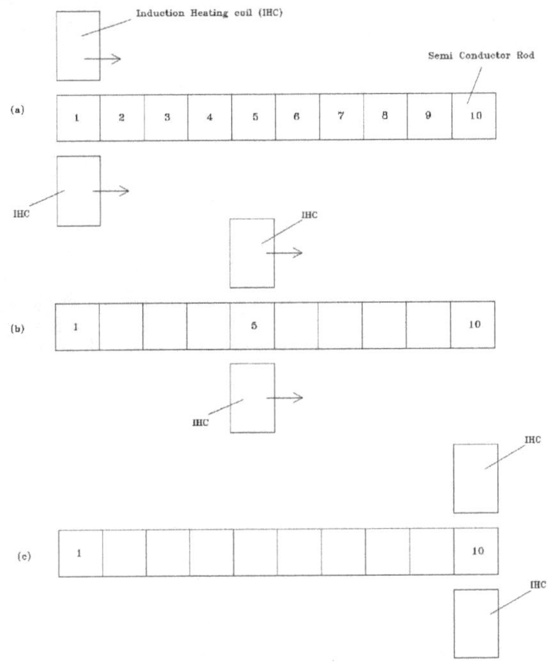

Fig.6.6(A) Stages in one pass of zone refining

(a) Start (b) Middle (c) End

6.1.8 SINGLE CRYSTAL GROWTH

The zone refined rod is molten in a crucible and a rod with a seed crystal [<100> orientation] at one end is dipped in the melt just touching it. It is pulled while rotating the crucible and the rod in opposite directions. The speed of rotation is 1 rev/second, the pulling rate is 2μm /sec. The whole set up is enclosed in an evacuated or inert gas filled chamber. The process is shown in Fig 6.8 in three stages. Si and Ga As can be grown by this technique. To prevent vaporization of As from molten GaAs a thick layer of B_2O_5 is maintained above the melt kept in a BN crucible (to prevent C pickup from crucible) The above technique is called **Czochralski technique.**

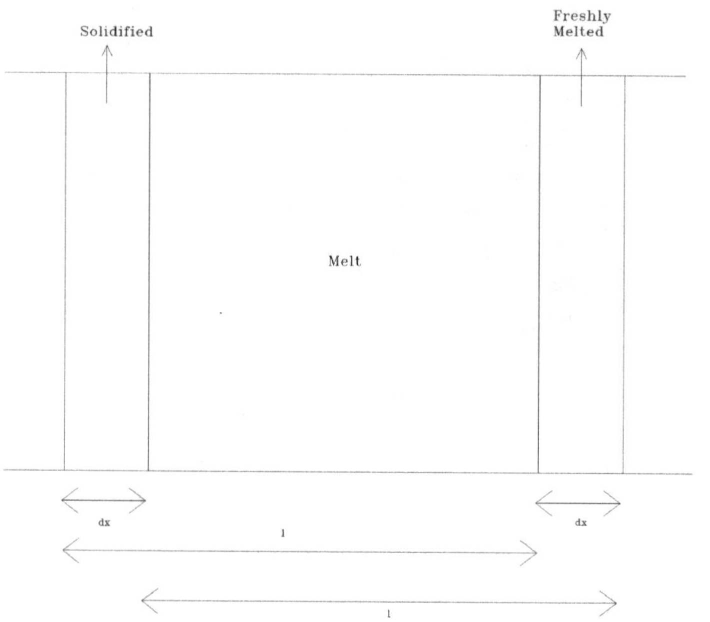

Fig.6.6(B) Geometry of zone refining

Another technique is explained in Fig 6.9 in which three stages are shown. There are two zones. One is above (top)and the other is below (bottom) the melting point of the semiconductor rod to be grown as a single crystal. A cylindrical crucible with a pointed conical end containing the rod is slowly pushed from above and vertically down at a speed of o.3-3.0μm/s so that the tip of the cone comes out first This process is called **vertical Bridgman method.**

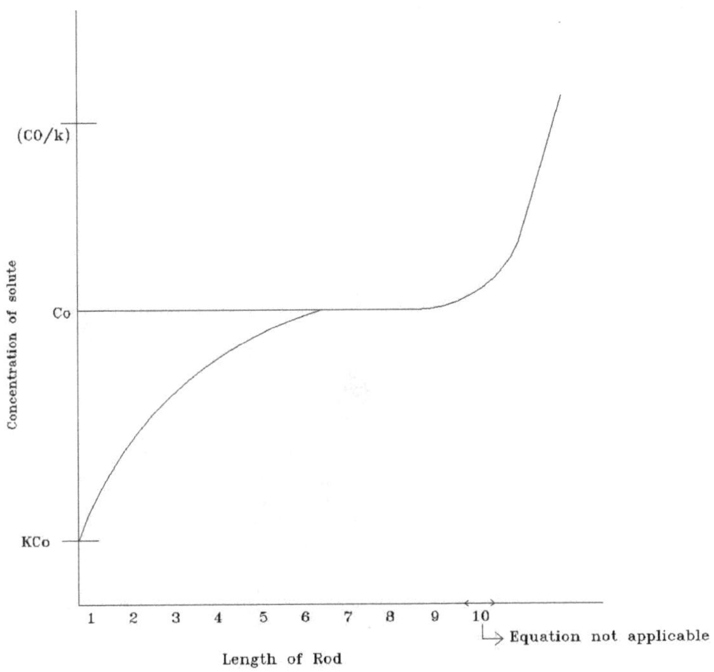

Fig.6.7 Concentration Profile in one pass of zone refining

Another variation of this technique is the horizontal **Bridgman method**. Here there are two zones one hot above the melting point (on the left) and another below the melting point (on the right) of the semiconductor rod. It is especially suited for GaAs. The melt is kept in a silicon nitride coated carbon crucible that is cylindrical with a pointed conical tip. Two zone furnace is moved horizontally from right to left at a speed of 2μm/sec.The tip comes out of the hot zone into the cold zone first as shown in Fig 6.10(A) GaAs is difficult to grow as single crystal from melt since the vapor pressure difference for Ga [0.0001atm] and As [1000atm] is large at 1523K.A convection barrier is kept in a corner of the chamber as shown in Fig 6.10(B).It is separated from the melt crucible lying in the other chamber. Diameter of crystal grown is 240-300 mm. the length is1000mm and it weighs about 140Kgms

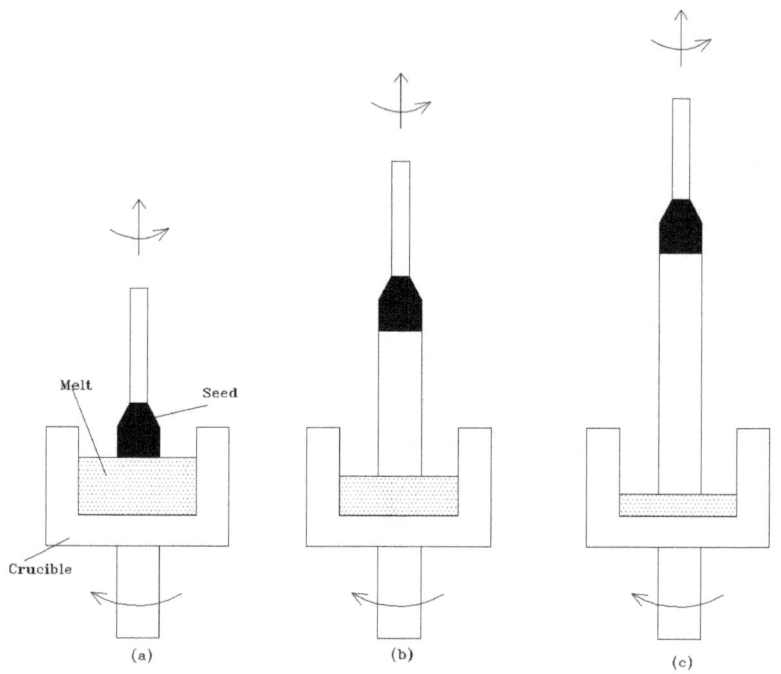

Fig.6.8 Three stages in single crystal growth by Czochralski technique

6.1.9 EPITAXIAL GROWTH

It is a technique of growing an oriented single crystal layer on a semiconductorsubstratewafer. Growth ofone layer ofsemiconductor on a substrate of the same semiconductor is called **homoepitaxial growth**. If a layer is grown on a substrate of another material it is called **heteroepitaxial growth.**

Silicon can be deposited on a silicon substrate to improve the flatness of the surface and reduce the electrical resistance. Thermal

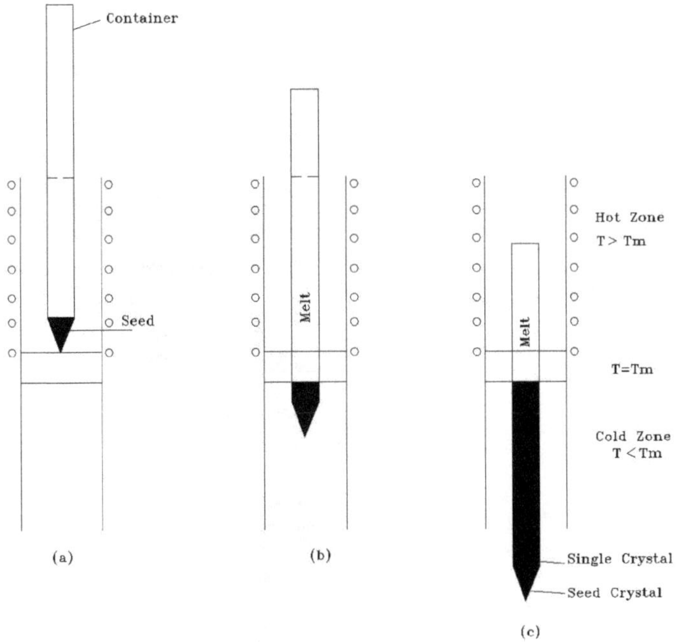

Fig.6.9 Three stages in single crystal growth by vertical Bridgeman Technique

conductivity of silicon is three times greater than that of gallium arsenide and thermal expansion of GaAs is 2.5 times greater than Si.GaAs can be grown on silicon. Lattice parameter of Si is 0.543nm and GaAs is 0.565 nm. Lattice mismatch is rather large. An innovative technique is used for growing this heteroepitaxial layer.At a temperature of 473-723K a thin layer (20 nm) of Ga is deposited on Si substrate. Then the substrate with a thin layer is raised to a higher temperature of 873-1023K to grow a second layer of GaAs. The amorphous first layer becomes crystalline when the heating is done for growing the second layer. AlAs having a lattice parameter of 0.566nm has a better lattice matching with GaAs.

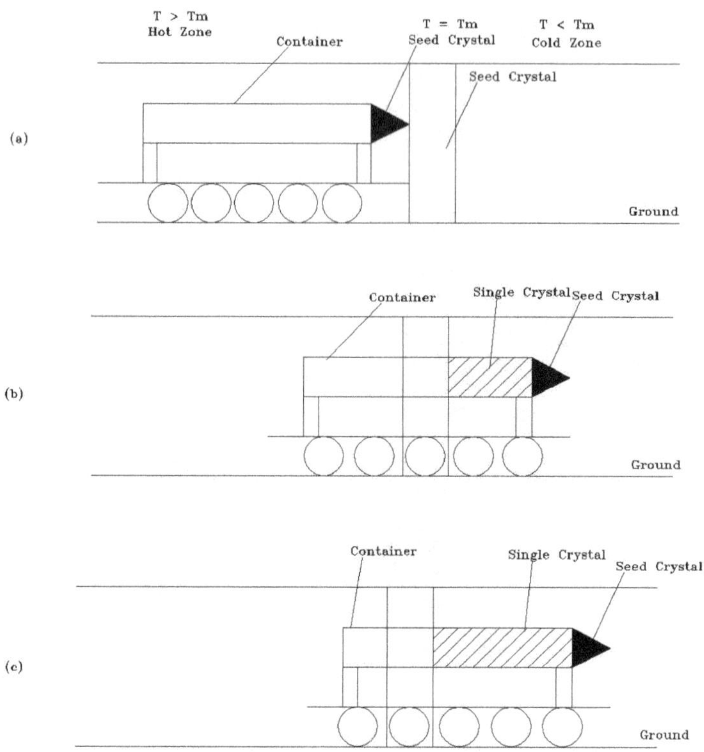

Fig.6.10 (A) Three stages in single crystal growth by Horizontal Bridgeman method

The ternary alloy AlGaAs has a better lattice matching with binary compounds AlAs and GaAs. One can choose any value of 'x' for the ternary compound $Al_x Ga_{1-x} As$ depending on the device to be manufactured. This ternary alloy layer can be epitaxially grown on GaAs substrate without strain. There are different techniques of epitaxial growth namely Liquid phase epitaxy, Vapour phase epitaxy etc. Molecular beam epitaxy is very promising as one can control the composition and doping. The growth rate is less than 1 μm/hour and the process is carried out at a relatively low temperature.It is a versatile process.It can be applied to different compounds $Ga_x In_1$-x As can be grown on InP with perfect lattice matching. A schematic illustration of the process is shown inFig6.11.Lattice mismatch can be investigated using inter planar distance (d) as it is related to lattice parameter (a). A slight mismatch can be accommodated in the epitaxial layer by straining the crystal provided that the thickness of the grown layer is less than a critical thickness t_c. If it is greater than t_c then dislocations have to be formed for matching. Later is undesirable in semiconductors.

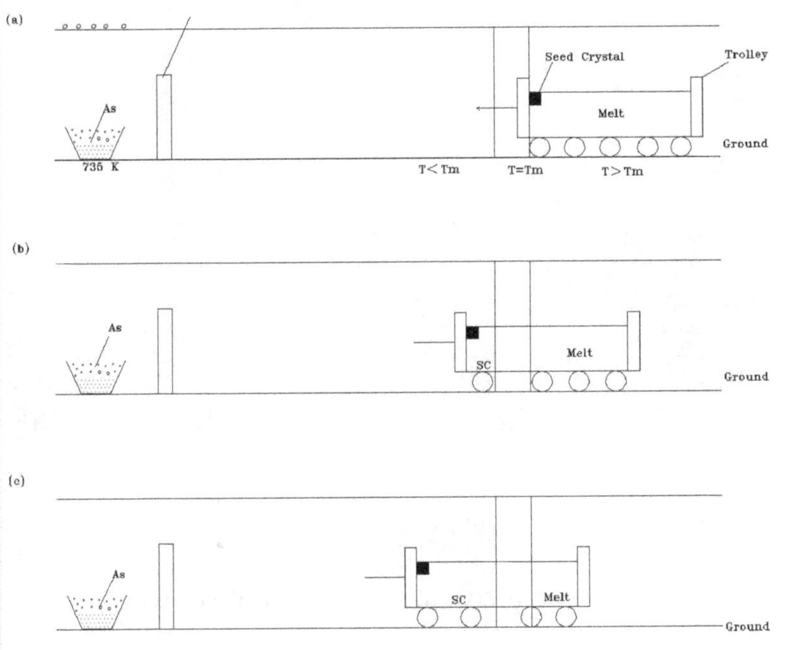

Fig.6.10 (B) Three stages in single crystal growth of GaAs by Horizontal Bridgeman Technique

$$t_c \approx 4\alpha b/f$$

where b is burgers vector, α is constant and f is lattice mismatch

It is equal to

$$2(d_l - d_s) / (d_l + d_s)$$

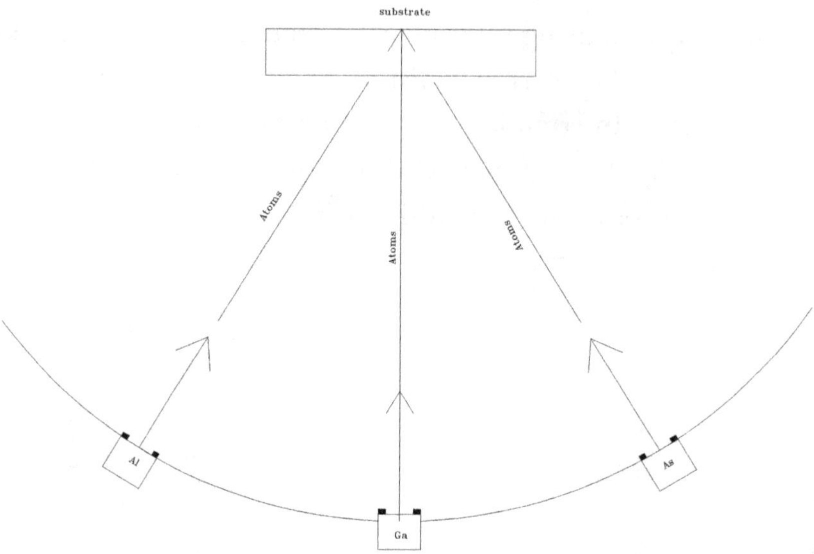

Fig.6.11 Schematic of Molecular Beam Epitaxial growth

l is layer and s is substrate. Atomic plane of layer material can be parallel with some other atomic plane of substrate or with the same atomic plane of substrate

(100)A//(111)B or(100)A//(100)B

where A & B are semiconductor layer and substrates

6.1.10 SUPERCONDUCTORS

Superconducting metals are well known but could not be put to use in everyday life due to technological problems. Superconducting organics and fullerenes are of recent origin. Super conducting intermetallic compounds are put to use in the form of wires and strips in a limited way. All the above materials have very low critical temperatures (15K)

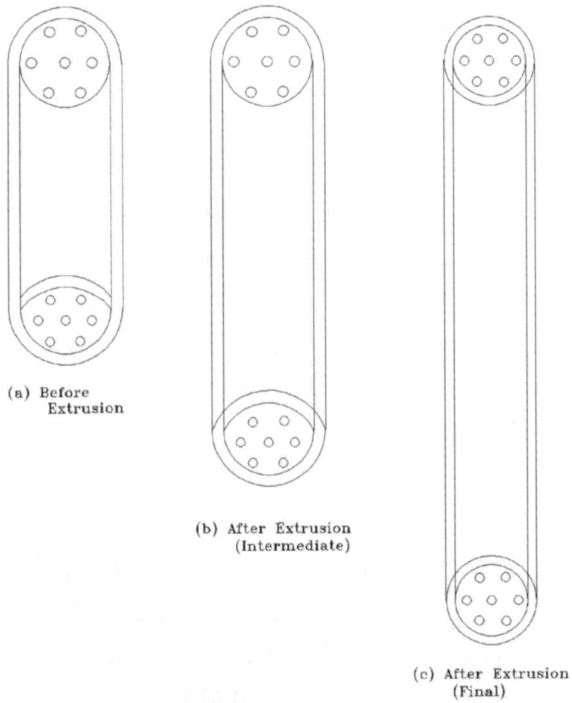

Fig.6.12 Production of Nb_3Sn superconducting multi filamentary cable

Super conducting Rare earth borides have T_c<40K.Liquid Helium refrigeration is a must. On the other hand Ceramic superconductors have high T_c and liquid Nitrogen cooling is sufficient. But production of wires, strips etc of required lengths is a formidable problem due to the brittleness of ceramics.

Intermetallic Nb_3Sn and V_3Ga are used in some critical applications. They are produced in long lengths (wires , tapes & strips) with consistent properties all along the length .Production of Nb_3Sn by a solid state process using diffusion has been illustrated in

Fig 6.12.It is popularly called ***bronze route.*** Holes are drilled in a cylindrical bronze block. Niobium rods of appropriate dimensions are inserted in the holes. The bronze block is pushed through a die to reduce its diameter and increase its length. Several such bronze blocks with reduced cross section are placed in a hollow cylindrical copper block. The void between outer copper block and inner bronze blocks is packed with Niobium. The copper block is pushed through a die to reduce the cross section and increase the length. This product from the previous operation is subjected to a heat treatment. Temperature is maintained at 873-1073K to cause diffusion of Tin that is present in bronze into Niobium. Sufficient time as given by the following equation

$$X= [(D_d) (t)]^{1/2}$$

is given[where X is penetration depth, D_d is Diffusion coefficient of tin in niobium and t is time]. The tin from bronze will not enter copper (outer sheath) due to the existence of a barrier for diffusion. This process is controlled by diffusion which depends on time and temperature. The super conducting properties will be excellent if the grain size of Nb_3Sn formed lies between 70 -90μm and the layer thickness is 2.5-3.5μm. It can be achieved at a diffusion temperature of 973K. Layer thickness and grain size of Nb_3Sn will decide the suitability of multi filamentary superconducting wire for the required applications. The mechanical properties are also important for handling. Volume fraction of filaments is a key factor. The diameter of filaments is of the order of a few microns.

Yittrium barium copper oxide is produced by P/M route and drawing. Powders of CuO, BaO_2 and $Y_2O_3$are taken in appropriate quantities and mixed thoroughly and blended. It is then compacted and sintered. This is then powdered and the process is repeated to arrive at the final stoichiometric composition. The chemical composition is checked by X-ray diffraction method. The sintering should be done in the oxygen atmosphere to supplement and compensate for the loss of oxygen that takes place. The compound is hard and brittle. It has orthorhombic crystal structure [a=0.388nm, b=0.384nm and c=1.163nm]. It has T_c=90K. Grainsize is small. Grain boundaries are useful in pinning the normally conducting regions in a superconducting matrix. In high temperature superconductors such as $YBa_2Cu_3O_7$ thermally induced lattice vibrations make the process of fluxoid pinning difficult. It cannot carry high current densities. It is environmentally unstable. By minimizing porosity stability can be improved. $YBa_2Cu_3O_6$ is an insulator and anti ferromagnetic. When oxygen content increases to 6.5the compound becomes conducting and magnetic. When oxygen becomes 6.64 it becomes superconducting. The molecular formula for superconducting compounds is appropriately given as $YBa_2Cu_3O_{7-X}$.

SOL-GEL method can be used for producing cuprate superconductors. It provides a homogeneous dispersion of the various component metals when a solution containing the metal ion is transformed into a gel by adding an organic solvent such as alcohol. The gel is then heated to a low temperature. It decomposes. Fine particles of desired oxide are obtained. To obtain the high critical temperature of cuprate superconductors the oxides obtained by this method are heated under an oxidizing atmosphere so that the correct stoichiometry of the superconducting compound is obtained.

Large scale production of cuprates is still a distant dream.

Thin films of cuprates are prepared by CVD by oxidizing organometallic compounds of suitable composition. By definition thin films are those with a thickness less than London penetration depth. Laser ablation technique, sputtering and epitaxial growth are other possibilities being explored for producing high temperature ceramic super conductors.

6.2 MAGNETIC MATERIALS

These materials are mostly based on the transition metals iron,nickel and cobalt.The magnetic properties are dependent on crystallographic directions in the solid.That is they are anisotropic.The easy direction of magnetization is that direction in which flux(B) is maximum for a minimum of applied field(H). It is shown in Fig6.13 for Fe, Ni & Co. When field strength is increased flux increases.It reaches a maximum of +B at +H and when the field is reversed it goes to maximum in opposite direction of -B at-H and again when the field is reversed in the opposite direction to + H it goes to + B completing a loop. The material undergoes a process called hysteresis. The area of the hysteresis loop represents loss in magnetic energy called hysteresis loss. Fig 6.14(A) shows such a loop for single phase single and polycrystalline material. The effect of grain boundaries is to increase the area of the loop. Fig 6.14(B) shows the loop for polycrystalline single and dual phase materials. For the latter, area is more in the loop. Magnetic materials are classified on the basis of the area of the loop as hard(large area) and soft(small area).Iron-silicon and Nickel-iron alloys and cubic ferrites are used for soft magnetic applications (continuously changing temporary field strengths).These are made available in single phase and coarse grained form. Al-Ni-Co-Fe alloys, Hexagonal ferrites and Rare Earth alloys are used for hard magnetic applications. (permanent and unchanging constant field strengths)These are made available in multiphase and fine grained form.

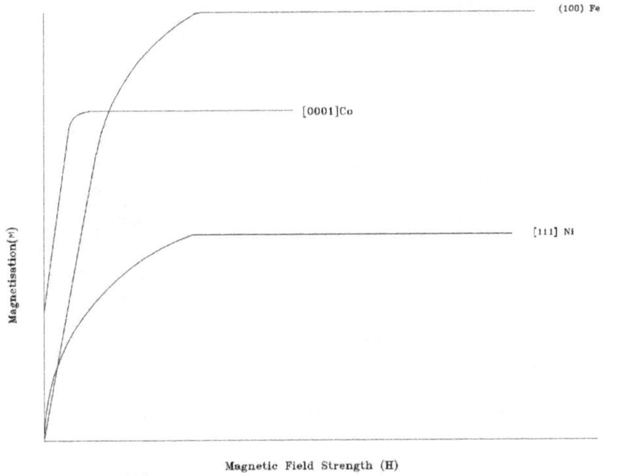

Fig.6.13 Magnetisation Curve for easy direction of magnetisation in Iron, Nickel & Cobalt.

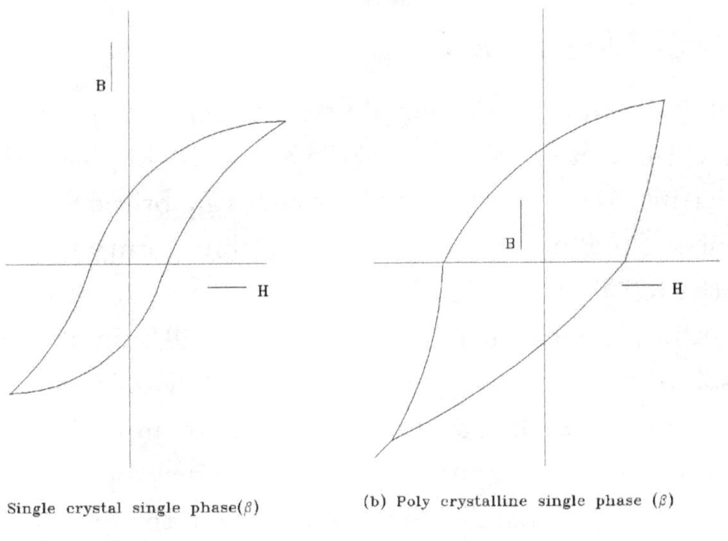

(a) Single crystal single phase(β)

(b) Poly crystalline single phase (β)

Fig.6.14(A) Ferro magnetic Hystersis loop

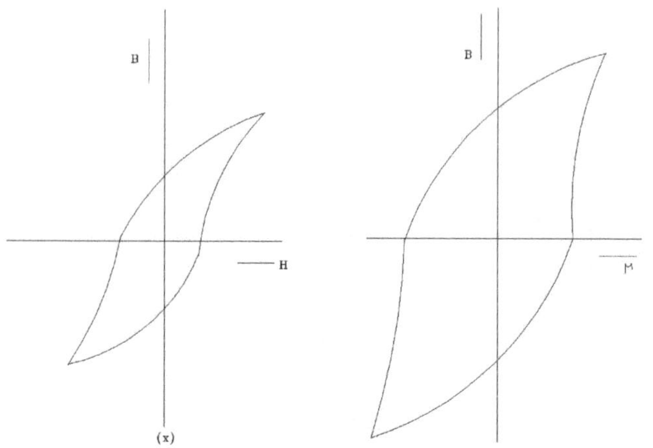

(a) Single phase (α) polycrystal sample (b) Polyphase polycrystal sample (α + B)

Fig.6.14(B) Ferro magnetic Hysteresis curve for soft & hard magnetic materials

6.2.1 SOFT MATERIALS

Iron silicon alloys are considered first. The phase diagram is shown in Fig 6.15. Upto 6.5% Si the alloys are single phase and have BCC ferrite. But beyond 4.5%Si the alloys are brittle and have low toughness. The alloys are used in polycrystalline form with few grains only. The resistance of the alloy is higher than that of iron. These alloys are produced by metal casting route. Si will be in substitutional solid solution in iron. Carbon will be low, only 0.01-0.02%.These alloys are hot rolled, then cold rolled followed by annealing and again cold rolling followed by annealing. Texture is developed. The rolling plane of the sheet is parallel to (100) plane and the rolling direction becomes [100].The texture developed is called ***cube texture*** .

The final heat treatment step is recrystallisation annealing to obtain a coarse grained microstructure as shown in Fig 6.16 with

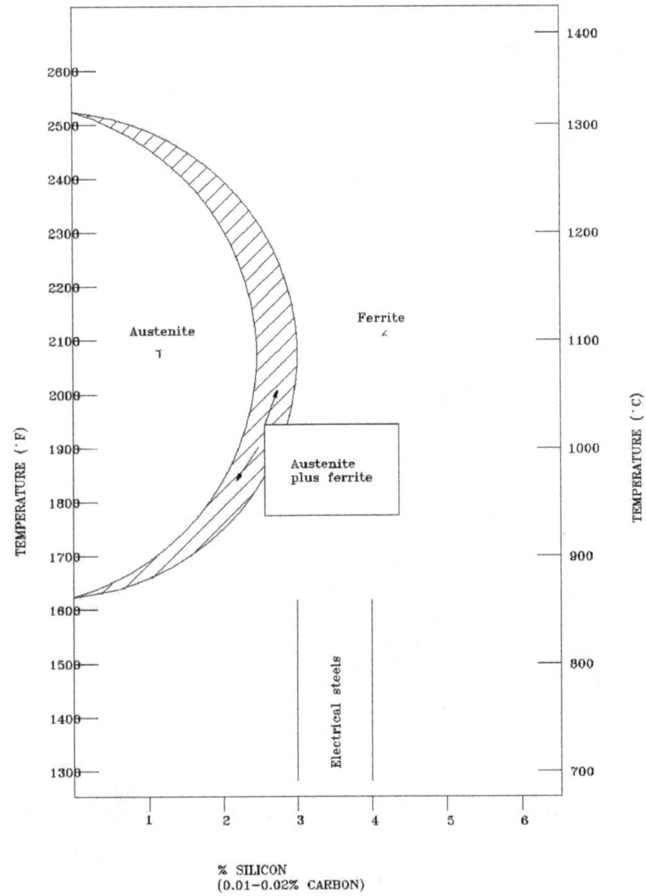

Fig.6.15 Fe–Si Phase Diagram

less number of grains. The recrystallisation temperature is greater than 0.6 times the melting point of the alloy(1823K). Developing cube texture (100)[001] is expensive compared to cube on edge texture (110)[001] but the former is advantageous from the point of view of minimizing hysteresis and eddy current losses. The grain oriented coarse grained alloy is cut into sheets and stacked with insulation in between sheets so that current path is restricted to individual stacked sheets and cannot go from one sheet to another sheet reducing the path length and minimising I^2R losses. Instead of using sheets if powder particles of <75μm size or diameter are used the current path can be restricted within the powder reducing the path length very much. Even though eddy current loss is reduced, hysteresis loss is increased by using powders.Also permeability of powder is greater than that of sheet.

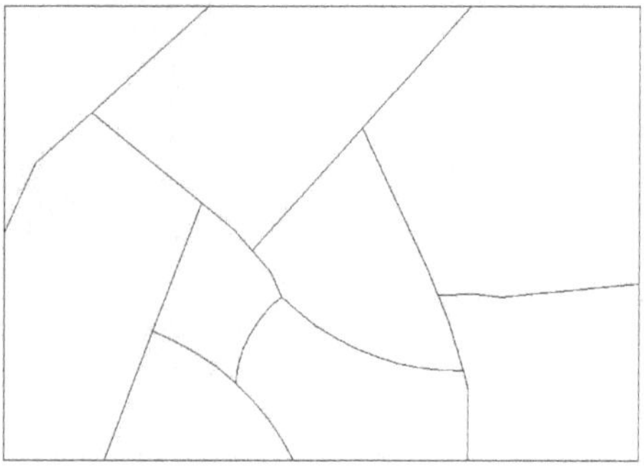

Fig.6.16 Coarse Grained Iron 4% Silicon Alloy – Schematic microstructure showing single phase of solid solution of Si in Fe

Nickel iron alloys are an improvement over iron silicon alloys. The phase diagram in Fig6.17 shows that the iron rich alloys will have BCC alpha iron and FeNi intermetallic compound.Nickel rich alloys will have FCC intermetallic compound Ni_3Fe and BCC alpha iron. Perm alloy has 75%Ni and 25%Fe. Superm alloy is an improvement over perm alloy and is superior in properties. It contains 78% Ni, 16% Feand5% Mo and 0.5%Mn.Mo increases the sensitivity of the alloy and makes it more amenable for heat treatment procedures to be followed. It has higher resistivity and permeability

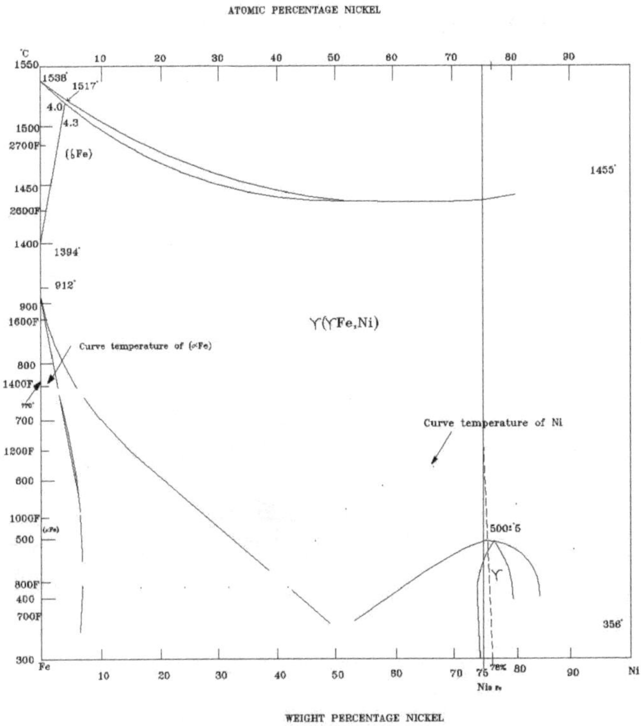

Fig.6.17 Fe–Ni Phase Diagram

(75 AT % Ni = 78 wt % Ni)

and lower magnetostriction and hysteresis loss compared to perm alloy.This alloy is produced by metal casting. Its microstructure is given schematically in Fig6.18.The permeability of Ni-Fe alloy is more compared with Fe-Si alloys as in Fig 6.19. Magnetic annealing can influence the B vs H curve of Ni_3Fe as shown in Fig6.20. Order-Disorder phase transformation occurs in nickel iron systems. It is taken advantage of in improving properties. Heat treatment schedule (T-t diagram) is shown in Fig 6.21 for obtaining single phase disordered Ni_3Fe with high permeability. The alloy is heated to above 873K and cooled to 673K very quickly in a magnetic field to prevent ordering and then cooled to 303K(room temperature) slowly. Fig6.22 shows the way to obtain a square hysteresis loop by magnetic annealing. Square loops are advantageous in computer memories.

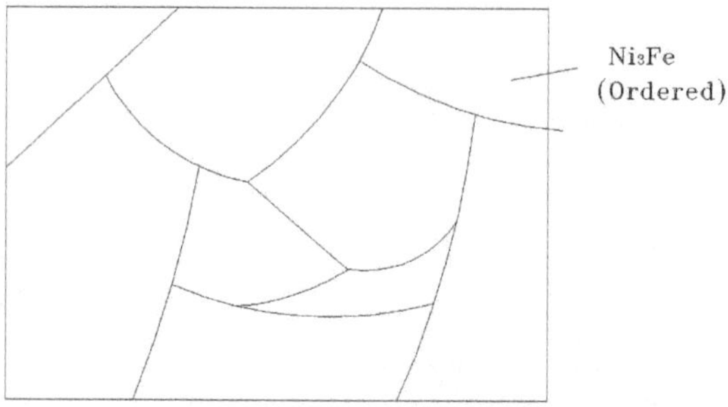

Fig.6.18 Nickel – Iron Alloy – schematic micro structure – FCC single phase ordered compoundNi_3Fe after magnetic annealing from 873K to RT

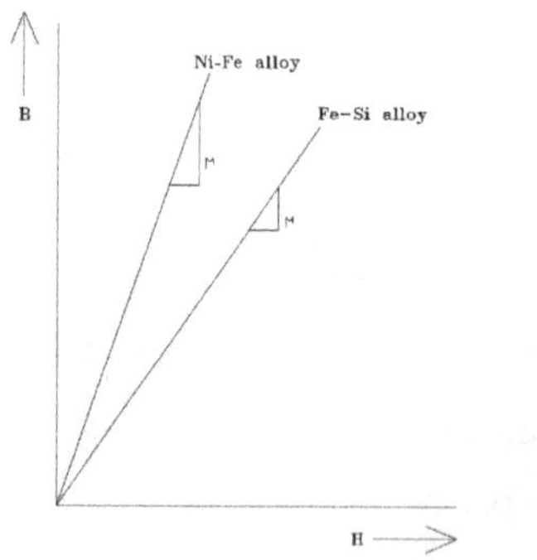

Fig.6.19 Permeability of soft magnetic alloys

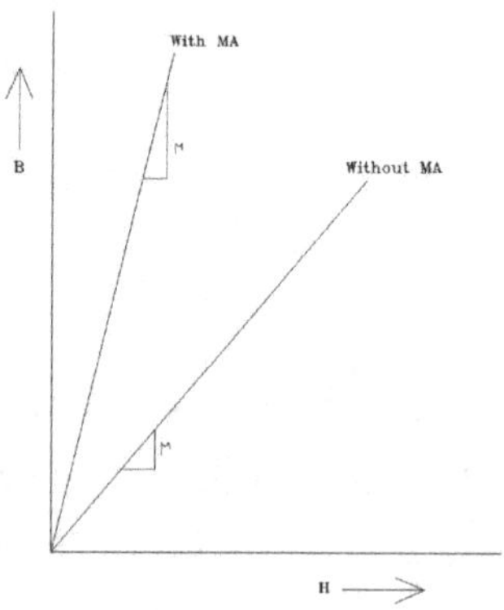

Fig.6.20 Effect of magnetic annealing (MA) on permeability

Cubic Ferrites have spinel crystal structure. There are two types of spinels namely normal [zinc ferrite]and inverse [iron ferrite]. Former contains 8divalent ions in tetrahedral sites while the later has them in octahedral sites. Trivalent ions are equally shared between tetrahedral and octahedral sites. Totally there are 56 ions in the unit cell of the lattice of which 24 are metallic and the remaining 32 oxygen . One unit cell contains 8 molecules of the formula AB_2O_4.

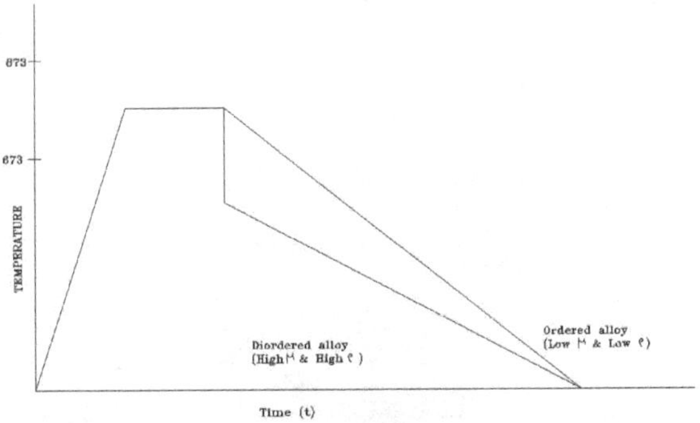

Fig.6.21 T–t diagram for Ni–Fe alloy heat treatment.

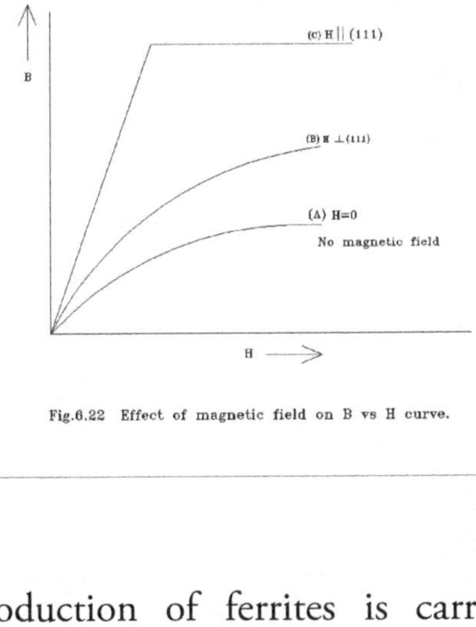

Fig.6.22 Effect of magnetic field on B vs H curve.

The production of ferrites is carried out using powder metallurgical techniques. A typical flowchart is given in Fig6.23. Cubic ferrites are soft magnetic materials and have higher squareness ratio for their hysteresis loops as shown in Fig 6.24. Ideal squareness ratio is one. Real materials have the ratio greater than one.It is estimated as given below:

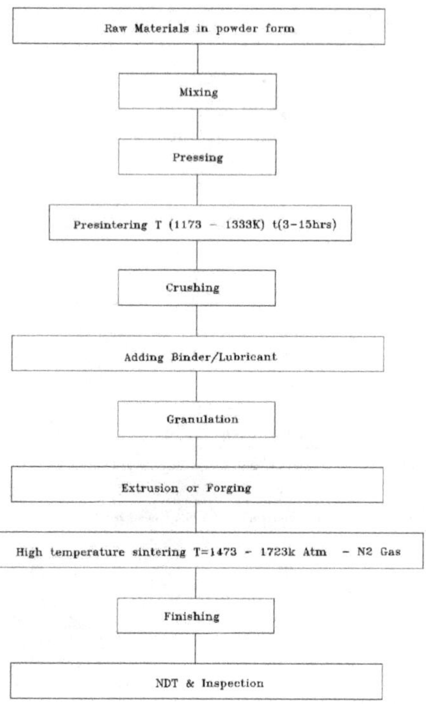

Fig.6.23 Flow chart for Ferrite Production

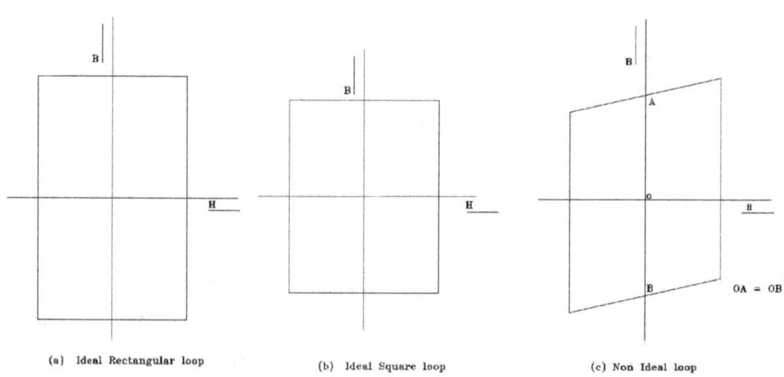

Fig.6.24 Different B vs H Curves to describe soft Ferrites

$$SR = \{[B_{max}] / [B(_{Hmax/2})]\}$$

Some ferrites have rectangular loops as shown in Fig 6.24(a). The desirable and undesirable microstructures of ferrites are shown in Figs 6.25and 6.26. The former has single phase polycrystalline coarse grained (>15μm)material with high amount of porosity. It may be as high as 50% due to the P/M technique employed for production. The permeability increases with increase in grain size and porosity. A simple calculation of the magnetic dipole moment arising in ferrites is shown in ***Appendix*** 7

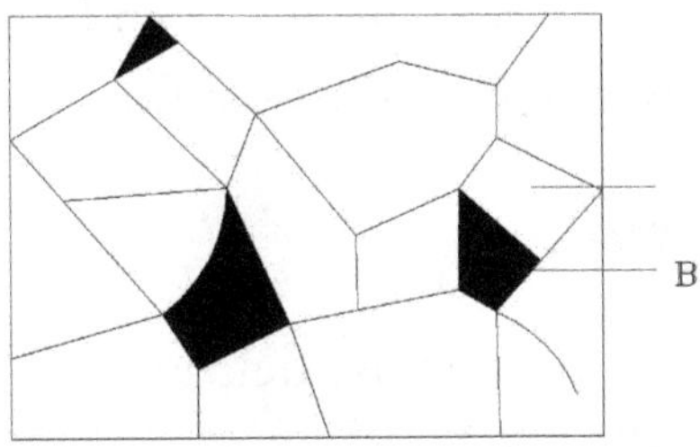

Fig.6.25 Microstructure of Ferrite with dual phase (Undesirable) Polycrystalline compound with the formula $[Meo(Fe_2O_3)]_8$

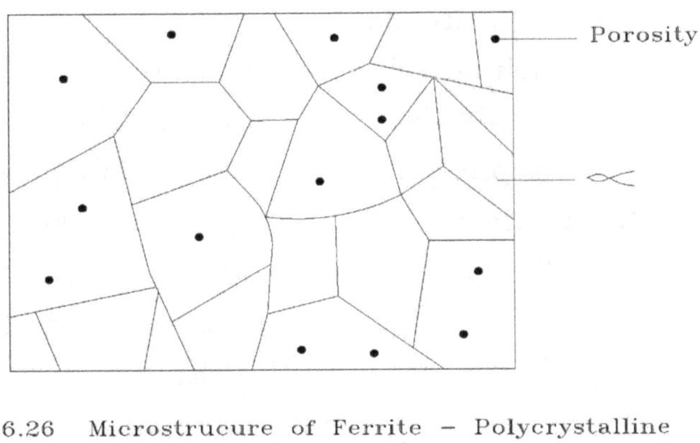

Fig.6.26 Microstrucure of Ferrite – Polycrystalline single phase (desirable) compound with the formula $[Meo\ (Fe_2O_3)]_8$

Very very pure iron has the lowest hysteresis loss. Ingot iron has a higher loss. Ordinary coarse grained silicon steel has a still higher loss. Grain oriented silicon steel (textured) has a lower loss than unoriented coarse grained silicon steel but more than very very pure iron and ingot iron. Ni_3Fe has a lower loss than G.O. silicon steel. Initial permeability of later is less than that of former. Resistivity is less for pure iron. Ingot iron has higher resistivity. Silicon steel has still higher resistivity. Saturation induction is lower forNi_3Fe than silicon steel. Cubic ferrites have higher resistivity than C.G Fe-Si alloy or Ni_3Fe. They have higher permeability but are more expensive. Amorphous iron silicon alloys containing boron and carbon have higher resistivity and no grain boundaries. Both eddy current and hysteresis losses are the least for these amorphous steels.

6.2.2 HARD MATERIALS

These materials have a high coercive field and high remnant magnetic flux. The energy product is high. Magnetically hard materials will be mechanically hard but the converse is not true. Magnetic alloys can undergo microstructural hardening by phase transformation or precipitation or ordering. Plain carbon steels with high carbon content and alloy steels with W, Cr, Co, or Al can transform from austenite at high temperature(austenitising) to martensite at room temperature by quenching followed by tempering(to relieve quench stresses).Cu-Ni-Co,Cu-Ni-Fe, Ag-Mn-Al, Bi-Mn-Al and Al-Ni-Co-Fe alloys undergo precipitation of second phase particles which hinder domain rotation and growth by pinning down the domain walls. Fe-Pt and Co-Pt alloys undergo disorder to order transformation at critical temperature on cooling from high temperature to room temperature. Superlattices are formed which have a high coercive force.

Al-Ni-Co alloys containing sufficient Fe are by far the most important of all in the category of hard magnetic materials. Large magnets are made by casting and solidification. Smaller magnets are made by P/M techniques. Easy direction of magnetization is [100]. By using directional solidification the energy product can be doubled. Columnar grains parallel to [100] are formed. If it is followed by annealing in magnetic field, the energy product can be raised further. It can still further increase by normal annealing at 823-873K for 10-15 hrs.

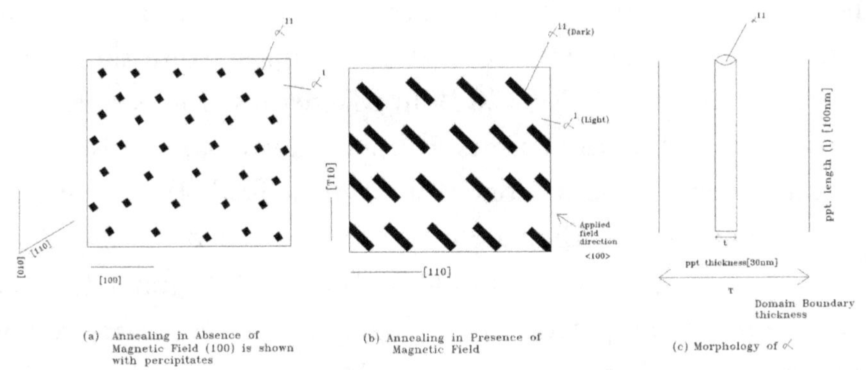

Fig.6.27 Hard Ferromagnetism in Al–Ni–Co alloy

The microstructure of this alloy is schematically given in Fig 6.27 (a) & (b)without and with magnetic annealing. The latter gives precipitates with shape anisotropy as in Fig 6.27(c). Before precipitation the crystal structure of the single phase (α) alloy above 1073K is BCC. It undergoes precipitation reaction to give products matrix α' (BCC & paramagnetic) rich in Ni & Al and precipitate with shape anisotropy α"(BCC & ferromagnetic) rich in Fe & Co[on cooling below 1073 K and followed by annealing at 853K].The precipitate is fine, less than the size of a domain and highly elongated in easy direction of magnetization. This microstructure obtained after final heat treatment is difficult to change and is almost permanent. They cannot be rotated.

Hexagonal ferrites are single phase and polycrystalline with a hexagonal unit cell containing two molecules of formula AB_2O_{19} and 64 atoms per cell A is divalent and B is trivalent. They have the crystal structure of magneto-plumbite. One unit cell has two sub repeat units each of five layers. Four layers have four oxygen atoms and the fifth layer contains three oxygen atoms and one divalent atom (Ba,Sr,). Totally there are 19 oxygen atoms, 12 ferric iron atoms and one Ba or Sr atom in one sub repeat unit. Among the 12 Ferric atoms 8 are having spin in one direction and 4 in opposite direction giving a net moment of (8-4) X 5=20 Bohr Magnetons. The permeability can be increased by three times if proper heat treatment is carried out. Annealing should be done in a magnetic field. These materials are hard and brittle. They are expensive compared to alloys.Easy direction of magnetization is [0001] .They are fine grained with a size of 1-5μm to keep permeability high. They are manufactured by P/M techniques. Porosity should be minimized.

Rare earth magnets are the most advanced commercialized permanent magnets. These are produced by P/M techniques. There are two types of compositions. One is Samarium cobalt alloys and the other is Neodymium Iron Boron alloys. In crystalline form these are fine grained single phase polycrystalline materials.

Polymer matrix composites containing Epoxy resin(2.5% by weight) as matrix and flaky & irregular powders of iron (5%) and Nd-Fe-B alloy (92.5%) as reinforcements are being powder metallurgically produced by uniaxial pressing with Zinc Stearate as lubricant followed by sintering at 453Kfor 2hrs.

Demagnetisation curve[plot of B vs(-H)] is used to find the energy product of a hard magnetic material. When H is zero B is B_r

and when H is H_c B is zero. The energy product (B) X (-H) omitting the –ve sign is plotted against B schematically in Fig 6.28.For actual materials it is schematically shown in Figs 6.29 (a) & (b) so as to relatively compare the materials for selection in applications. The energy product for a hard magnetic material should be as high as possible. It can be increased by annealing the material in a magnetic field as shown in Fig 6.30. If there is a material with an unsymmetric crystal structure then the properties will be different in various crystal directions. It is shown in Fig 6.31. The isotropic material will have higher energy product and higher coercive field. The anisotropic material is better suited for soft magnetic applications. Remnant magnetic flux is high but the coercive field is small and the hysteresis loop will be narrow enclosing a smaller area.

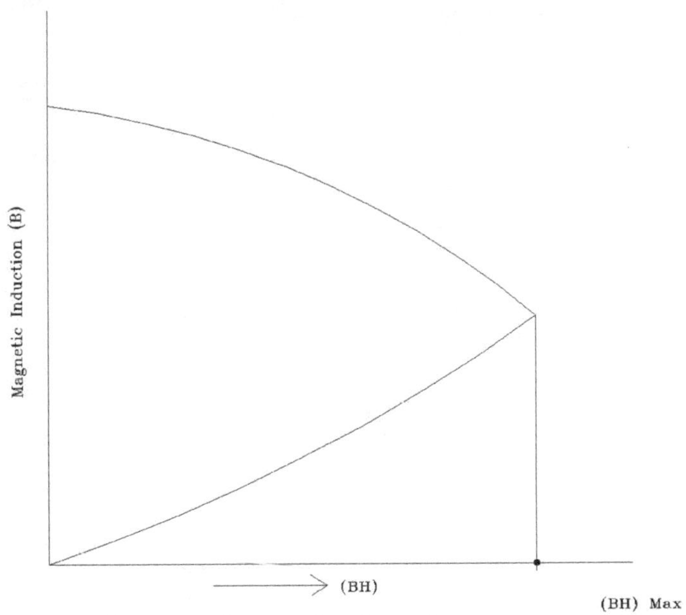

Fig.6.28 Energy Product Curve

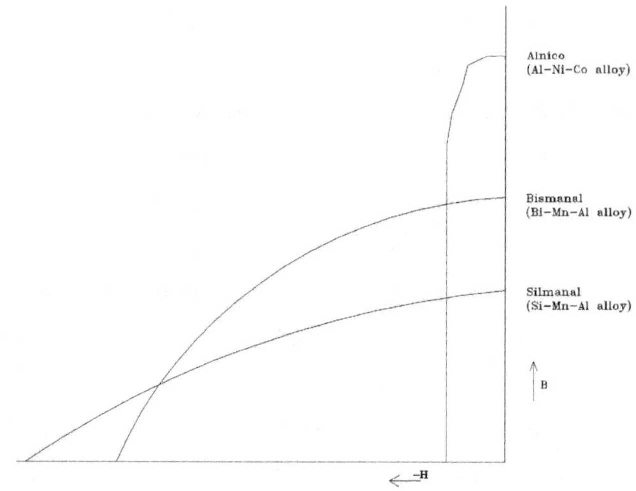

Fig.6.29(a) Demagnetisation Curve of some hard alloys (schematic)

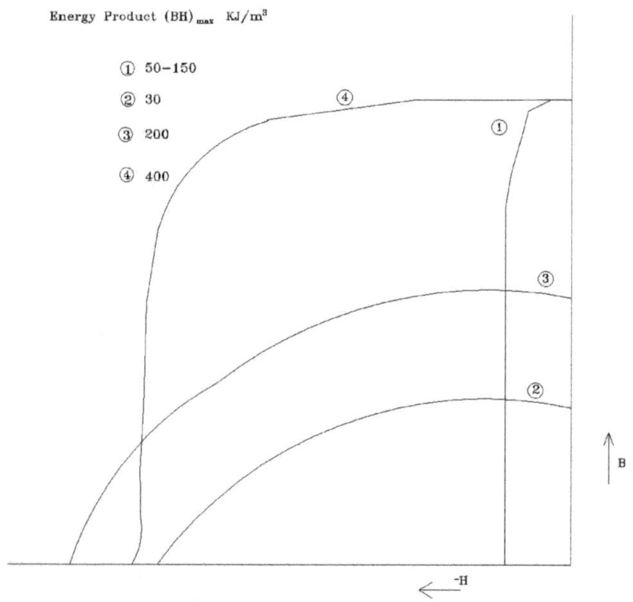

Fig.6.29(b) Demagnetisation Curve for hard magnetic materials
(1) Al Ni Co_5 alloy
(2) Ba 0.6 Fe_2O_3
(3) $SmCo_5$
(4) $Nd_2Fe_{14}B$

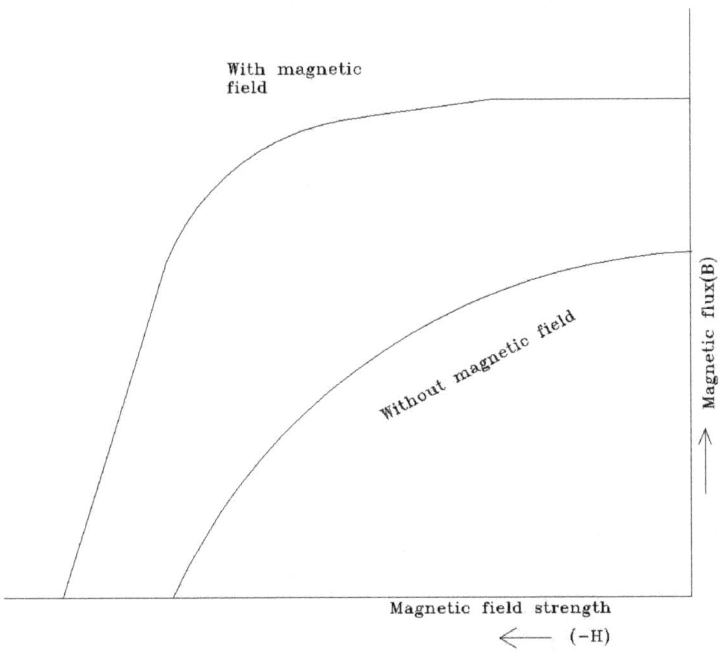

Fig.6.30 Effect of Heat treatment in a magnetic field on demagnetination curve for a hard magnetic material

6.2.3 AMORPHOUS MATERIALS

Amorphous materials can consist of a single metallic element or more than one element. The former is understood with dense random packing of hard spheres called the Bernal model. The latter if it has a transition metal-metalloid combination can be understood with the Bernal-Polk model which assumes that the metalloid atoms occupy the interstitial gaps formed by the dense random packing arrangement of metal atoms. These amorphous materials are called metallic glasses but unlike the silicate or borate glasses are not transparent and brittle.

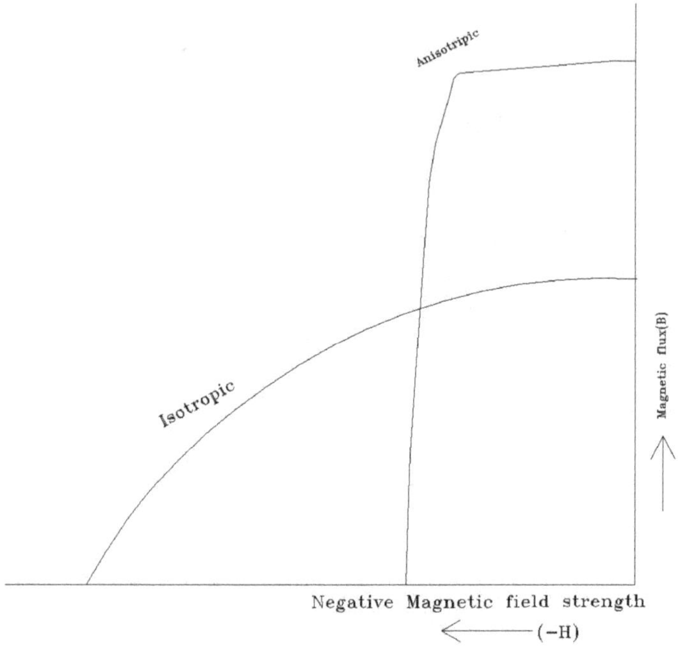

Fig.6.31 Demagnetisation Curves for isotropic and anisotropic hexagonal ferrite BaO. $6Fe_2O_3$

In recent years several systems have been identified for glass formation. Ease of glass formation depends on the following: (T_g/T_m) should be high. Eutectic alloys are highly suitable. Pure metal has not been produced as metallic glass. Only binary and ternary alloys have been formed as glass. The size difference between one atom A and another atom B should be minimum. The atomic radii ratio should fall in between 0.59 and 0.88. There should be chemical short range order in the metallic melt. Enthalpy of hole formation should be high.

Popular techniques of glass production are Melt spinning, Melt extraction, Planar flow casting and Twin rolling. Tapes, wires, ribbons and foils can be produced. Melt spinning is illustrated in Fig6.32.It is a popular method of producing ribbons of metallic

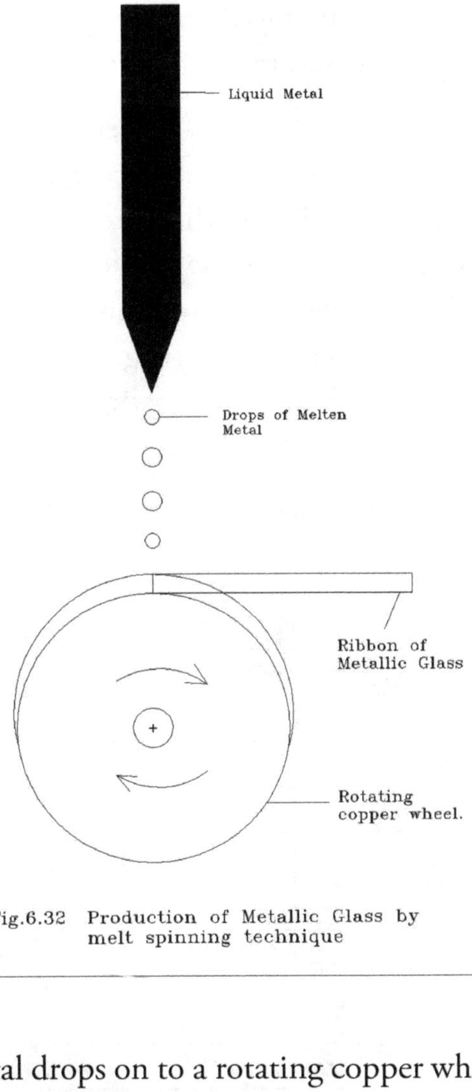

Fig.6.32 Production of Metallic Glass by melt spinning technique

glass. Liquid metal drops on to a rotating copper wheel and cooling rates as high as 10^5-10^6degree/s are achieved. Rapid quenching and solidification takes place. Recently (BMG) bulk metallic glasses have been produced. Techniques used are unidirectional zone melting,arc melting , injection moulding and suction casting in a copper mould. Mechanical alloying can also be employed. Lanthanum based BMGs are very popular metallic glass systems. BMGs have high yield strength and elastic limit.Near net shape forming is possible.

They deform by viscous flow below the crystallization temperature. Deformation processes employed for polymers can be used. BMGs have attractive electrical and magnetic properties.

Metallic glasses have 2-3 times higher electrical resistivity and excellent magnetic properties such as low coercive field high remnant flux and zero magnetostriction.They are magnetically isotropic. Metallic glasses for soft magnetic applications are $Fe_{80}B_{20}$ and $Fe_{79}B_{12}Si_{9}$.For hard magnetic applications $Nd_{40}Fe_{60}$ and $Sm_{40}Fe_{60}$ are available. These are hard and strong. The magnetic properties appropriate to soft and hard magnetic materials are given in Table 6.2

Table 6.2 Magnetic properties

(a) Soft materials

Material	**Resistivity μΩm(10 ³)**	**Permeability(10 ³)**
Low carbon steel	10	5
Fe-Si alloy	60	7
Grain oriented Fe-Si alloy	47	40
78 Permalloy	16	100
Superm alloy	60	1000
Met Glas(Fe +Si+B+C)	200	300

(b) Hard materials

Material	**Remnance(T)**	**Coercivity(A/m)x10 ³**
Fe-1%C steel	0.9	4.0
Al-Ni-Co-Fe alloy	1.2	570.0
(BaO)(6)(Fe_2O_3)	0.4	190.0
Co-Sm alloy	0.9	690.0
Fe-Nd-B alloy	1.3	1100.0
PtCo alloy	0.6	340.0

6.3 THERMAL MATERIALS

6.3.1 THERMAL CONDUCTORS AND INSULATORS

Low thermal conductivity ceramic materials such as fireclay, dolomite magnesite etc are used as insulating bricks to line furnaces and convertors used in extraction and refining of metals. These bricks are having sufficient porosity (>25%) to increase insulation. Air in the pores are poor thermal conductors. Vacuum is the best as heat cannot be conducted or convected through vacuum. For optimal thermal resistance, pores should be continuous and small in size. Alloying additions decrease thermal conductivity. Additions of Cr_2O_3 to Al_2O_3 reduces the thermal conductivity. Solids with open and highly ordered crystal structures made of atoms of similar size and mass have higher thermal conductivity. Excellent examples are SiC & AlN. Spinels with complex crystal structure and UO_2 & $ZrO_2$with a great difference in mass of constituent atoms have lower thermal conductivity. Ceramics [which have no free electrons] conduct heat by phonons. In metals thermal conduction by electrons is significant since they are present in large numbers. Cu, Ag and Al are good conductors of heat while wood and rubber are good insulators of heat

Aluminium oxide has low permittivity, low dielectric loss, high thermal conductivity, excellent mechanical properties and ease of metallization.It is widely used for substrates of integrated circuits. It can conduct away the heat generated in circuit elements due to I^2R heating. It prevents short circuiting due to expansion of circuit element materials and coming into contact with each other. Therefore alumina is the most preferred material for electronic circuit substrate boards.

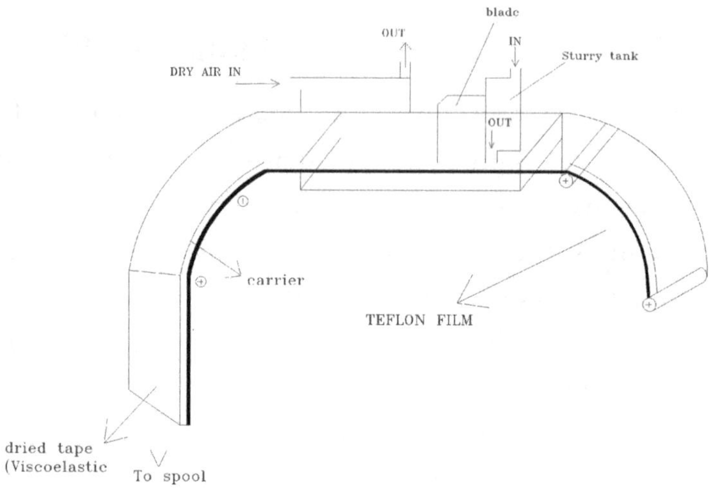

Fig 6.33 Schematic to Tape casting

Alumina substrates are produced by tape casting as shown in Fig 6.32. A film ofcontrolled thickness is formed on a supporting mobile TEFLON tape under a stationary blade, when a slurry containing alumina powder, Trichloroethylene (solvent), PVB (binder), Ethanol (deflocculant), Menhade fish oil(dispersant), and Octylphthalate (surfactant) is cast on the clean ,smooth, impervious and insoluble moving tape surface. It is a continuous high productivity process. The tape produced is 0.01-1.0 mm thick, flat, uniform and compressible to some extent. The casting speed is 0.001to0.002m/s. The viscosity of slurry is 2500-5000mPa

Among the oxide ceramics, alumina is the hardest, strongest and stiffest. It has good chemical resistance to air, water and sulphurous atmospheres. It is both corrosion and wear resistant. It is available in plenty and easily manufactured in the form and shape required at low cost It has attractive mechanical, chemical, electrical and thermal properties. Heat removal is the critical problem in electronic circuitry miniaturization and alumina is very useful in this regard. Better still is aluminium nitride. Its thermal conductivity is 5-10 times larger than alumina. Its thermal expansion coefficient matches better with Silicon than that of alumina. In future aluminium nitride is likely to replace alumina in furthering miniaturization of electronic devices.

6.3.2 DILATATION MATERIALS

Materials undergo dimensional changes with rise and fall of temperature. It is characterized by a coefficient called thermal expansion coefficient. It increases up to Debye temperature (T_D) rapidly and thereafter remains constant. Cubic crystals are isotropic and changes in dimension are symmetrical. For other crystals like HCP, thermal expansion and contraction depends on crystallographic direction and are anisotropic. Alloys can be designed to have a particular and suitable thermal expansion coefficient depending on the requirement. INVAR is an alloy of Ni and Fe and possesses zero expansion coefficient. Al_m-SiC_p composite can have various values depending on the volume fraction of SiC.It can be tailor made to match any material such as brass, bronze etc. Carbon-Carbon composite can be made to have zero expansion coefficient

The thermal conductivity and coefficient of linear expansion of some materials are given in Table 6.3(a)

Table 6.3(a) Thermal properties of materials

Material	Thermal conductivityW/m.K	Thermal expansion(/K) x10 $^{-5}$
Al	230	2.39
Cu	39	1.67
Ag	430	1.95
Ingot Fe	66	1.23
0.1%C steel	47	5.5

18-8 Stainless steel	16	1.73
Si	180	0.26
GaAs	50	0.68
Rubber	0.12	15-40.0
Wood	0.25(av)	3.0
Cork	0.04	15.0
PTFE	0.225	10.0
Si3N4	25	0.32
SiC	90	0.45
AlN	150-250	0.45
Al2O3	30	0.85
SiO2	1.4	0.005
Mo2Si	30	0.7-0.8
BaTiO3	60	0.85
Polyethylene	0.33	12.5 -20.0

6.3.3 THERMAL CAPACITANCE MATERIALS

Thermal capacity increases with increase in temperature from absolute zero to room temperature and remains constant at 6.0cals/mole/K with further increase in temperature. $T>T_D$ is termed high temperature and vice versa. The temperature after which thermal capacity of a material remains constant depends on bond strength, elastic constants and melting point of that material and varies widely for different materials. Debye temperature is one fifth of the melting point in Kelvin. For oxide and carbide ceramics thermal capacity increases from a low value at low temperatures to 6.0cal/mole/K at about 1273K.It remains constant at that value further on.

6.3.4 THERMAL DEFORMATION/SHOCK RESISTANT MATERIALS

It is defined as the ratio of thermal conductivity to thermal expansion coefficient of the material. A high thermal conducting material will not develop steep and large thermal gradients and will be resistant to thermal shock. A similar effect is caused by high thermal capacity and high heat transfer coefficient between solid and surrounding. A material with zero thermal expansion coefficient will not be prone to thermal shock and failure. SiC and Si_3N_4 are excellent examples for possessing high thermal shock resistance compared to oxides of Silicon. Fused Silica has good thermal shock resistance due to extremely low thermal expansion coefficient. Mg_m-$C_f$composite has a 6000% increase in Thermal deformation resistance over Mg due to zero longitudinal thermal expansion coefficient of the carbon fibre used as reinforcement in magnesium matrix.

6.3.5 THERMOELECTRIC MATERIALS

These materials are used in thermocouples to measure temperature by contacting the hot material (molten metal in a crucible or furnace).Two dissimilar thermoelectric materials should be used for that purpose. They will be soldered at one end to provide he hot junction and the other end is connected to a voltmeter to complete the loop.The thermocouple can measure the EMF generated. Thermal EMF arises due to composition difference of the two dissimilar wires and the temperature difference between hot and cold ends. These thermoelectric materials are characterized by three factors namely seeback coefficient(S),Thompson coefficient(μ_T) and Peltier heat(π). These three variables are not independent of each other. If one is known the other two can be known using the second law of thermodynamics.It is small for metals and alloys and high for semiconductors (Two orders of magnitude larger). S is negative for n type and positive for p type semiconductors. In the former, carriers (electrons) will be above the Fermi energy and in the conduction band. In the later, carriers (holes) lie well below the Fermi energy and in the valence band. Semiconductors with diamond cubic crystal structure having high thermal conductivity are not used in thermocouples as the figure of merit and therefore efficiency will be less. It is high if seeback coefficient(S) and electrical conductivity (σ) are high and thermal conductivity (λ) is low. It is given by the following:

$$\mathbf{Z=S^2(\sigma/\lambda) \text{ where } S=(\Delta V/\Delta T)}$$

Where Z is a figure of merit. Metals and alloys have low Z and semiconductors have high Z. It cannot be improved for metals as the ratio (σ/λ) is constant, but can be improved for semiconductors by decreasing thermal conductivity of the alloy and keeping electrical conductivity the same as the individual component. Example for this is (Bi_2Te_3+Bi_2Se_3) semiconductor alloy. It has higher Z compared to that of Bi_2Te_3 andBi_2Se_3.Some of the thermoelectric materials used in thermocouples are iron, copper, constantan, chromel, alumel, platinum, platinum-rhodium alloy, tungsten, rhenium, lead telluride, lead selenide, bismuth telluride, bismuth selenide and antimony telluride. Thermocouples made of metals and alloys have sensitivity of the order of microvolts per degree while those of semiconductors of milli volts per degree. S is a measure of sensitivity.

6.3.6 THERMIONIC MATERIALS

Tungsten is a widely used thermionic material. Its work function is 4.5eV. It has low vapor pressure and is chemically stable.Therefore lower vacuum of the order of 10^{-3} is sufficient. Pure tungsten filament will creep under its own weight. Thoriated tungsten is used to prevent this. The thorium in its oxide coats the tungsten filament and reduces the work function to 2.6 eV due to the electric dipole layer formed at the surface. If work function is less, operating temperature decreases and brightness increases. Lower temperature will prevent environmental deterioration of filament and prolong the life of the filament. Operating temperature is 2500-3500K. If temperature is high emission of electrons is more.The work function of some materials are given in Table 6.3(b)

Table 6.3(b) Thermionic Work function of materials

Material	Ag	Al	Au	Be	Ca	Cs	Cu	K	Na	Li	Zn	W	Ta	Mo	Th	Ba
Work function(φ)eV	4.4	4.2	4.9	3.9	3.2	1.9	4.5	2.2	2.3	2.48	4.3	4.5	4.2	4.2	3.4	2.5

Barium has a work function of 2.5eV.If it is deposited on tungsten by evaporation, the barium coated tungsten has a lower work function of 1.1eV.

Calcium also has the same effect.

Lanthanum hexaboride with a work function of 2.7 eV has become an attractive option for thermionic emission. Operating temperature is low 1400-2000K. But it is very expensive. The vacuum required is 10^{-6} as it is chemically less stable and a few traces of oxygen will spoil the filament. LaB_6 is prone to thermal shock. Heating and cooling should be done gradually.

6.4 OPTICAL MATERIALS

These are classified as linear and nonlinear. The refractive index of the former will not change with intensity of light falling on it while in the later it undergoes change. Optical materials are required for LEDs, long distance fibre communications, solar cells and optical memory and switching devices.

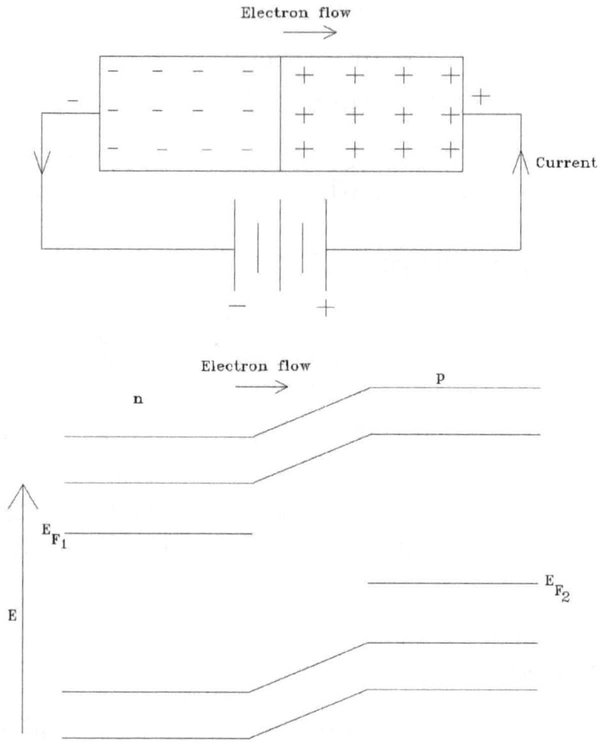

Fig.6.34 Principle of LED

Light Emitting Diodes are compact, efficient, cheap and rugged. The principle of operation is illustrated in fig6.34. A Forward biased p-n junction will provide light in a LED. Electrons flow from high energy level to lower energy level emitting photons. GaN is widely used for this. Si doped gallium nitride material is n type and Mg doped one is p type. GaN is a wide band gap semiconductor material. It can be used at higher temperatures compared to Si.It is a direct band gap material with an energy gap of 3.4eV (Si has 1.12 eV, Ge has 1.43 eV).The bond between Ga and N is strong. It improves service life, operating frequency and output power. It is mechanically very hard ,is stable and has high heat capacity. It can be deposited as thin films on SiC or Al_2O_3 despite the lattice mismatch. It crystallizes in hexagonal form similar to wurtzite [a=3.18A^0 and c=5.186A^0] under normal temperatures and pressures. It has a refractive index of 2.3.It is usually obtained by epitaxial growth. It emits blue light. It is more efficient and consumes less power compared to GaAs or Si. It is chemically stable and inert. It is used in electronic devices for space exploration. It is sensitive to environment and therefore a good sensor material. It is resistant to radiation.It is used in devices for detecting various types of atmospheres and waves. Its output power is high and is used in communication and antimissile operations in chemical and electronic warfare.

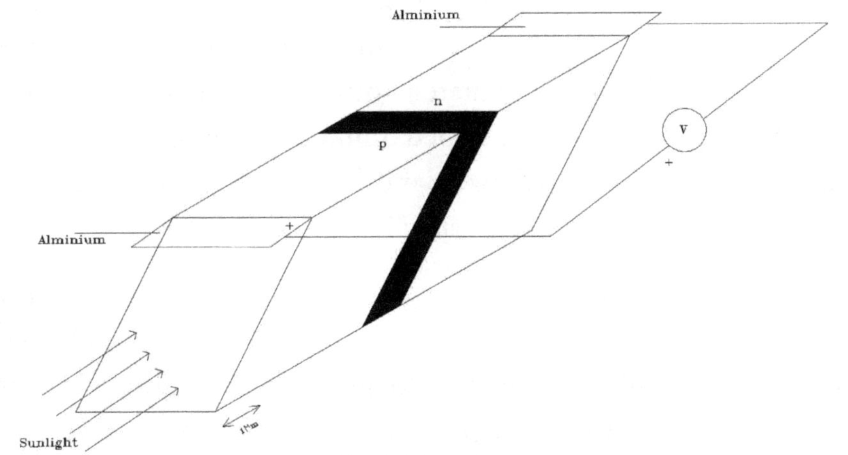

Fig.6.35 Principle of Solar cell

Photo voltaic materials are used in solar cells. A typical solar cell is shown in Fig6.35. Sun light (Photons) falls on p layer, travels through it to the transition region and knocks off electrons from valence band into conduction band. These electrons flow into the n region while holes are flowing into the p region. This gives rise to voltage and current in the external circuit. The voltage is around 0.6V in a silicon solar cell. Si is the widely used material. It can be a single crystal or polycrystalline or amorphous Silicon. The theoretical thermodynamic efficiency is 33.5%. This the maximum limit for solar cells. So far 26%efficiency has been reached routinely and recently it has been improved upon to 28%. Photons falling on a solar cell not only knock electrons but also generate photons which are usually absorbed and prevented from coming out of the cell. By avoiding this, the efficiency is improved from 26 to 28%. Oflate hydrogenated amorphous silicon is being tried out. It consists of a random network of covalently bonded atoms of Si lattice with randomly dangling bonds. It is similar to crystalline Si with vacancies. They have no long range order but having correlations of ordering up to third and fourth nearest neighbours. One cannot apply the Bloch Theorem to amorphous materials. Alternate technique is to be used. It is called cluster model approach. By adding hydrogen to silicon the dangling bonds can be saturated and neutralize the unsaturated vacancies. It is called Hydrogenated amorphous silicon. It is similar to crystalline silicon. It can be doped unlike amorphous silicon. HAS is a good candidate material for solar cells. It is cheap at only half the cost of crystalline silicon. Efficiency is around 8-14%.

High quality silica glass fibres are used for long distance audio and video communications. These fibres are very pure and fine (core diameter is 50μm) with low loss(<20dB/Km). The fibres are produced by vapor transport process. Concentration of transition metal ions like Cu, Co, Fe etc. should be very low (<1ppm). Still repeaters and signal regenerators are required. With the development of Er doped glass this need has been eliminated. Wavelength of laser used is 1.3μm(1.2 to 1.6μm range). The Er doped fibres will not interfere with or intercept the path of light propagating through the optical glass fiber.

Lithium Niobate, a crystalline and transparent material is a versatile nonlinear optical material. It is electro and acousto optic and also photo conductive. It is an intermediate solid solution of

50%Li_2O and 50%Nb_2O_5.It can be used for optical switching which takes place in picoseconds.

Electric, Ferroelectric, ferroagnetic, ferrimagnetic and super conducting switches will take milli or micro seconds. Optical switching is by far the quickest.

Indium antimonide is a semiconducting nonlinear optical material with an energy gap of 0.2eV. Optical computers are being proposed to be built with such materials. The refractive index and reflectivity of some materials are given in 6.4 (a) & (b).The efficiency of some photovoltaic materials are given in Table 6.4 (c). Table 6.5 gives the electronic properties of vacuum,air and water.

Table 6.4 Optical properties

(a) Refractive index of materials)

Material	Cu	Al	Ag	Al2O3	Silica glass	PE	PTFE	Si	GaAs	Ge	LiNbO3
Refractive index	0.14	0.97	0.05	1.76	1.5	1.51	1.35	3.94	3.91	4.0	2.29

(b) Reflectivity of materials

Material	Cu	Al	Ag	SI	Al2O3	Silica glass	PE	PTFE	GaAs
Reflectivity	0.956	0.903	0.985	0.3542	0.0758	0.0413	0.0413	0.222	0.3526

(c) Efficiency of photovoltaic materials

Material	Efficiency (%)
Thermodynamic limit	33.5
Single crystal Si	24
Polycrystalline Si	20
Amorphous Hydrogenated Si(thin film)	12
Cd-Te thin film	12-15
Cu-Se	12-15
Organic cells	5

Table6.5 Electronic properties of some standard materials

Property	Vacuum	Air	Water
Permittivity	1.0	1.000576	81.1
Permeability	1.0	1.0	0.9999
Susceptibility	0.0	0.0	-9.14×10^{-6}
Refractive index	1.0	1.00029	1.333
Thermal conductivity	0.0	2.41×10^{-6}	0.136
Electrical resistivity	∞	$(1.3\text{-}3.3)10^{16}$	10^{5}
Electrical conductivity	0	$(3\text{-}8)\times10^{-15}$	1×10^{-5}

7

RECENT DEVELOPMENTS

7.1 SPINTRONICS

Instead of using the charge of the electrons and their direction of flow one can utilize the direction of spin of the electron for working of solid state devices. Consider a ferromagnetic material (with a net moment) F and a non ferromagnetic material(in which net moment is zero in the absence of a field) that are joined together as shown in Fig7.1(a). Assume that in material F the majority of electrons have spin up(anticlockwise spinning of electron with magnetic moment positive) and in NF the spin up and spin down (clockwise spinning of electron with magnetic moment negative)electrons are equal in number. Now apply a voltage in the manner shown in above figure. The spin up electrons from material F will flow into material NF in which originally there were equal number of spin up and spin down electrons. At the interface of F and NF there is a positive change in M It is denoted as ΔM. It is shown in Fig 7.1(b). This excess magnetization gives rise to a resistance. It will be appreciable. If the change is by a factor of two it is termed a giant change or colossal change. This principle can be used to make a F1-NF-F2. device similar to a p-n-p or n-p-n transistor.

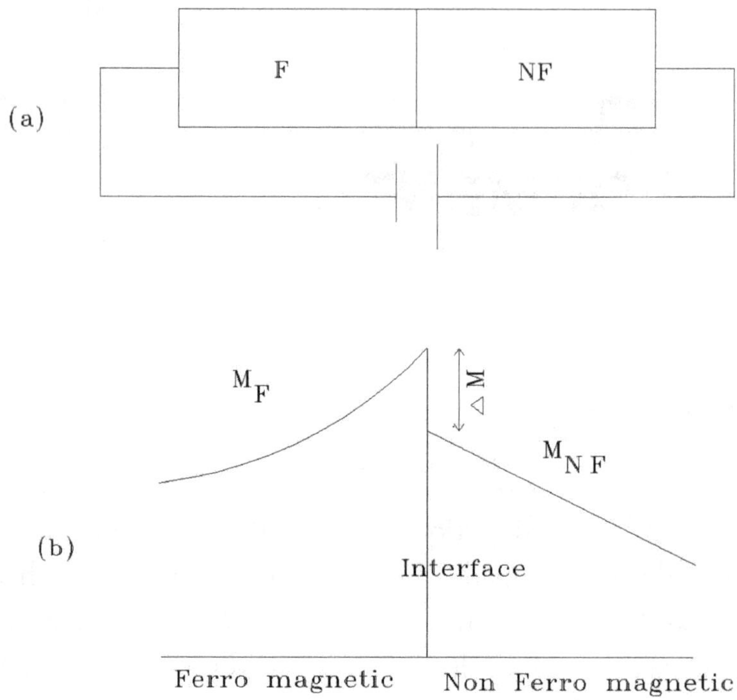

Fig.7.1 Principle of Magnetic Resistance

In such a device two situations can arise as shown in Fig7.2(a) & (b) In the first case both materials F1 and F2 can have excess spin up electrons (as majority carriers)In this case when a voltage is applied as shown flow of electrons will be unhindered and resistance will be minimum. In the second case F2 has excess spin down electrons (majority carriers) while F1 has excess spin up electrons (as majority carriers) when a voltage is applied as shown flow of electrons is hindered due to higher resistance. Current in the circuit will be less compared to the previous case. This is due to the higher scattering of spin up electrons in a spin down material compared to a spin up material. Like spins involve less scatter and less resistance to flow while unlike spins cause more scatter and more resistance to flow of current.

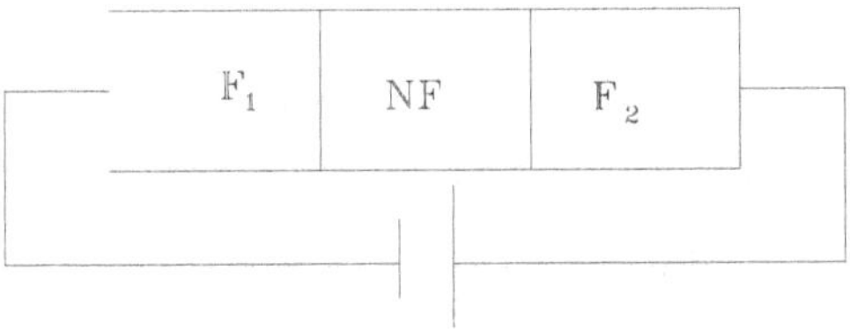

(a) F_1 & F_2 have same polarization – spin up or spin down

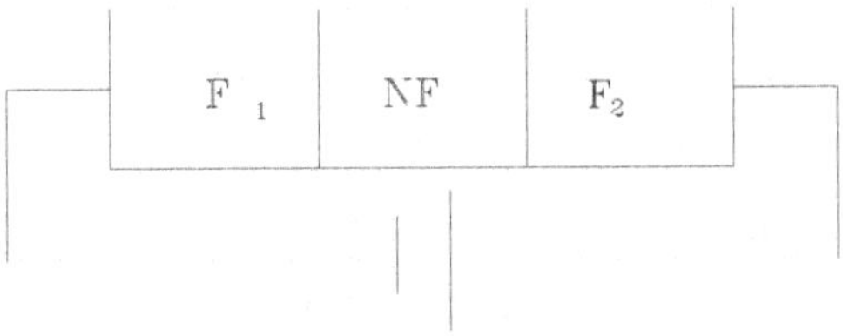

(b) F_1 & F_2 have opposite spin polarization

Fig.7.2 Illustration of Transistor based on spintronics

7.2 PHOTONICS

Photons are particles moving with the speed of light. One can do with photons whatever one does with electrons. Photons are associated with electromagnetic waves while electrons are associated with what are called matter waves. Based on the properties of electrons one can make solid state devices called transistors. Similarly one can make transphasors based on the properties of photons. It is an optical transistor in which an incident beam of laser light with a low intensity is amplified to higher intensity. These devices can work in picoseconds unlike electronic devices which take milli or micro seconds. It is made of nonlinear opticl materials. These photons can be diffracted by gratings ruled with diamond marker. One can also engineer a material with a dielectric constant varying periodically to diffract photons of visible light (with wavelength of 500nm) similar to a periodic atomic lattice of a solid that can diffract X-rays, electrons and neutrons. Such materials are produced by microlithography.One should use Maxwell's equations for photons similar to Schrodingr's for electrons. The Brillouin zone concept is applicable to photons and one gets photonic bands similar to electronic bands. (see Appendix-5)

7.3 GMR AND CMR MATERIALS

If a conductor is exposed to a magnetic field that is perpendicular to the electric field resistivity increases. If in a material the increase is by about20% it is called a giant magnetic resistance material. MnFe,MnNi andNiO are examples for such materials. The principle behind such materials is illustrated in Fig 7.3 If the increase is by about 50% it is called a colossal magnetic resistance material. $LaMnO_4$ (lanthanum manganate) is an example for such a material. The increase in resistivity is directly proportional to the square of magnetic flux of the applied field.

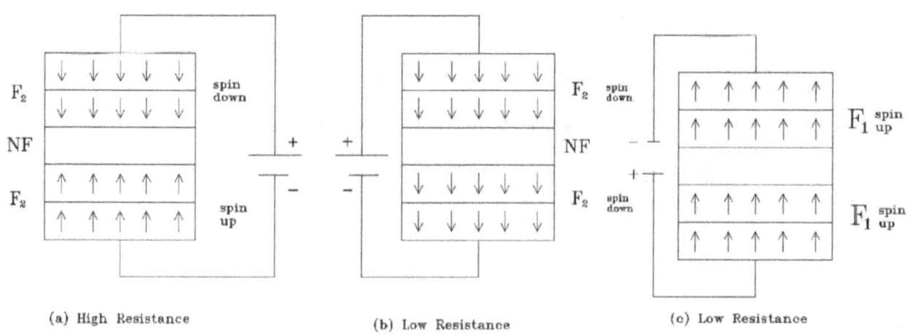

Fig.7.3 Principle of GMR materials

$$(\Delta\rho) \alpha (\mathbf{B})^{2.}$$

The resistance can be increased or decreased at will (manipulated by proper stacking up) by building the material layer by layer as shown in Fig7.4

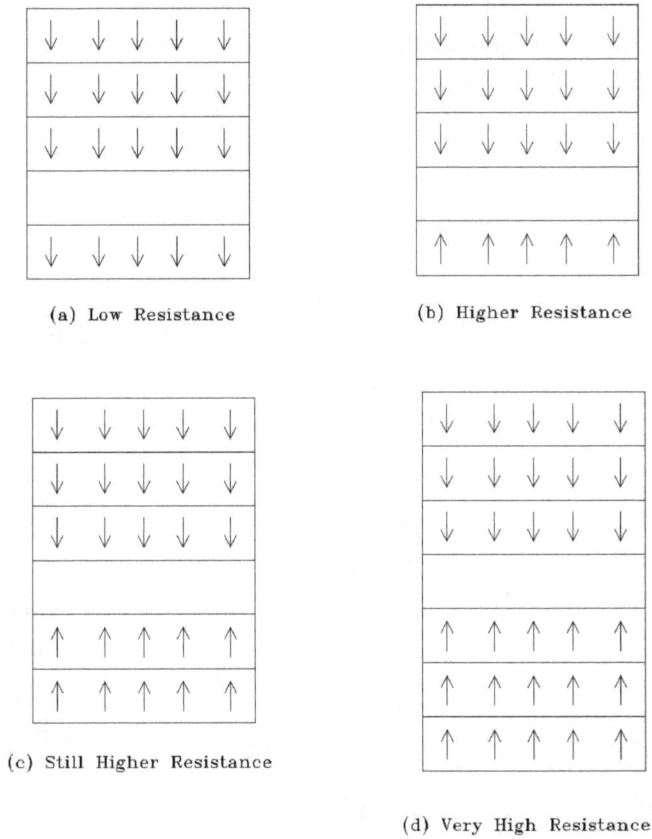

Fig.7.4 Illustration of how resistance can be made a variable using spin of electrons.

7.4 NANOELECTRONIC MATERIALS

A nano particle is a molecule of 'n' atoms. An aluminium nano particle consists of 13 atoms, copper 20 atoms gold 55 atoms etc. The particle size is 1 to 100 nm. This particle will be highly reactive due to high surface area to volume ratio. The stability of the particle depends on a number called the magic number. For smaller particles it is called electronic magic number and for a bigger particle structural magic number. The former can be 3,9,20,36,61 etc and the later for fcc crystal 1,13,55,147 etc and for hcp crystal 1,13,57,153 etc. Nano aluminium has fcc structure which is same as bulk aluminium but for nano gold the crystal structure is different from bulk gold. The former takes the icosahedral shape while later has fcc structure. Therefore, as the particle size decreases to nano dimensions there may be a crystal structure change.

Metals and alloy nanoparticles can be produced by chemical synthesis(precipitation from aqueous and nonaqueous solutions), atomisation, mechanical alloying, laser evaporation (from the surface of a bulk rod)etc. Chemical, thermal and plasma evaporation processes are also used. Nanoparticles can be made into useful components by powder metallurgy techniques(compaction and sintering). Electrode position can be used to produce sheets and rapid solidification techniques(melt spinning) to produce ribbons and thin foils. Nano grain structured bulk material can be produced by severe plastic deformation (extrusion, rolling etc) by imparting large deformation at optimum strain rate and temperature.

A nano particle of less than 'n' atoms will have discrete energy levels like a molecule having energy levels corresponding to bonding and antibonding orbitals. The energy gap is larger than the thermal energy. It gives rise to interesting electronic properties with the possibility of several applications. The electronic structure can be studied with UV Photo Electron spectroscopy. The spectrum gives a series of peaks corresponding to discrete energy levels. The average energy does not depend on chemical nature of atoms but on the dimensions of the particle. It is called the quantum size effect. The particles are separated by distances of the order of wavelength of electrons. The electronic properties depend on the number and kind of atoms that make up the nano particle.

Nano particle of nonmagnetic atoms can exhibit a net magnetic moment. Rhodium Nanoparticle with 20 atoms show such a magnetism. The net moment is larger as the size becomes smaller. Nano particle of silicon and germanium are not intrinsic semiconductors like bulk material. Their optical behaviour is also unlike bulk silicon and germanium. In their optical spectrum the blue line shifts towards higher energy and lower wavelength implying an increase in their band gap energy. It is also the case with intensity of absorption. It increases as the size of particles decreases. It is explained on the basis of the behaviour of excitons(Electron - Hole pair).

7.5 ORGANIC ELECTRONIC MATERIALS

These materials are attracting a lot of attention for their possible applications in solid state devices. Poly acetylene, Poly aniline, Pyrrole and Thiophene are good conductors of electricity. Poly aniline is electro chronic and chemo chronic. It can be used for Light Emitting Diodes. Anthracene, Perylene de, 4-BCMU and DCHD posses nonlinear optical properties. These are produced by reprecipitation from their rich solution mixed with poor solvent(water) under sonic agitation. The scattered droplets nucleated into nanoparticles and grow into single crystals and thin films. Their size depends on temperature, concentration, mixing procedure and the surface modifiers added at the beginning. The thin films produced are flexible, can be rolled and stretched again. This helps in taking them from one place to another within a room or building or to another place. It is very useful for making large display screens. Organic superconductors have been discovered. These are large molecules. One molecule is separated from another by a small distance. The molecules are arranged in two dimensions. The electrons and holes jump from one molecule to next molecule. They posses anomalous superconducting behaviour. The molecules attain the superconducting state when a magnetic field of sufficient strength is applied. This is due to the different momentum of a spin up and spin down electron which on forming a pair possess a nonzero net momentum.

7.6 GRAPHENE

It is a single sheet of graphite as shown in Fig 7.5. It is the thinnest substance in the world as on date. The carbon atoms are arranged in a hexagonal two dimensional lattice .It is of very high quality. It is chemically simple.It can be produced from pencil leader using Scotch tape to peel away a single layer of graphite. Its strength is the highest among all materials known to the humans (120-130GPa). It is 6.2 times stronger than iron whisker (21GPa).Structural steel has a tensile strength of 400 MPa. Grapheme is an electrical conductor. It dissipates the heat generated due to electric current flowing through it very efficiently. Electrons move with a high velocity in it,30 times faster than in Silicon. Superfast computers and smartphones can be fabricated using it. It can be used to produce heavy water at low cost compared to present methods available. It can be used as a super sieve to filter deuterium from a mixture of hydrogen containing the three isotopes.Magnetic grapheme can be produced by partially hydrogenating it. Magnetic strength depends on the amount of hydrogen. By controlling it one can fine tune the magnetic strength. Another way to get magnetic graphene without compromising its electrical properties is to have a graphene layer on a substrate of ferromagnetic YIG(yttrium iron garnet).

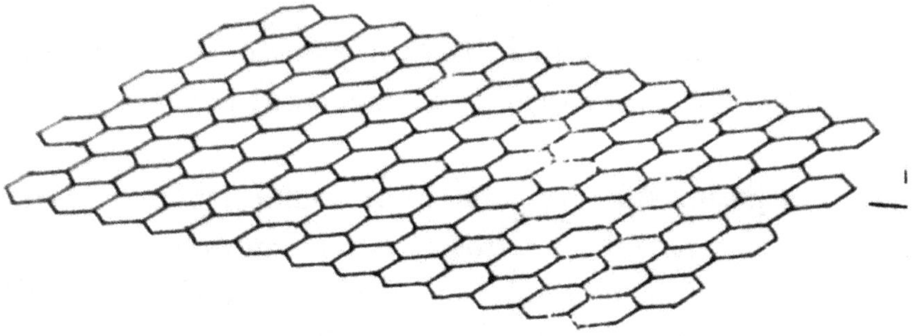

Fig 7. 5 A single layer of graphene sheet.

7.7 CARBON NANOTUBES

A carbon nanotube is a graphene sheet curled into a hollow cylinder. The curling can be done symmetrically around a straight axis or at various angles to give tubes of different helicity as indicated in Fig 7.6. Each one is unique giving rise to variation in the electronic properties. Chirality refers to the angle of variation of the sheet around the axis. The tubes can be single or multiple walled. A SWT(single walled tube) will be a few nms in diameter and several microns in length. A MWT (multi walled tube) will have several concentric coaxial tubes separated by a fraction of a nm usually equal to the interlaced distance in graphite. The nanotubes of carbon are produced as follows. Two graphite electrodes are kept in a chamber of inert gas at a particular pressure and an arc is struck between them at controlled current and voltage. The soot deposited on the cathode contains nanotubes. One can use laser evaporation or chemical vapour deposition also to produce nanotubes. The tubes can be metallic or semiconducting. It depends on the chirality of the tube which determines its electronic structure. Presence of defects in the tube can alter the electronic structure. In the same tube one region can be metallic and the adjacent region semiconducting. These tubes are very light. Their strength to weight ratio is high, 100 times that of steel and 3 times that of carbon fiber. Their oxidation temperature is higher than that of carbon fiber, thermal conductivity comparable to diamond and surface area greater than that of graphite. Solid state devices made of CNTs are comparable in performance to semiconductor devices. It is tedious and time consuming to produce ICs of CNTs. CNTs can be used as probe tips in Atomic force Microscopes and Scanning Tunnelling Microscopes , display screens, gas flow sensors and liquid flow sensors.

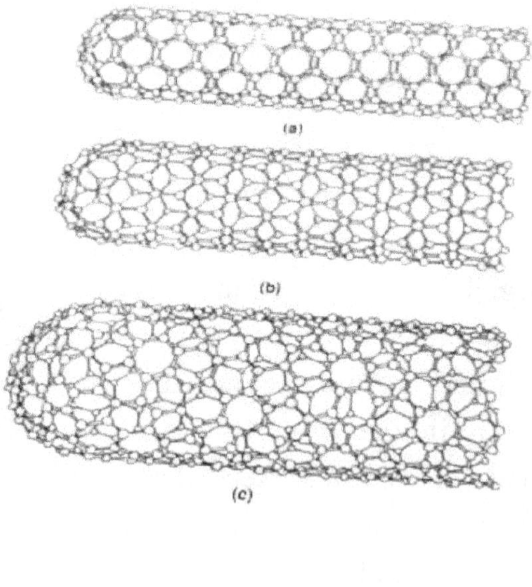

Fig 7. 6 Graphene rolled in different ways to get carbon nanotubes of various types.

7.8 FULLERENES

Fullerene is a molecule of 60 carbon atoms and spherical in shape as shown in Fig 7.7. The sphere can be constructed with 12 pentagons and 20 hexagons. Atoms are located in their corners. The molecule crystallises in FCC structure as illustrated in Fig 7.8. The unit cell has 8 fullerene molecules in its eight corners and 6 molecules in its six faces at their centre. In effect the unit cell will contain a total of [(8×1/8)+(6×1/2)]4 Molecules. It takes a few hours to produce 1 gm of fullerene.Two graphite electrodes are placed in a chamber of inert gas at proper pressure and an arc is struck at a controlled voltage and current. A soot is deposited on the chamber walls . It is collected .It contains fullerene molecules. Using tolling it is separated. The fullerene molecule can be made super conducting by doping it with all alkali metals except sodium and lithium. Doping

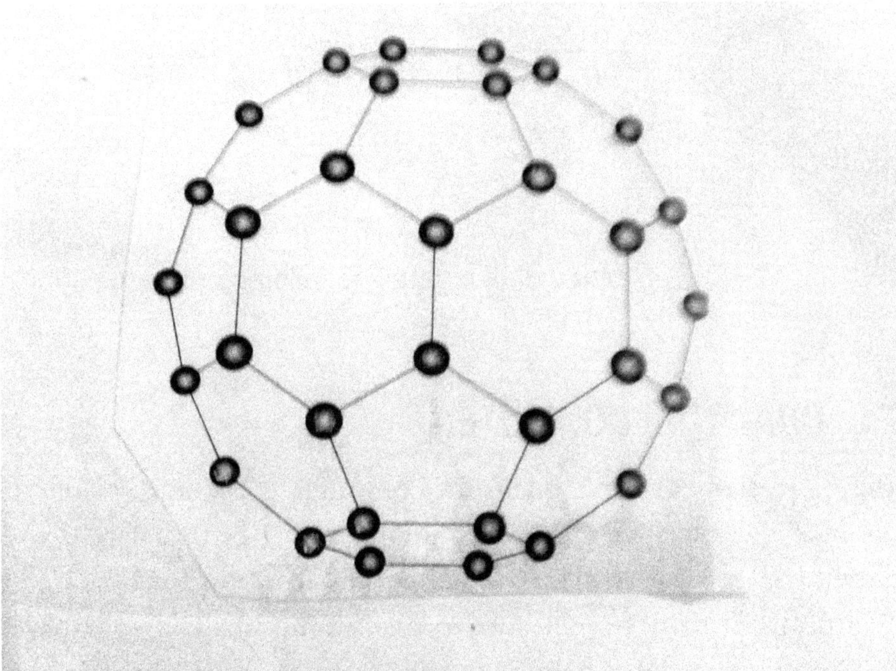

Fig 7.7 A molecule of fullerene showing the arrangement of carbon atoms.

with TDAE (tetrad dimethylamino ethylene) gives a ferromagnetic fullerene. It's critical temperature is 16.1K. Its crystal structure is monoclinic. Fullerene is a nonlinear optic material.

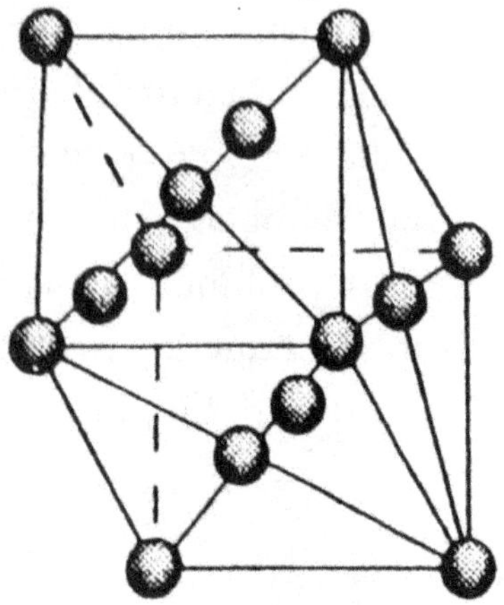

Fig 7.8 FCC unit cell of crystalline fullerene molecule.

7.9 QUANTUM COMPUTER

The basic element for a quantum computer is a quantum bit. It can hold a vast array of values simultaneously 1 or 0 or 1 & 0 and everything in between all at the same time. It is possible because of quantum mechanics applicable to an infinitesimally small space. Subatomic particles inhabit a range of States. Between two such particles different relationships can exist. The property of matter in one quantum state called superposition as well as a second quantum state called an entanglement are both required and are achieved by a variety of ways to carry out computing. Ions can be suspended in a magnetic field or a photon can be entrapped or a phosphorus atom can be manipulated in a silicon substrate. A prototype of quantum computing processor has been built with superconducting wires at a temperature of near about 0K.This approach is called adiabatic quantum computing.

7.10 BIOLOGICAL COMPUTER

It is made of biological molecules and can decipher images encrypted on DNA chips. All the four components required for a computer are in this case molecules. These molecules interact logically with each other. The hardware and software are complex biological molecules. They activate one another to carry out a well planned chemical work. This computer is transparent solution in a tube consisting of various small DNA molecules with select DNA enzymes and ATP. The ATP provides the energy. The molecules interact with each other and one simply watches what is going on in the tube. It can decipher separately the fluorescent images of logos and emblems of organisations and institutions. It is the first computer to be based on the molecular crypto system of images by DNA computing. All living organisms are biological computers including human beings.

7.11 ELECTRONIC WASTE

e-waste as it is called is a major problem as well as an opportunity the world over. The problem is what to do with toxic materials in the waste and how to handle it.The opportunity is to recover and reuse precious and scarce Materials. In the former category comes Pb, Hg, Sb, As, CA, F, S etc while in the later category comes Cu, Au, Ag, Al etc. India comes in the top five countries among e-waste producers in the world. e-waste is increasing every year due to discarding of electronic goods, devices, instruments, equipments etc. In the next five years it may increase by 25%.India produced 1.7 million tons of e-waste in the year 2014.In that year total e-waste was 40 million tons of which only 7% was mobile phones, computers, printers, office equipment, electric shavers etc. Majority of the waste was washing machines, dish washer, microwave ovens and other kitchen, laundry and bathroom equipments. E-waste management is very important from environmental pollution and degradation. The health and safety of all life forms including flora and fauna depend on it.

7.12 ZERO GRAVITY PROCESSING

Semiconductor crystals are grown in spaceships under zerogravity (weightlessness) conditions. Density of elements will not play any role. Homogeneous materials can be obtained. Ga and Mo can be alloyed even though their densities are vastly different. Gravity segregation is eliminated. GaS crystal of 25 mm length has been grown in space whereas on earth one can get a crystal of 2 to 3 mm. CdTe, CdS and CdHgTe (CMT) are grown under zero gravity conditions. The last one mentioned, if made on earth, will give a highly inhomogeneous alloy with 3 layers. In space one can get a homogeneous crystal. CMT is a solid solution of CdTe & HgTe. Under terrestrial conditions influence of density on homogeneity is a real challenge. GaSb & InSb crystals have also been grown under conditions of weightlessness. The future for this field is bright and challenging.

7.13 SOLID STATE ELECTRONICS

Solid state microelectronics has changed our life beyond expectations. It all started in1947 with the development of Germanium transistor. Vacuum tubes used till then from 1907 onwards and rectifiers developed upto 1947 went out of circulation. Silicon transistor was developed a few years later around 1950. The first integrated circuit came in1959. Ultra large scale integration was developed with millions of circuit elements in one chip. Gig scale integration has been developed with one billion transistors in one chip. Trillion circuit elements in one chip is currently being developed. Integration permits complex circuits consisting of many diodes, resistors, transistors, capacitors, inductors etc. in a single chip. It greatly advances miniaturisation, reduces cost and increase reliability.

SSI-100 devices in one chip

MSI-100to1,000 " "

LSI-1,000to1,00,000 " " ™

VLSI-10,000to1,0,00,000" "

UVSLI-1,00,000 to 10,0,0,0,00,000 " "

GSI-10,0,0,0,00,000 devices (10^{+9})onwards in one chip

Moore's law was held to be valid for several decades. It states that every 10 years the number of circuit elements in a chip doubles. It is no longer held to be valid\. However one drawback of miniaturisation is that the heat generated will short circuit the elements due to thermal expansion unless and until it is efficiently and quickly conducted away by the substrate. Integrated electronic circuits consist of only electrical elements such as resistors, rectifiers, diodes etc. Integrated optoelectronic circuits consist of optical elements like lasers and electrical elements like diodes.

APPENDICES

1. Particles and Quasi particles

Elementary excitations lead to oscillations in a solid. These can be dealt with wave mechanics and associated interacting quanta .These quanta are called particles or normal particles. These can be divided into two types called Fermions and Bosons. The former obey Fermi-Dirac statistics and the later Bose -Einstein statistics. Fermions have half integral spin quantum number [± {(1/2),(3/2),(5/2).....}] and obey Pauli's exclusion principle. Their number is conserved. Examples are electrons, protons, neutrons, Hydrogen atom etc. They can not be created or destroyed. The bosons have integral quantum number [±(1,2,3....)].They do not obey Pauli's exclusion principle. Their number need not be conserved. Examples are phonons, photons, magnons, alpha particle etc. Quasi particles are non interacting particles which can replace a system of interacting particles but obey a different dynamics compared to particles. The quasi particle that can possibly replace an electron is shown in Fig A.1.

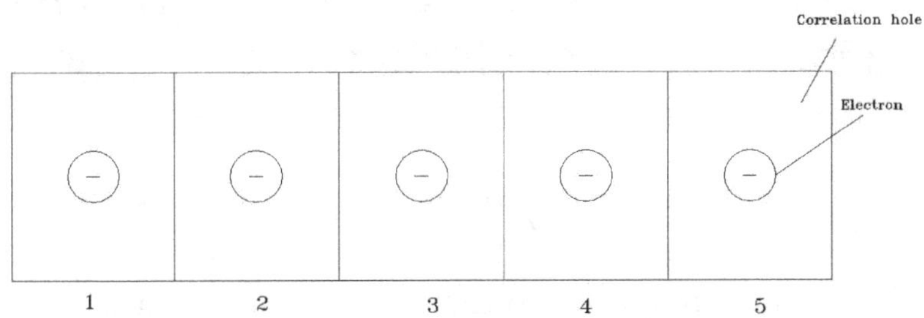

Fig.A..1.1 Quasi particles – Electrically neutral & non interacting [Five are shown]

2. Calculation of Fermi energy

The expression for fermi energy is given below:

$$E_F=(h^2/2m)(3/8\pi)^{2/3}(Ne/V)^{2/3}$$

$$=3.65x10^{-19}(n)$$

n=(Ne/V)= [(Valence of element)x(Number of atoms in unit cell)/(Volume of unit cell)]

A few examples are given below:

For FCC Aluminium

n=[(4x3)10^{30}] / (4.05x4.05x4.05)

For BCC Ferrous iron

n=[(2x2)10^{30}] / (2.87x2.87x2.87)

For HCP Zinc

n=[(6x2x2)10^{30}]/ (2.66x2.66x4.95x3x1.732)

For DC Silicon

n=[(8x4)10^{30}] / (5.43x5.43x5.43)

3. Brillouin zone and electron movement under the influence of an electric field

(a) At absolute zero

Electron with a momentum in the absence of an electric field is shown in Fig A3.1(a) represented by its wave number vector in a brillouin zone. Now a field is applied in the direction shown in FigA 3.1(b). The electron is accelerated by the field E in the opposite direction and its velocity and momentum increases steadily as represented by wave number vectors k2, k3, k4, k5, k6 and so on. At the point when the electron has touched the boundary of the zone as shown by k7 diffraction/reflection to a position k7' occurs. Again it is accelerated and wave number vector becomes k7' gets reflected to k7" and again it is accelerated and so on. This process goes on and on. Similarly for vectors k8 &k9.This is how an electron moves even at absolute zero temperature. It cannot cross the boundary. If the field becomes extremely high the situation is different.

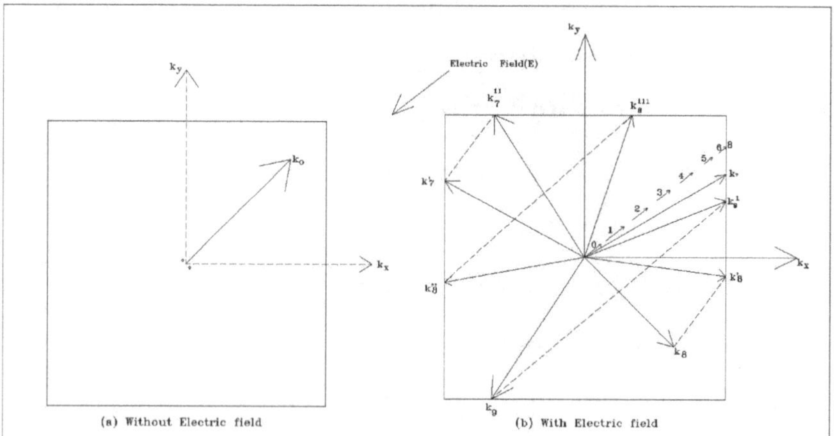

Fig.A..3.1 Electron Movement in Brilluoin zone
(a) Without electric field (b) With electric field

(b) At a higher temperature

An electron of energy E_0 will acquire a higher energy E_0+kT. If the temperature is sufficiently high the new energy may be able to bridge the energy gap E_g between conduction zone and valence zone and the electron will jump into conduction zone and the process explained in the previous section will be repeated in the higher zone.

4. Brillouin Zone and Phonons

Phonons are associated with waves of length given by

$$\lambda_{phon} = (2\pi / \mathbf{k}_{phon})$$

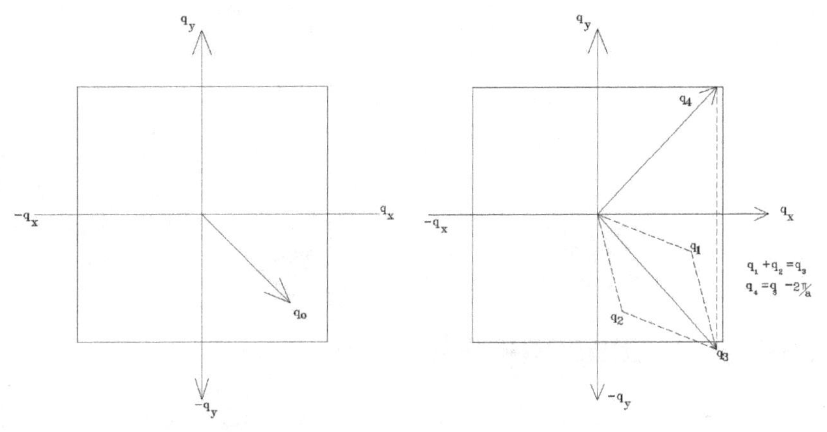

Fig.A..4.1 Phonon Movement in Brillouin zone

The corresponding wave number vector is represented as q. Fig A.4.1 (a) shows a phonon with wave number vector q_0 in a brillouin zone for a 2D lattice.Fig A4.1(b) shows two phonons with wave number vectors q_1 and q_2 interacting to give a third phonon of wave number vector q_3 which falls outside the brillouin zone .It is not permitted and the new phonon will undergo reflection so that it has a wave number vector q4 falling inside the zone. This process is called Umklapp process in contrast to the normal process which is explained below. The two phonons interacting and producing a third phonon with a wave number vector that falls well within the zone .It can then move freely inside the zone. A phonon will move from hot end or region in a solid to a cold end or region. The frequency ω (related to energy) of a phonon plotted against q is shown in Fig A4.2. (a) and the dispersion curve D(ω) against E the energy of phonons in FigA4. 2(b). Similar to electrons there are acoustical and optical zones separated by forbidden region as shown in FigA4.2(c).

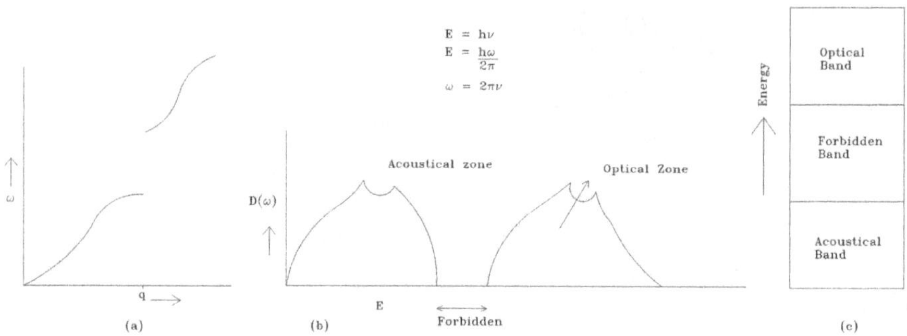

Fig.A.4.2 (a) ω Vs q (b) D(ω) Vs E (c) Energy Band diagram for phonons

5. Brillouin Zone and Photons

Similar to electrons and phonons, photons can also be studied with construction of Brillouin zones.

$$\lambda_{phot} = (2\pi / k_{phot})$$

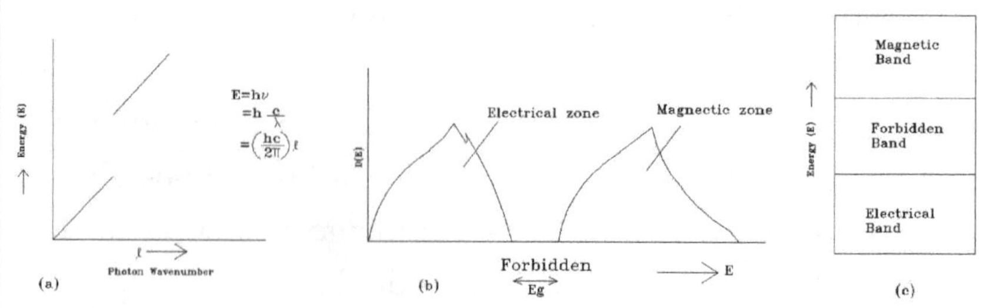

Fig.A.5.1 (a) E Vs ℓ (b) D(E) Vs E (c) Energy Band diagram for photons

The energy against wave number vector[(E vs k_{phot}) which is linear] and the dispersion curve [D(υ) vs E] for photons are shown in Fig A5.1(a)&(b).There are two zones namely electrical and magnetic separated by a forbidden region as shown in Fig A5.1(c).

6 Effective mass of an electron

The mass of an electron is different at the zone boundary compared to that in the interior due to diffraction effects. It is given by

$$\mathbf{m^*=[(h)^2/(4)(\pi)^{2]}/(d^2E/dk^2)}$$

$m^*=m_e$ the actual mass of electron in the interior of the zone. This is the case for electrical conductors as the valence zone is not filled completely. But in semiconductors and insulators the valence zone is filled to the brim and m* is different from me. The curvature of Evs k curve (the second derivative) may become negative. Electrons may have positive mass (m*is positive) in the interior and negative mass(m* is negative) near the zone boundary. Therefore near the boundary electron will move in the direction of applied field which is termed as anomalous behaviour.

7. Magnetic moments of ferrites

A spinel has the molecular formula$[R^{2+}R^{3+}O_4]_8$ where R^{2+} is in tetragonal site and R^{3+} in octahedral sites for normal spinel and R^{2+} in octahedral sites and R^{3+} shared equally by octa &tetra sites.

Zinc Ferrite is a normal spinel and Zn is diamagnetic. The eight ferric iron atoms in octa and the eight in tetra will have their magnetic moments cancelled due to opposite spins. Therefore this ferrite is not ferrimagnetic. In inverse spinels the ferric atom moments cancel off. A few examples are given below: Consider manganese ferrite. Mn atom has a magnetic moment of 5 BM and the eight atoms in octa site will add up to a net moment of 40 BM. The ferric iron atom moments cancel off.For ferrous iron ferrite. The ferrous atom has a magnetic moment of 4BM.So the eight atoms will contribute 32 BM and the ferric moments cancel off. So the net value is 32BM.Similarly for cobalt ferrite (3x8=24BM) and nickel ferrite (2x8=16BM) will be the net magnetic moment. In a mixed ferrite of zinc (3 atoms) and nickel (5atoms) the nickel atoms that are in octahedral site will contribute 5x2=10 and ferric iron (11 atoms in octahedral and 5 atoms in tetra sites) will contribute [(11-5)=6] x5=30 to add up to 40BM. The ferric iron atom has a net magnetic moment of 5 BM. Similarly one can have Zn-Mn and Zn-Ni-Cu mixed ferrites with high magnetic moments. [a ferric iron atom has lost two 4s electrons and one 3 d electron to give 5 electrons of same spin while a ferrous iron atom has lost two 4s electrons and has 6 3d electrons of which 4 or not paired. In hexagonal ferrite such as barium ferrite 8 Ferric ions are having magnetic moment pointing in one direction and 4 in opposite direction giving a net moment of 4x5=20 BM. Similarly one can calculate for strontium ferrite etc.

8. Electron atom ratio and density of state curves

(A) When the Fermi sphere just touches zone boundary

In any metal of volume V containing N_e electrons

$(4/3)\pi(p_{max})^3 = (4/3)\pi(h/\lambda)^3 = N_e(h)^3/2V$

$\lambda = (8\pi V/3N_e)^{(1/3)}$

Consider a BCC metal.

Volume [V] of unit cell is $(a)^3$ and number of atoms $[N_a]$ is 2.

$a=(V/N_a)^{(1/3)}$

In BCC metal the first plane to diffract electrons is (110) and

$(n)\lambda = 2d\sin\theta$

When Fermi sphere touches tangentially the zone boundary the angle of inclination is 90°.

$\lambda = a\sqrt{2}$

$= (2V/N_a)(1/3)\sqrt{2}$

(N_e/N_a) is obtained by equating $(8\pi V/3N_e)$ and $(2V/N_a)2\sqrt{2}$ which gives a value of 1.48

(B) When the zone is completely filled

Number of energy states per unit volume of k space=$V/8(\pi)^3$ and $N_e = 2\ V/8(\pi)^3$

Volume of I Brillouin zone = $2x8(\pi)^3/(a^3)$

N_e to fill the above volume = $4V/(a^3)$

N_a in a block of volume V = $2V/(a^3)$

$(N_e/N_a)=[4V/(a^3)]/[2V/(a^3)] =2$

Similarly one can do for other crystal structures such as simple cubic, face centered cubic and diamond cubic

9 Lasers &masers

Uncertainty principle states that $(\Delta E)(\Delta t) \geq h$. If ΔE is small Δt is large. More electrons can be made to stay longer at a higher energy level if thc energy level is sharp ie population inversion is long lasting. On the other hand pumping efficiency will be large if ΔE is large. This precludes stable population inversion as Δt is small. Two level configuration is not conducive for laser action since both optical pumping and laser action is between the same two levels. A three level configuration or a four level laser configuration is conducive for lasers since optical pumping and laser action are between a set of two different levels as shown in Fig A9.1(a)(b) & (c). Cr doped Al_2O_3 (Ruby) was the earliest material used for producing laser beams. Nowadays semiconducting compounds (binary, ternary and quarternary compounds) are commonly used.

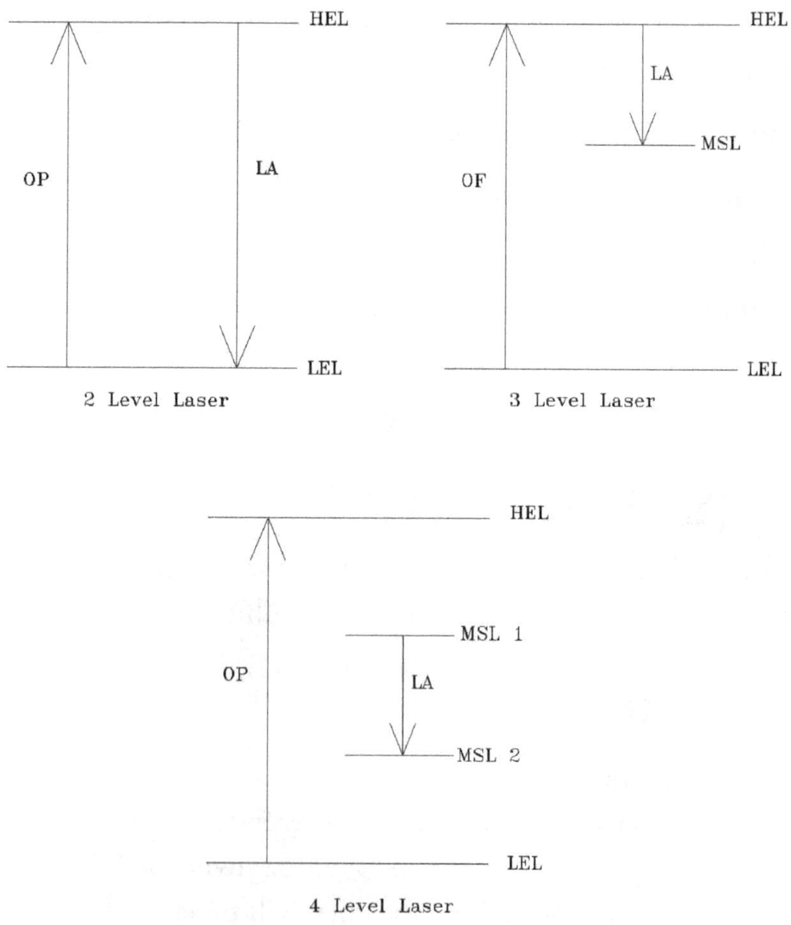

Fig.A.9.1 Principle of Laser

The maser action is similar to laser action but the difference lies in the splitting of energy levels. The masers use Zeeman splitting of energy states of a paramagnetic ion by a magnetic field while the laser uses crystal field splitting. Continuous operation of a maser system requires a three level configuration. Er doped Al_2O_3 is useful for such maser action.

10 Applications

A. Electrical
  a. Conduction
    1. Wiring in offices, factories, industries, homes, hospitals, colleges, public buildings like museums etc
    2. Transmission and distribution from power stations to distributors.
  b. Insulation
    1. Plug heads,
    2. Handles for testing instruments
    3. Gloves and boots for personnel
  c. Resistance
    1. Heating elements
    2. Resistors
  d. Dielectric
    1. Microwave ovens
    2. Microwave sensors
    3. Stealth coating
    4. Capacitors
  e. Piezoelectric
    1. Ultrasonic transducers
    2. Actuators in inkjet printers

f. Pyroelectric
   1. Thermal imaging
   2. IR cameras

g. Ferroelectric
   1. Actuator for fuel injector
   2. Capacitors

h. Super conduction
   1. SolenoidCoils,   2. MagneticInsulation,
   3. Wires,   4. Cryotrons

i. Semi conduction
   1. Thermo couples   2. Rectifiers   3. Transistors
   4. Photo cells   5. Sensors

B. Magnetic
   a. Soft materials
      Temporary magnets of all types
   b. Hard materials
      Permanent magnets of all types

C. Thermal
   a. Conduction
      (1) Sensors
      (2) Furnaces
      (3) Cooking utensils
   b. Insulation
      (1) Refractory bricks
   c. Expansion and contraction
      (1) Length standards
      (2) Container seals
   d. Shock resistance
      (1) Space vehicle fuel chamber
      (2) Refractory bricks for furnaces and convertors

e. Emission
   (1) Electron microscope
   (2) Field ion microscope

f. Capacity
   (1) Sensors
   (2) Heat Storage Materials
   (3) Cooking utensils

D. Optical
1. Lasers,
2. LEDs
3. Solar batteries
4. Optical fibres
5. Optical storage devices
6. Optical computers

9. QUESTIONS

CHAPTER 1

1. Explain what you understand by the dual nature of matter.
2. What is a matter wave ?
3. What is a fermion ?Give examples
4. What is a boson ?Give examples
5. What is a quasiparticle ? Give examples
6. Write briefly on the of M-B, F-D & B-E statistics
7. Give an expression for de Broglie wavelength
8. a)Give an expression for Schrodinger's wave equation for a particle (electron) in a box (solid)
   b)Give the three equations relating E with (T, v,V) temperature frequency & velocity.
9. Show tetrahedral void & octahedral void in FCC,BCC & HCP lattices.
10. Name the four interstitial elements that can fit into such voids.
11. How do you broadly classify properties of solids into two types and why ?

CHAPTER 2

1. What are the assumptions about an atom in Free electron theory?
2. For a 2D square lattice define & sketch Fermi circle in momentum space (Px, Py)

3. What is Fermi Energy (E_F)?
4. Derive an expression relating E_F & p
5. Define Fermi a) temperature and b) velocity
6. What is the Fermi distribution function f(E) ?
7. Show f(E) Vs E at three different temperatures OK, T1 & T2 where OK <T1<T2
8. Derive an expression for N(E)
9. How does it vary with temperature?
   Show at OK, T1 & T2 where OK < T1<T2
10. How does E vary with k the wave number vector?
11. Discuss Kronig - Penney model
12. How does the potential depend on velocity and atomic size?
13. How does the energy gap (Eg) depend on electro negativity of A & B in an alloy of A & B
14. What is the significance of energy bands as given by the Kronig-Penny Model.
15. Sketch the energy for four different cases with high V and low P, high V and high P, low V and high P and low V & low P in solids
16. Anisotropy of electronic properties of solids cannot be accounted for in FET. Explain
17. What are the advantages and disadvantages of FET?
18. What are the limitations of K -P model?
19. What are the advantages of K-P model?

CHAPTER 3

1. What is electron diffraction?
2. State Bragg's Law.
3. Give an expression relating E vs. k as given by BZT. Show that in a sketch. How is it different from FET?

4. Draw the first Brillouin Zone of a square 2D lattice and show how Fermi circles get distorted near the boundaries of the Zone.
5. What is the diffraction condition for FCC, BCC, HCP & DC solid crystals?
6. Show how the density of states of energy N(E) varry with E for (a) 2D square lattice (b)2D hexagonal lattice using the Fermi circles of increasing radius in the first Brillouion Zone.
7. What is the electron to atom ratio (Ne/Na) when N(E) vs. E corresponding to I BZ is packed upto a) to peak b) Fully in SC, FCC, BCC DC & HCP lattices.
8. What is a super lattice? Give examples.
9. How will you identify a super lattice by XRD?
10. What are ordered & disordered alloys ? Give examples.
11. Determine the boundaries of IBZ for 2D a) Square and b) Hexagonal lattices
12. Do the same thing for 3D a)SC b) DC c) FCC d) BCC and e) HCP lattices
13. Sketch the shape of IBZ in SC, FCC, BC HCP & DC crystals.
14. What is the difference between ordered and disordered a) FCC lattices b) BCC lattices in the shape of I BZ
15. Draw N(E) Vs E curve in Si as per BZT for the valence & conduction zones
16. How N (E) vs E differs at three different temperatures, say OK. T1 & T2 where OK < T1 < T2
17. What are the assumption of BZT?
18. What are the advantages & disadvantages of BZT?
19. What are the limitation of BZT?
20. How can anisotropy of electronic properties be accounted for in BZT?
21. What is the variation of Electric potential in real crystalline solids.

22. Show schematically for a 2D square lattice the same.
23. Show in different sketches the effect of atomic size and velence on the energy in an atom.
24. How will you simulate by modelling N(E) vs. E curve. Explain

CHAPTER 4

1. What are the assumptions made in Density Functional Theory.
2. What do you understand by Local Density Approximation.
3. Why high speed high capacity computation facilities are required for applying the above theory?
4. How the total energy in a crystallite solid is divided into parts? Is it correct?
5. Does it appeal to your intelligence and satisfy your logical requirements.
6. Explain electron-electron interaction ion-ion interaction and electron ion interaction in a solid.

CHAPTER 5

1. How do you account for high conductivity of metals?
2. Why conductivity of semiconductor increases with increase in temperature?
3. Alloying decreases the conductivity of a pure metal. Explain why?
4. State Nordheim's rule.
5. State Matthiesen's rule.
6. Why ordered alloys such as Cu Au & Cu_3Au have lower resistivity than normal alloys.
7. Why cold working increases resistivity of a metal or alloy?
8. How do you account for insulating property of a crystalline material?
9. Ideal insulators cannot be polarized. Why?

10. What is a soliton? How it helps conduction in polymers?
11. Why rubber gloves are used for handling electrical equipment?
12. What is electro striction?
13. Define Polarisation.
14. Name the four types of Polarisation.
15. Why electrical properties of a crystalline material are anisotropic?
16. What is an electrical dipole? What is its moment?
17. What is a domain in a ferroelectric material?
18. What is the dependence of permittivity on temperature for (a) Polyethylene and (b) PVC (Polyvinyl Chloride)?
19. Explain the process of electrical conduction in crystalline ceramics.
20. Explain conductivity of amorphous materials.
21. Define super conductivity.
22. Explain why good electrical conductors are not good materials for super conduction.
23. Show a cooper pair of electron in a Fermi circle.
24. Define T_C, M_C, J_C Hc of a super conductor.
25. What are Type I & Type II super conductors?
26. What is Meissner Effect?
27. What are hard and soft super conductors?
28. State Londons Equation for penetration depth is a super conducting material.
29. What are thin and thick films in super conductivity?
30. Is their insulation for a magnetic field? Explain.
31. Explain BCS theory of super conductivity in metals.
32. Is BCS theory valid for ceramics and polymers? Explain.
33. What is T_C for $YBa_2Cu_3O_7$? Is it above or below liquid N_2 temperature?
34. What is photo conduction?
35. State a few applications of piezoelectric effect.

36. Define para, dia, ferro, ferri and antiferromagnetism.
37. How does Zone Theory explain Paramagnetism? Explain.
38. How does Zone Theory explain Ferromagnetism? Explain.
39. What is Piezomagnetism.
40. Why BCC Iron is ferromagenitic but FCC Iron is not?
41. Why Chromium and manganese are not ferromagnetic even though their 3d shell is incompletely filled? Explain.
42. What is a Bohr Magneton?
43. What is magnetic an nealing?
44. Define Permeability.
45. Define Susceptibility.
46. What is magneto striction?
47. What is the easy direction of magnetization in Fe, Ni & Co?
48. Derive an expressions relating permeability of a material and its Susceptibility.
49. Show that for an ideal diamagnetic material susceptibility is -1 and magnetic induction B = 0.
50. If T_C of a ferromagnetic material is high does it imply that magnetic moment per atom will be high?
51. Why there is a B_S for a ferromagnetic hystersis loop but no Ps for a ferroelectric hystersis loop?
52. The speed of switching in a computer memory is less than 1 μs. Will you use a Ni-Fe or a Fe-Si alloy. Otherwise what other material will you use and why?
53. In the valency band of Si if the curvature is convex downward at the curie point will the region be populated by holes or electrons. [(d^2E / dk^2) is-ve]?
54. In the conduction band of silicon if the curvature in convex upward will the region be populated by holes or electrons. [(d^2E / dk^2) is +ve]?

55. A bivalent metal like Zinc has more free electrons (infact double) that of a monovalent material like Copper. But conductivity of Copper is more than Zinc. Explain.
56. Why metals are opaque to light?
57. Sketch a schematic optical reflectivity spectrum for (a) Metal (b) Semi conductor and (c) insulator.
58. What are inter and intraband transition?
59. What are direct and indirect band gap materials?
60. State Snells Law.
61. What is the wavelength of light emitted by red and blue laser?
62. What is the colour of light emitted and corresponding wavelength for the following compounds (a) GaAs (b) GaP and (c) GaN?
63. Explain spontaneous and stimulated emission of light.
64. Explain the terms homo and hetero junction lasers.
65. Write briefly on the dependence of refractive index of a material on its permittivity and permeability.
66. State the mathematical equation relating the three.
67. Compare the thermal expansion of metals, ceramics, and polymers.
68. Compare the thermal conductivity of copper and Bronze. What is the effect of allying?
69. Thermal conductivity of metals is 2 to 3 times more than that found in dielectric materials. Why?
70. The range of electrical conductivity is 6 times more than thermal conductivity if one considers all the materials. Explain.
71. Plot the heat capacity of solids schematically from 0 K to 303 K (RT) according to classical Boltzman, Quantum Einstein and Debye theories.
72. Why beyond R.T. specific heat capacity reaches a constant value of 6.0 Cals / mole assymptotically?

73. Dielectrics are phono heat conductors and metals are electron heat conductors. State true or false giving reasons.
74. What are the assumptions of Einntein Model in estimating heat capacity of a material?
75. How is the above model improved by Debye in his model?
76. Explain what you understand by wave function in thermionic emission of electrons.
77. What are the variables influencing emission of electrons when a material is heated to a high temperature?
78. What is Seebrack effect?
79. What is the importance of (ΔV / ΔT) in thermo couples?
80. What is the translucent solid? How is it different from the transparent solid?
81. What is the (N_e/N_a) ratio in (a) FCC (b) BCC lattice when the first Zone is filled upto the peak in N(E)in E curve and completely filled?
82. Why in Cu-Zn alloy there is a change in crystal structure from FCC to BCC at 50 atomic percent of Zink [i.e. (N_e/N_a) = 3/2]?
83. Why some metals crystallize in BCC, others in FCC and some others in HCP? Explain on the basis of (N_e/N_a) ratio.

CHAPTER 6

1. Explain how wires are produced by (a) wire draiwing (b) Hydrostatic extrusion.
2. Compare Copper and aluminium as conductors.
3. Name a few resistors.
4. Name a few insulators.
5. Why is Nichrome used as a heating element but not Nickel or Chromium?
6. Why is constantan used as a resistor but not Copper or Nickel?

7. Give the composition of the following alloys (a) Manganin (b) Nichrome and (c) Constantan.
8. Ideal Insulators cannot be polarized. Why?
9. How are dielectrics classified according to permittivity?
10. What is the desirable microstructure of a ferro electric? Why?
11. How would you produce $BaTio_3$ on a large scale? Explain. Why electrical annealing is done for this material.
12. All ferro electric materials are dielectric. But the converse is not true. Explain.
13. Draw the schematic microstructure of $BaTio_3$.
14. Sketch the unit cell of a $BaTio_3$ crystal.
15. What is an intrinsic semi conductor? Give examples.
16. What are p - type and n - type semi conductors?
17. How do you produce n - type Si and p - type Si?
18. What is a compound semi conductor? Give examples.
19. How do you produce p type and n type GaAs?
20. What is the range of dopant concentration in an impurity (extrinsic) semi conductor?
21. What is the concentration limit of undesriable impurity in a semi conductor?
22. What are metallurgical grade Silicon and electronic grade Silicon?
23. Why Semi conductors should not have grain boundaries and undesirable impurities?
24. Compare and contrast Silicon and Gallium Arsenide as semi conducting materials with respect to cost, availability and properties.
25. Compare Silicon & Germanium similarly.
26. Explain Chockralsky technique for producing single crystals of Si, GaAs & Ge.
27. Describe horizontal and vertical Bridgman methods of semi conductor production for Si, Ge, &GaAs.

28. Explain what you understand by lattice matching.
29. What is hetero epitaxy?
30. Discuss the method of epitaxial growth for producing semi conductors like GaAs.
31. Highlight the salient features of Zone Refining.
32. Give the governing equation for the above process.
33. Sketch the unit cell of Si and GaAs.
34. Sketch the micro structures of a single crystal Si and GaAs.
35. Name a few intermetallic and ceramic super conductors.
36. How Bronze Route is used to produce multifilamentary Nb_3Sn super conductor?
37. How is $YBa_2Cu_3O_7$ produce by (a) PM route (b) Sol-Gel method?
38. What is the significance of liq N2 and liq He in super conductivity?
39. State the crystal structure of $YBa_2Cu_3O_7$ with unit cell dimensions.
40. What is the purpose of Silicon in Fe 4% Si Alloy?
41. Why it should be greater than 3 and less than 4.5%?
42. Sketch the schematic microstructure of Fe 4% Si alloy?
43. Sketch hysterics loop of the above alloy schematically.
44. Why Molybdenum is added to super malloy?
45. What is the composition of super malloy?
46. What is the heat treatment gives to Fe-Si alloy and Ni-Fe alloy? Describe with T t diagram.
47. What is the hysterisis loop of Ni-Fe alloy with and without magnetic annealing? Why are the former alloys used for computer memory applications?
48. Compare the magnetic properties of the above two alloys. Explain how Hysteresis losses and Eddy Current losses are minimized?
49. What are cube and cube on edge texture? Explain.

50. Discuss the production of ferrites by PM route?
51. What are ESD magnets?
52. What is the desirable micro structure of Al-Ni-Co alloy? How is it achieved? Sketch it and explain.
53. How these alloys are manufactured?
54. Describe the production and properties of a Samarium Cobalt and Iron Neodymium - Boron magnetic materials.
55. Discuss the composite material magnetic materials briefly.
56. What is a metallic glass? How is it produced? Give examples.
57. What is a BMG? Give examples.
58. Discuss Melt spinning method of producing metallic glass materials.
59. Describe the advantages and disadvantages of metallic glass materials as magnetic materials.
60. Sketch the demagnatisation curve for a few hard magnetic materials.
61. What are the application of square loop ferrites?
62. How do you produce a hexagonal ferrite. Sketch the unit cells of cubic and hexagonal ferrite systematically?
63. What is the thickness of domain wall in (a) Ferroelectric and (b) Ferro magnetic materials?
64. What is the domain wall energy in (a) Ferro electric and (b) Ferro magnetic materials?
65. What is a mixed ferrite? Give examples.
66. Which of the ferrites are more suitable for microwave applications?
67. Compare and contrast the properties of Al_2O_3 and AlN.
68. Describe the tape casting process.
69. Why Al_2O_3 is used as substrate material for Integrated Circuits?
70. Why vaccum is the best thermal insulator?
71. Porous refractory bricks are used in furnace lining. Why?

72. What is the composition of the alloy INVAR? Why is it called INVAR?
73. Discuss the thermal expansion of Iron and Nickel and how it varies with temperature.
74. Write about the importance of Al_m SiC_p composite as a dilation material.
75. What is the use of low thermal capacity materials?
76. What is thermal shock resistance of SiC and Si_3N_4?
77. State the best combination of the thermocouple materials.
78. How semi conductors are very useful in this regard? Give a few examples.
79. Write about W, Ba, La B_6 as thermionic materials.
80. Discuss Si and GaAs an optical materials stating their advantages and disadvantages.
81. What is a linear optical material. Give examples.
82. What is a non-linear optical material. Give examples.
83. What is a photo voltaic material. Give examples.
84. InGAAsP material is suitable for lasers and in optical fibre communications. Why?
85. PbSbTe is useful for lasers over a wide range of wavelength (7-30μm)? Where is it used?
86. InGaSb lasers can be used to generate coherent light in the wavelength range of 1.55 7μm. State True or False.
87. Write about GaAs / AlGaAs junction layer.
88. InGaAsP / InP lasers are very useful for generating 1.3 1.55μm IR light. State True or False.
89. What do you understand by the term opto electronics.
90. Discuss GaN is an optical material.
91. How Silica optical fibres are produced for the communication applications? Explain.
92. Describe the working principle of (a) Solar cell and (b) LED.

93. Discuss Silicon (crystalline and amorphous) as photo voltaic materials.
94. Write about Lithium Niobate and Indium Antimonide as non linear optical materials.
95. What are homo junction and hetro junction lasers / transistors.

CHAPTER 7

1. Explain what you understand by the term spintronics.
2. Describe the principle of working of a F-NF-F device.
3. What is photonics?
4. What is a transphasor?
5. Define the terms GMR and CMR.
6. What are the uses of such materials?
7. Explain what you understand by an optical computer?
8. What is the speed of switching of a electrical (valves), electronic (SS transistor), ferro electric, ferromagnetic and optical devices use in memory applications of computers and microprocessors
9. What do you understand by nano structure?
10. What is a magic number?
11. What are the interesting property changes that occur when one go from ordinary material to a nanostructured material.?
12. How do you get a carbon nanotube?
13. What is the future of organo electronic materials
14. Show the structure of graphene sheet.
15. What are the electronic properties of graphene sheet?
16. What are the possible applications in electronic devices?
17. What is the crystal structure of fullerene?
18. How many carbon atoms are there in a fullerene molecule?
19. What are the attractive properties of fullerene?
20. Compare optical and biological computers.
21. What is the importance of recycling electronic devices?

22. How can you obtain zero gravity?
23. What is the advantage of processing an alloy under zero gravity?
24. What is a solid state electronic device?
25. Expand' VLSI'?
26. What is a femto second?

10 NUMERICAL PROBLEMS

Chapter 2

1. Calculate the wavelength of an electron moving at a velocity of $1.3x10^6$ m/s
2. Determine the wavelength of a photon having an energy of 3eV
3. What is the energy of an X-ray photon with a wavelength of 0.25 nm?
4. What is the energy of an optical photon having a wavelength of 400nm
5. Determine the frequency of a photon with an energy of 4eV
6. Estimate the frequency of a phonon at a temperature of 1000K (Hint: Use formulas E=hυ, E=kT, λ=(h/mv), c=λυ) for the above problems where he is Planck constant, υ is frequency, k is Boltzman constant, m is mass and v is velocity of subatomic particle, λ is wavelength and c is velocity of light.)
7. Calculate the Fermi velocity and Fermi temperature for aluminium with E_F=11.63eV. can such a temperature occur in a metal? Explain.
8. For aluminium with a Fermi energy of 11.63eV find the energy spread of a free electron above and below E_F AT 303K (R.T)
9. Calculate the number of free electrons for the following metals:

   Metal valence Atomic weight density

$X10^{-6}$Mg/mole Mg/m^3

Copper	1	63.5	8.9
Aluminium	3	26.98	2.79
Zinc	2	65.37	7.13

Take Avagadro Number as $6.023x10^{23}$/mole

10. E_F for copper is 7eV.At what energy f(E) will be equal to 0. 2eV for the maximum energy(E_F+kT) to be 7.4ev. (Hint: Plot f(E) vs E)
11. What is the average energy of an electron if E_F for silver is 5.5eV?What is the Fermi velocity and temperature?
12. Determine the Fermi energy of BCC ferrous iron if the Lattice parameter is 2.87A^0 and valecy is 2
13. Calculate the Fermi energy of copper. **Use appropriate data**

Chapter 5

5.1 Conductors

1. A wire of diameter $5x10^{-3}$ m should carry a current of 15A in a particular device. Maximum heat loss allowed is4W/m. What is the maximum permissible resistivity for the wire?
2. Calculate the resistivity of aluminium at 303K if$(\rho)_0$ is $8x10^8$ ohm.m and temperature coefficient of resistivity(α) is0.0042
3. Calculate the increase in resistivity of copper metal and nichrome alloy if their temperature is raised from 0K to 973K by heating. α_{cu}=0.0043, α_{nic} =0.0001, ρ_{cu} =$1.7x10^{-8}$ and ρ_{nic} =$108x10^{-8}$.Hint: $\Delta\rho=\rho_T-\rho_0$ and $\rho_T = \rho_0 + (\alpha)T$, Where Tis temperature (ρ) is resistivity and α is temperature coefficient of resistivity.
4. Copper and Nickel are is omorphous forming a series of solid solutions from 100%Cu to 100%Ni.If$(\rho)_{cu}$ is$1.7x10^{-8}$ and $(\rho)_{Ni}$ is $59x10^{-8}$ ohm.m. Take the resistivity of 96%Cu4%Ni alloy to be

$7x10^{-8}$ ohm.m and find the constant 'A' in Nordheims rule. Find the resistivity of a solid solution alloy of 80%Cu and 20%Ni

5. A copper wire of cross sectional area $6x10^{-6}$ m^2 carries a current of 55A.Calculate its resistivity. Desity is 8.9Mg/m^3 ,valence is1 and atomic weight is $64x10^{-6}$ Mg/mole. Avagadro number equals $6.023x10^{23}$. What is the number density of free electrons and their drift velocity?
6. Find the constant 'A' in Nordheim's equation of a dilute hypothetical alloyof Au in Ag. Concentration of Gold is0.05% in the alloy and $(\rho)_{Au}$ is $2.2x10^{-8}$ and $(\rho)_{Ag}$ is $1.61x10^{-8}$ ohm.m The alloy has a resistivity of $1.71x10^{-8}$ ohm.m.

7 A hypothetical solid solution alloy of A in B has a composition of 99.99% A and 0.01% of B.If ρ_A =$1.6x10^{-8}$ $(\rho)_B$ is$3x10^{-8}$ and $(\rho)_{AB}$ is $2.0X10^{-8}$ ohm.m. Find the constant 'A'. [Nordheim's rule states that $(\rho)_{AB}$ =$X_A(\rho)_A$+$X_B(\rho)_B$ +A X_A X_B]

8. Calculate the resistance of an aluminium wire of length 12m and cross sectional area $6x10^{-6}$ m^2 if resistivity is$2.47x10^{-8}$ ohm.m.
9. Copper wres of diameter of cross section 2,5 and10 mm are to be made into heating elements.Length of the wire is to be 5m. Find resistance of the wires if ρ_{cu} is $1.7x10^{-8}$ ohm.m. What is the heat generated and rise in temperature in each case if the current is 15 A and voltage is 220V. Take any d and find. The Fermi energy for copper. Use appropriate data.

5.2 SEMICONDUCTORS

1. Electrical resistivity of germanium varies with temperature as given below:

Temperature(T),Kelvin	**310**	**330**	**355**	**385**	**420**
Resistivity(ρ)	11.8	5.9	2.3	0.9	0.35

   Is germanium a metal or semiconductor or an insulator?

2. Estimate the energy gap in Germanium using the data given below:

Temperature(T),Kelvin	**303**	**353**	**373**	**420**	**423**
Resistivity(ρ)	**11.75**	**2.33**	**0.89**	**0.35**	**0.34**

3. A wire of germanium doped with a p type impurity is 0.02m long and has a diameter of 0.002m. It has a resistance of 120 ohms.What is the percentage of the dopant?

4. Determine the energy gap Eg at room temperature using the data given below:

Material	**AX10^{-4}**	**B**	**Eg(eV)**
Silicon	4.73	636	1.17
Germanium	5.05	204	1.52

   Hint:

$$Eg_T = [Eg_0] - [(A)(T^{2)}/(B+T)]$$

5. Determine the Eg for Si and Ge at a pressure of 19 k bar if Eg at absolute zero and at atmospheric pressure[10^{-3} k bar] is 1.17 and 1.52 eV and [(ΔE)/(ΔP)] is ($-2\text{x}10^{-3}$) and ($+15$)x10^{-3} eV/k bar respectively.

   Hint:

$$[(\Delta E)/(\Delta P)] = \{[Eg_p - Eg_{atm}]/[\Delta P]\}$$

6. The temperature dependence of the energy gap of a InSb semiconductor is given by

$$Eg_T = Eg_0 + (\alpha)T$$

Eg is 0.3 ev and (α) is $-2.9x10^{-4}$ eV/K. Find out Eg_T at room temperature (303K)

7. The mobility of electrons at room temperature in Si, Ge, GaAs &SiC are 0.135,0.36,0.65 & 0.09 respectively. Find their conductivities taking dopant concentration to be 10^9 atoms/m^2 and charge of electron to be $1.6x10^{-19}$ C
8. Calculate the electrical conductivity of a n type semiconductor material at room temperature. The mobility of electrons is $0.15m^2$ /V.s and concentration is 10^{18} /m^3. Charge of electron is $1.602x10^{-19}$ C. Assume number of donor atoms =number of electrons.

   Hint:

   $(\sigma) = (e)(\mu_e)(N_{de})$
9. A silicon single crystal is doped with 10^{23} atoms/m^3 of arsenic. The crystal wires has an area of cross section equal to 100(μm^2) and a length of 0.01m.Calculate its conductivity. Mobility of electron is $0.07m^2$/V.s.If it is doped with phosphorous atoms numbering 10^{23} /m^3 determine the conductivity. Assume the same mobility. Take electric charge from above problem. If a voltage of 100V is applied find the current.
10. 0.01 Kg of silicon is doped with aluminium and another 0.01 Kg with arsenic and both are melted together and solidified. What is the conductivity of the resulting alloy. Assume the conductivity of p type and n type semiconductor to be the same and is equal to 10 mho/m.
11. A silicon single crystal contains 10^{15} phosphorous atoms/m^3 as donor impurity.Find the conductivity at 303, 373, 473, 573 and 673K. What is your inference from the values.Mobility of electron in silicon is $0.15m^2$ /V.s and number of free electrons with energy equal to E_F is $5X10^{44\,i}$ i.e[N_e (E_F)]

12. Determine the conductivity of n type germanium containing $5x10^{22}$ arsenic atoms/m^3 if the mobility of electrons is $0.39m^2$ /V.s in germanium and charge is $1.6x10^{-19}$
13. Silicon is an intrinsic semiconductor with mobility of electrons and holes equal to 0.135 m^2/V.sand $0.048m^2$/V.s. Number of conduction electrons and conduction holes are same and equal to 10^{16}/m^3 .Take electric charge from previous problem. Calculate the conductivity.
14. Calculate the electrical conductivity of P doped Si at room temperature.Dopant concentration is 10^{23}/m^3 and mobility of electrons and holes are 0.14 and 0.05 m^2/V.s.Take electron charge as in previous case.
    Hint:
    $(\sigma)=(n)(e)(\mu_e)$
15. InP has an energy gap of 1.29Ev.It is an intrinsic semi conductor with mobility of electrons and holes equal to 0.46 and $0.15m^2$/V.s . Concentration of charge carriers (N_e) equals 10^{25}/m^3 at 0K.Calculate its conductivity.
    Hint:
    $N=N_0$ EXP[(-Eg)/($2k_B$ T)]
16. At room temperature extrinsic p type silicon semiconductor has an electrical resistivity of 0.02 ohm.m and majority carrier (hole) concentration of$1.6x10^{21}$ /m^3 .What is the mobility of holes in Silicon?
17. At room temperature extrinsic n type Ge semiconductor has an electrical resistivity of 0.015 ohm.m and majority carrier (electrons) concentration of $1.6x10^{21}$ /m^3 .What is the mobility of electrons in Germanium.
18. Calculate the concentration of electrons in Si if one in every million (10^6) of Si atoms is replaced with a n type P atom. Desity of Si is 2.3 Mg/m^3 and atomic number is 28.

19. A silicon single crystal containing P as dopant is to be grown. Concentration of dopant should be 10^{22} atoms/m^3.Assume K=0.35.Weight of Si is 2.5 Kg in the melt in a crucible. Using the concentration of P find the weight of P to be added to the melt. Density of Si is 2.33Mg/m^3 and the atomic weight of P is 31.

    Hint:

    $C_S = K.C_L$

20. Determine C_S after 5,6,8,10 passes in zone refining of a semiconductor rod of 0.1m length if the initial concentration of impurity atom is 0.1.The length of the zone is 0.01m and the segregation coefficient K is 0.1.

    Hint:

    $C_S = C_0 [1-(1-K)EXP\{1-(Kx)/(l)\}]$

21. For an is omorphous semiconductor alloy activation energy (ΔE) is 0.55eV and conductivity (σ_0) is 10 mho/m at absolute zero (0K).Find the conductivity

5.3 DIEELECTRICS

1) Determine the capacitance of a SiC capacitor with two parallel plates of area 10^{-10} sq.ms separated by a distance of $5x10^{-7}$ m when it is subjected to a voltage of 1V.What is the quantity of charge on the plates. ε_r=3.9 [Hint:Use the Formula C=(ε_r) (A) /(d)] where C is capacitance, A is area of plate, d is distance between plates and ε_r is relative permittivity.
2) Estimate the capacitance of an Al_2O_3 capacitor with two parallel plates of area $3x10^{-3}$ sq.ms separated by a distance of $o.8x10^{-6}$ m. ε_r=8.0.
3) A parallel plate capacitor is subjected to a potential of 20V.The dielectric material between the plates has a relative permittivity of

7.0.The two plates are separated by 0.005m and the Area of the plates is 6x10 $^{-4}$ sq.ms. Find the polarisation (P), displacement (D), capacitance (C), and the charge on the plates (Q).

4) Determine the relative permittivity of a ferroelectric material used in between two parallel plates of a capacitor if the capacitance of a device is 11x10 $^{-10}$F.Area of the plates is 2x10-4 sq.ms and distance of separation is 0.003 m.
5) A parallel plate capacitor has dimensions of o.1mxo.5mx0.005m. Reqired capacitance is 100F. Three materials are available for using between the plates. They have relative permitivities of 20,100and120.Find the distance of separation in each case and identify the best material of your choice stating the reason.
6) $BaTiO_3$, a widely used ferroelectric material has an ε_r of 4000.It is used in a capacitor which is subjected to an electric field (E) of 10000V/m. Calculate the extent of polarisation in the material. ε_0=8.8x10 $^{-12}$F/m or A.s/V. m . [Hint: Use $P=\varepsilon_0 E(\varepsilon_r-1)$]
7) Plot on a graph sheet P Vs. E for the three hypothetical materials A,B and C using the data given in table below and suggest the best material for a capacitor stating the reason for your choice.

E(V/m)	P(C/m²) A B C
100	150 1500 1000
200	300 6000 3000
300	450 12000 6000
400	550 14000 7000
500	650 15000 8000
600	690 16000 8500
E_c	-200 -300 -400

P_r= 500, 1300,6500

5.4 SUPERCONDUCTIVITY

1) Lead has a critical temperature of 7.2K and critical field strength of 6400A/m. Calculate the field strength at a temperature of 7.0K
2) Determine the superconducting temperature of mercury subjected to a magnetic field of 10000A/m. Critical temperature for superconductivity is 4.5K.Critical flux is 0.0411T at 0K & permeability of vacuum is $1.257X10^{-6}$V.s/A.m. {HINT: Use the following equations:
   {$B_{cT}=B_{c0}$ [1-(T/T_c)2]
   H_{cT}= {B_{cT}/μ_0}8
3) Lead is subjected to a magnetic field of 20000A/m. At what temperature will it become superconducting if T_c=7.2K, B_{c0}=0.8T at 0K and $\mu_0=1.257x10^{-6}$V.s/A.m.
4) Use BCS theory to determine the energy gap of lead if critical temperature is 7.2K and for $YBa_2Cu_3O_7$ if T_c is 92K.[Hint:Use the formula Eg=3.5(k_B)(T_c)].
5) Afield of 50000A/m exists at the surface and 40000 A/m at a distance of'x' from the surface in a superconducting wire. The London penetration depth(λ) in Tin is $5x10^{-8}$ m.Calculate 'x'. {HINT:Use the formula $H_x=H_0$ EXP[-(x/λ)]}.
6) H_c=20A/m,Jc=100 andT_c=170K. Plot in 3D on a graph sheet a line sketch and demarcate the super and nonsuper conducting regions in the plot.
7) Determine the London penetration depth of a hypothetical superconducting material which is 500nm in diameter and subjected to a field of 1500A/m on the surface which decreases to 1000A/m at a distance of 30nm exponentially

5.5 Magnetic Properties

1) Determine the permeability of elemental metals Bismuth &Aluminium and Fe-4%Si alloy if their magnetic susceptibilities are $-165x10^{-6}$, $20.7x10^{-6}$ and $1.x10^{-6}$.What do you conclude from the answers?
2) The saturation magnetisation of BCC iron is 1750 k.A/m and its lattice parameter is 0.287 nm. Its unit cell has 2 atoms. What is the magnetic moment per atom in Bohr magnetons?
3) There are 9 electrons in the outermost shell of a particular atom. Five have positive and four have negative spins. What is the net magnetic field of moment per atom?
4) Density of nickel is $8.9Mg/m^3$ and its atomic weight is$58.7X10^{-6}$Mg/mole. Saturation induction of nickel is 0.65W/Sq.m. Calculate the magnetic moment of nickel atom in Bohr magnetons.
5) The Curie temperature of magnetic iron is 1041K.Find its exchange energy.
6) Draw the hysteresis loop of pure elemental nickel at 575K & 723 K. Curie temperature is 630K. Do similarly for iron at 1000K&1075K if curie temperature is 1041K and for cobalt at 1350K&1450K if Tc is 1400K.
7) The magnetic moment for elemental nickel is $0.6\mu_B$/atom and its atomic weight is $58.7x10^{-6}$Mg/mole. Density is 8.75 Mg/Cu.m Take the Avagadro number as $6.023x10^{23}$.Find the magnetisation per unit weight and unit volume.
8) The magnetic moment for iron is $2.2\mu_B$/atom and for cobalt $1.7\mu_B$/atom. Take the relevant data and calculate magnetisation per unit weight and unit volume like in the previous problem.
9) Calculate the net magnetisation of the following mixed ferrites used in memory of computers:
   $[(MnMg)OFe_2O_3]_{8,}$ $[(MnCu)OFe_2O_3]_8$ and $[(LiNi)OFe_2O_3]_8$.

10) A soft magnetic material is used at a frequency of 50 Cycles/sec in an application. The magnetic specimen weighs 30 Kg and the area of hysteresis loop is 150 J/cu.m. Its density is 7.5Mg/cu.m. Determine the energy loss/hr/unit volume in the specimen.
11) Determine the hysteresis loss/unit volume of a magnetic material which has H_c=500A/m,B_s=2T and a volume of $25x10^{-5}$ cu.m
12) For the three hypothetical materials A,B&C magnetic flux at different field strengths are given below in the table.If B_r is 6,600 &60 and H_c -75,-80 & -85 is for the materials A,B&C, Plot on a graph sheet the hysteresis curves for the materials. What do you conclude about the suitability of the materials for being used as permanent magnet material in applications?State the reasons for your selection.

H(A/m)	B(T) A	B	C
10	1	5	2
20	2	15	4
30	3	45	8
40	4	135	16
50	5	405	32
60	5.8	700	55
70	6.4	900	65
80	6.6	1000	70
90	6.7	1025	72
100	6.8	1050	73

13) Draw the demagnetisation curves and calculate the energy product for the three hypothetical materials A, B & C using the data given in table below.

Material	B_r(T)	H_c(A/m)

A	200	-500
B	400	-800
C	600	-1000

14) Calculate the squareness ratio for the following hypothetical materials from data given in table below. Which is best suited for computer memories and why?

Material	B_r	B_{max}
A	9	10
B	14.5	15
C	17.75	18

15) Draw on a graph sheet the hysteresis loop for the two hypothetical materials A & B with permeabilities of 0.1 & 0.01. Calculate the energy loss per cycle. Comment on the usefulness of the two materials.

Material	B_{max}	μ_{max}	B_r	H_c
A B	50 60	10 30	20 40	-5 -2.5

16) Draw the hysteresis loop for the materials A &B on a graph sheet from the data given below. What is your inference & conclusion?

    Material A-B r=B_{max}=-B_{min}=50T,H_{max}= -H_{min}=20A/m
    Material B- " " " =80T, " " " =50A/m

5.6 Thermal Properties

1) Calculate the linear thermal expansion coefficient of a bar of length 2 m if it is increased in length by 0.002m when temperature is raised from 293 K to 353K.
2) A bar of steel with an elastic modulus of 210GPa and yield stress of 50 MPa is fixed between two ends at a minimum

temperature of 293K in winter. In summer the temperature rises to a maximum of308K.Calculate the change in length if the linear thermal expansion coefficient is $1.1x10^{-5}$.Also calculate the stress in beam. Will it cause permanent deformation?

3) Rails of 10 m length are placed on a railway track at a RT of 283K in winter. During summer the temperature reaches a maximum of 318K.What gap should be maintained between two rails so as to avoid stress on them?
4) The thermal expansion coefficient of copper is $17x10^{-6}$ K^{-1}. A wire of length 1.5 m is heated from 273K to 573K. Calculate the stress and strain in the wire. Take elastic modulus to be 117GPa
5) Determine the specific heat of copper with E_F=7.0eV at 303K (RT).N_a =6.02x1023atoms/mole and k_B=1.381x10 $^{-23}$J/K. [HINT: Use $Cv_{el}=5N_A k_B(T/T_F)$ & $E_F=k_BT_F$].
6) The heat capacity of aluminium is 913J/Kg.K. What is the rise in energy stored in a component made of aluminium having a mass of 1Kg if the temperature rises from 303K to 430K?
7) Determine the Weidmann-Franz ratio(L) for copper if its electrical and thermal conductivities are 5.85x10 ^{7} mho.m and 3.9x10 ^{2} W/m.K at room temperature. [HINT: Use $L=(\sigma_t)/(\sigma_e)(T)$]
8) Determine the thermal shock/deformation resistance. For the following materials.

Material	$(\sigma)_T$ W/m.K	(α) 10^{-6} K-1	E GPa	$(\sigma)_b$ MPa
Copper	385	17	120	150
Bronze	180	17	100	550

White cast iron	75	11	110	230
Alumina	29	9	345	150

Hint: TSR/TDR=($\sigma_b\sigma_t/\alpha$ E) σ_b-fracture strength, σ_t-thermal conductivity, α thermal expansion coefficient, E-Youngs Modulus

9. What is the rise in temperature during ideal deformation for the materials given in table below ?

Material	ρ Ohms/m	C J/Kg.K	(σ) MPa	(ε)
Titanium	4.58	520	600	0.3
Aluminium	2.69	900	80	0.6

Hint: $\Delta T=(\sigma\varepsilon/C\rho)$whereC is hear capacity anρ is density

10) Calculate the thermoelectric figure of merit for Copper, Silver and Indium Antimonide from the data given in table below: [HINT: Use $Z=\{S^2(\sigma)_e/(\sigma)_{t\}}$]

Material	S(μV/K)	$[(\sigma)_e]^{-1}=(\rho)\times10^{-8}$ Ohm.m	$(\sigma)_t$ W/m.K
Al	-0.20	2.85	210
Cu	+3.98	1.7	390
Ag	+3.68	1.5	420
InSb	-130	450	7.5

11) What will be the energy of electrons emitted by a tungsten filament at 2000Kif the Work function is 4.5eV for tungsten.
12) A copper-constantan thermocouple has the hot end at 800Kand cold end at303K. Calculate the thermal E.M.F generated.
13) If an iron-constantan thermocouple is used in the above problem what will be the result?
14) The variation of E.M.F against temperature is given for three popular thermocouples in table below. Calculate the sensitivity ($\{\Delta V\}/\{\Delta T\}$) of each.

Temperature(K)	273	283	293	303	313	323	333	343	353	363	373	

Platinum-PlatinumRhodium alloy	0.0	0.06	0.11	0.17	0.23	0.30	0.36	-	0.5	-	0.64	E.M.F (mV)
Copper-Constantan	0.0	0.39	0.79	1.19	1.61	2.03	2.47	2.91	3.36	-	4.28	"
Iron- Constantan	0.0	0.52	1.05	1.58	2.12	2.66	3.20	3.75	4.3	4.85	5.40	"

5.7 Optical Properties

1) Refractive index of water is 1.33 and relative permittivity varies with frequency as follows:
   $(\varepsilon)_r$ 7.0 3.3. 2.8
   f 1.5 8.3 25
   What do you infer about the material water as a dielectric?
2) For Silicon refractive index is 3.45. Calculate its permittivity. Assume Silicon is nonmagnetic.
3) Calculate for magnetic iron its refractive index. Its permittivity is 11.8 and permeability is $-4.1\text{x}10^{-6}$
4) What is the velocity of light in a material that possesses a permeability of 0.99999 and permittivity of 11.8? Also calculate the refractive index of the material.
5) What is the velocity of light in a material if the permeability and permittivity are 1.00002 and 6.9? Also find its index of refraction.
6) The dielectric constant of four different materials Si, Ge, SiC & GaAs are 11.9,16.0,10.0 and 13.1. Assume they are nonmagnetic and calculate their refractive index.
7) Si has an energy gap of 1.12 eV.If a beam of photons of energy 2eV impinges on its surface estimate the energy of electros at the bottom of the conduction band.
8) Permittivity of Silicon Nitride is 6.5. If it is nonmagnetic find its index of refraction.

9) The shortest wavelength limit is 380 nm and the longest wavelength limit is 700nm.Find the energy band gap maximum and minimum.[HINT: Use E_g = hν= (hc/λ). λ=hc/E_g].
10) For emission of light of wavelength 600nm (which is visible to the eye) what should be the energy of the band gap in the material?[h=6.63x10^{-34} J.s and c=3x10^8m/s].
11) If the band gap energy of GaAs is 1.43 eV and InAs is 0.36 eV what will be the wavelength of emitted light for each. If the two compounds form a series of continuous solid solutions[isomorphous] and the energy gap varies linearly with composition for Ga_x In_{1-x} As calculate at what composition of InAs will the emitted light have a wavelength of 1.0μm. [HINT: Use Eg=0.36+1.06(x)].
12) For a ternary compound/alloy the energy gap depends on temperature,pressure and composition.For Al_x Ga_{1-x} As the relationship with composition is given below at constant temperature [RT]&pressure[atm.pressure]: Eg=1.424+1.247(x) when x<0.45 and >0.0).Find the energy gap for the compound if x=0.2.
13) GaAs is a direct band gap material.AlAs is an indirect band gap material.Al_x Ga_{1-x} As is a direct band gap material up to x=0.38 and an indirect band gap material above 0.38. Calculate the energy gap when x=0.2.HINT:Use the following relationship:Eg=1.424+1.455(x).
14) GaAs is a direct band gap material and GaP is an indirect band gap material.Calculate the energy gap of $GaAs_{1-x}$ P_x using the following equation which is valid upto x=0.45.
Eg=1.424+1.5(x) + 0.176(x^2).

CHAPTER 6

1) In an ideal wire drawing process maximum reduction per pass is 63% [$r = A_f/A_o$].If a wire of 0.005m diameter is required what should be the initial diameter of the work piece. Initial length is 0.8 m. What is the final length [HINT: Use volume constancy i.e. $A_f L_f = A_o L_o$].
2) 0.160 Kg of copper powder is taken and compacted and sintered. The density of the P/M product is 7.95Mg/cu.m. Theoretical density is 8Mg/cu.m. What is the amount/volume of porosity in the component?
3) Theoretical density of soft ferrite is 4.8Mg/cu.m. Compacted &sintered ferrite has a porosity of 5% and weighs 0.18 Kg. What is the density of the P/M product?
4) $YBa_2Cu_3O_{7-x}$ is produced by P/M route. If the theoretical density is ~6.9Mg/cu.m and the product weighs 0.55Kg and shows a density of 5.65Mg/cu.m what is the percentage of porosity in the product?
5) $BaTiO_3$ is manufactured by P/M method. After compaction and sintering the component weighs 2.5 Kg with a density of 5.6 Mg/cu.m. If the porosity is 3% what is the initial density.
6) Distance between two (100) atomic planes in a single crystal is 0.3nm. If the crystal is deformed in such a way that the above distance becomes 0.33nm find the strain in the crystal.

Miscellaneous questions

1) At RT which of the following will be an insulator and why? GaSb, Al and AlN [Eg is 1.95, 0.0 and 6.3 eV respectively]
2) State the wavelength of laser light emitted by AlGaAs, InGaAs, PbSnTe and InGaSb.

3) A p type dopant is added to Ge. If the concentration of dopant is increased what will happen to a) hole concentration, b) electron concentration and c) conductivity.
4) Answer the same questions in the previous problem if a n type dopant is added.
5) Answer the same questions in problems 4 & 5 if instead of Ge, Si is used.
6) What is the importance of cobalt magnetic tapes? State its uses.
7) Plot the heat capacity of solids from 0to303K according to classical, Quantum Einstein's and Debye's theories.
8) Sensitivity of copper-constantan, iron-constantan thermocouples are same at 0.054mV/K. Compare the temperature range of use of both.
9) Chromel- Alumel thermocouple has a sensitivity of 0.046mV/K & Platinum-Platinum Rhodium alloy thermocouple has 0.0095 mV/K. Which one is more responsive to change in temperature and why?
10) CFET doesn't explain the variation of specific heat with temperature correctly. State true or false. Why is it so?
11) CFET gives a wrong dependence relationship between electrical conductivity and temperature. State true or false and give reasons.
12) Two semiconducting compounds form a series of continuous solid solutions [isomorphous]. How will the lattice parameter and gap vary over the entire composition range? [HINT: Use Vegard's Law which states $a_{AB} = X_A a_A + X_B a_B$ & $Eg_{AB} = X_A Eg_A + X_B Eg_B$].
13) The first commercial bulk metallic glass has the following composition:
Zr = 41.2%, Ti = 13.8%, Cu = 12.5%, Ni = 10.0% and Be = 22.0%. It requires a fast cooling rate of 1K/S & several

cms thick plate can be made. What is the trade name given to this bulk metallic glass.

Ans: [Vitrealoy]

14) Draw the potential vs atomic diameter for a single atom, for two atoms arranged on a straight line and several atoms arranged similarly.
15) Tabulate the energy gap in eV against lattice parameter for 1.GaP 2 Ga As 3,Ga Sb, 9 AlSb.

REFERENCES

1. W. HumeRothery & B.R Coles, Atomic theory for students of Metallurgy, IOM, London,1969.
2. G.V. Raynor, An introduction to the electron theory of metals, IOM, London, 1953.
3. A. Cottrell, Introduction to the modern theory of metals, IOM, London,1988.
4. A. Cottrell, Concepts in the electron theory of alloys, IOM, London, 1998.
5. A.H. Cottrell & D.G. Pettifor, Electron theory in alloy design, IOM, London, 1992.
6. Dan Wei, Solid state physics, Cengage learning, India, 2008.
7. Rolf. E. Hummel, Electronic properties of materials, Springer-Verlag , U.S.A, 2001.
8. DavidJiles, Electronic properties of materials, Nelson Thornes Ltd, 2001
9. L. Solymar & D.Walsh, Electrical properties of materials, Oxford University Press,U.K, 2010.
10. Offied Madelung, Introduction to solid state theory, Springer, 1995.
11. James W.Mayer & S.S.Lau, Electronic materials science, Maxwell Macmillan, U.S.A, 1990.
12. Ben. G. Streetman & Sanjay Kumar Banerjee, Solid state electronic devices, PHI Learning, 2010.

13. C. Kittel, Introduction to solid state physics, John Wiley (Asia), 2005.
14. A.R. West, Solid state chemistry and its applications, John Wiley (Asia), 2003.
15. G.I. Epifanor, Solid state physics, Mir Publishers, Moscow, 1979.
16. W.D. Kingery et.al, Introduction to ceramics, John Wiley(Asia), 2004
17. Michel Barsoum, Fundamentals of ceramics, Mc Graw Hill, New York,1997.
18. John Wulff et.al,The strcture and properties of materials,Wiley Eastern Ltd, India,1980.
19. R.E. Reed Hill, Physical metallurgy principles, East West Press, India, 1974.
20. D.SClark & W.R. Varney, Physical Metallurgy for Engineers, Affiliated East West Press, India, Chapter4.1962
21. Sir Alan Cottrell,An Introductio to Metallurgy, Universities Press, Hyderabad, India, 2000, pp470-508
22. V. Azaroff Introduction to Solids, Tata McGraw Hill, New Delhi, India, 1960
23. Carl. C Josh, Nanostructured Materials, Jaico publishing house, Mumbai, India, 2009.
24. T.Pradeep, NANO The essentials, Tata McGraw HILL, New Delhi, India, 2007.
25. Charles P Poole Jr., Frank J Owen's, Introduction to Nanotechnology, WileyStudent Edition, New Delhi India, 2006

INDEX

CPSIA information can be obtained
at www.ICGtesting.com
Printed in the USA
LVHW042033021222
734242LV00013B/87

9 789356 481770